The Outsmarting of Criminals

Also by Steven Rigolosi

Who Gets the Apartment?

Circle of Assassins

Androgynous Murder House Party

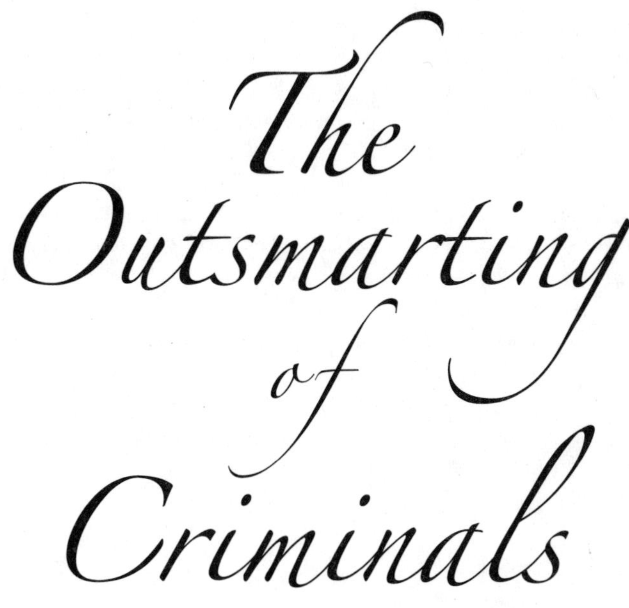

The Outsmarting of Criminals

STEVEN RIGOLOSI

Ransom Note Press
Ridgewood, NJ

10 9 8 7 6 5 4 3 2 1

Ransom Note Press, LLC
143 East Ridgewood Avenue, Box 419
Ridgewood, NJ 07451

Typeset and printed in the United States of America

Library of Congress Cataloging-in-Publication Data

Rigolosi, Steven A.
The outsmarting of criminals / by Steven Rigolosi.—First U.S. Edition.
pages cm
Summary: "A cozy introducing Miss Felicity Prim, who believes her ample experience in reading mystery novels has prepared her for a new career in private detection"—Provided by publisher.
ISBN 978-0-9773787-9-1 (hardback : alk. paper)
1. Women private investigators—Fiction. 2. Detective and mystery stories. I. Title.
PS3618.I43O98 2014
813'.6--dc23

2013031030

Acknowledgments

I offer my sincerest thanks to Christian Alighieri (*il miglior fabbro*), Cathy Lee Morrison, Marc Lieberman, Dorothy McIntosh, Emily Marlowe, Max St. John, Cheryl Solimini, everyone at Deadly Ink, and, of course, The Partridge. I would also like to thank J. E. Larson, the immensely talented artist who illustrated and designed the cover and book jacket. Finally, to Chris and Debbie, Dave and Annie, Jules and Katie: Much gratitude for showing me how it should be done.

"Mystery has energy.
It pours energy into whoever seeks the answer to it."

—John Fowles, *The Magus*

1

A House in the Country

When, after many years of living quite peacefully in New York City, Miss Felicity Prim felt herself being mugged for the first time, her initial thought was: *My handbag is caught on something*. As she lay in the hospital, watching Doctor Poe set her fractured arm, she wondered: *Why did the mugger choose me?* Then she vowed: *This will never happen again.*

But she had to recover before taking action. The doctor had prescribed an intense regimen of relaxation and inactivity (a challenging requirement for a busy New Yorker). She was to remain at home for a month, in her bright, rent-controlled, one-bedroom apartment on East 26th Street, and focus on getting better. Her sister, friends, and coworkers would run her errands, pick up her dry cleaning, and bring her whatever she needed or wanted: meals, groceries, magazines.

And what she wanted most, she found, were the books she'd scoped out during her last visit to the Union Square Barnes & Noble. She'd scribbled the titles on the notepad she kept in her handbag—the same handbag that had contained her wallet, which the mugger had probably tossed in a trash can after removing the cash from it. Fortunately, she didn't need the notepad to remember the books she'd planned to purchase. She'd been awaiting payday, turning the titles over in her head, thinking about the hints they provided regarding plot and character. Miss Prim rattled off the list to Dolly, who returned several hours later, apologizing that she'd lost track of time. As if such apologies were necessary! Because that is what one *does* in a bookstore: One loses track of time.

With one arm in a sling and a book in her hand, Miss Prim looked out of the window of her front room. Ten stories beneath her, city workers were situating the latest art installation in Madison Square Park. A man wearing a cowboy hat (the artist?) waved frantically at the installers. As Miss Prim settled into her easy chair near the window, she thought: *Perhaps getting mugged was a blessing in disguise. At last, I have time to read as much as I want to. Over the next month, I shall read without being jostled, poked, and prodded on buses and subway cars. I shall read* what *I like,* when *I like, and not just for an hour before I go to sleep, or at my desk while I hurry through lunch.*

How she admired the protagonists of her books, those worthy men and women of crime fiction! *They* did not work in a doctor's office ten hours a day, five or six days a week. *They* did not get mugged while walking along city streets and minding their own business. *They* took charge of their lives. When they encountered a mysterious situation, they took matters into their own hands. Uncooperative politicians, corrupt corporate raiders, overworked policemen, those who insisted that everything was perfectly lovely despite the heroine's fears: None of these stood in the sleuth's way. In the end, justice was served and the universe was restored to balance. Why? Because, by the end of the novel, the sleuth had used her superior intelligence—not common violence—to outsmart the criminal.

A month passed and the sling was removed from her arm. The evening before she was due to return to Doctor Poe's office, she reminded herself of her vow—*This will never happen again*—and studied herself in the mirror.

She needed to get in shape. Once an athletic young woman who could hold her own in a badminton tournament, she had allowed a certain thickness to set in around the waist and ankles. She'd become lax about walking when cabs were plentiful, and she'd begun indulging in her favorite New York caloriefest, the black-and-white cookie, rather too often. The confection was, she was forced to admit, nothing more than a sugar-slathered, fat- and cholesterol-laden cake masquerading as something less insidious. She marched into her kitchen, located the cookies Celia had given her a day earlier, and pitched them into the garbage pail.

The next day she took her usual route to Doctor Poe's office, looking over her shoulder often; much more frequently, in fact, than she'd done in the 1970s, when New York City was much more dangerous, or in the stressful days after 9/11. In the past, she'd enjoyed watching people, wondering about the lives and loves of those she passed on the streets. Now she found herself wondering why *this one* looked so suspicious, *that one* appeared dangerous, and *the other one* seemed to be up to no good.

That night, after her joyous return to Doctor Poe's office—for everyone acknowledged that they simply could not have gone on any longer without her—Miss Prim stopped at Chelsea Piers, a co-ed gym on the Hudson River. The time had come to join a health club, and her goal was to find one in an inconvenient location. Walking to and from a somewhat distant health club, she reasoned, would provide more of a workout than taking a cab to a local one.

While receiving a tour of the facility she nearly fled in embarrassment, almost believing she'd stumbled into a Victoria's Secret or *Playboy* "Women of Manhattan" photo shoot, what with all the well-coiffed, perfectly lipsticked and mascara'ed young women so provocatively dressed in skintight Spandex leggings and sausage-casing bras. Yes, these are the models, Miss Prim thought; and the young men with the large biceps in tank tops and skinny legs in cargo shorts were the photographers or tech crew. But no, all of the males appeared to be working out on intricate machinery or with various weight bars, stopping every few minutes to admire themselves in the mirrors. At Doctor Poe's office she'd become aware of the narcissism of the younger generation, that hyperconnected yet disaffected cohort attempting to find its way in the big city. But until she stepped foot into Chelsea Piers she hadn't realized quite how out of control things had become.

She signed a contract for a shockingly expensive three-month trial membership.

At a women's center in Greenwich Village, she enrolled in a self-defense course taught by a tough-looking man named Sal who, Miss Prim discovered during the fourth class, was actually a woman. She learned how to perform an arm twist to extricate herself from an unwanted grip, as well as effective methods to prevent herself from being strangled.

Still, it is one thing to take on a trained instructor within the confines of a controlled classroom, quite another to confront a crack or meth addict. (Yes, Miss Prim knew about these substances. One does not work in a doctor's office for decades without learning about life on the streets.) In certain situations—those in which charm and intelligence do not succeed in disarming attackers, and those in which one is outnumbered—more drastic measures might be necessary.

Miss Prim drew a nonnegotiable line at firearms, however. She'd been raised to believe that violence creates more problems than it solves, and as she'd matured she had found her own belief system mirrored by that particular piece of indoctrination.

A taser, Miss Prim decided, was the answer. She asked Dolly to purchase one for her, as Dolly was quite facile with using computers to purchase hard-to-find items. Dolly, still shaken by Miss Prim's recent misfortune, agreed, and a week later she handed her friend the latest in electrical self-protection technology, the Laser Taser 3000. Miss Prim took ownership of the device while vowing never to use it. Unless absolutely necessary.

Several weeks after taking possession of the Laser Taser 3000, Miss Prim arrived at her apartment building on East 26th Street and headed for the staircase, which was tucked into a remote corner of the lobby. Taking a deep breath, she began walking up the ten flights of stairs. This was part of her new physical fitness regimen. Walking up the stairs, she'd read, is much, much better for the waistline than standing in an elevator.

She'd reached the third floor when she thought she heard a staircase door open behind her. And then … the sounds of someone climbing the staircase aggressively, perhaps two stairs at a time.

Miss Prim picked up her pace. It was fanciful to think someone was chasing her up the staircase. Wasn't it?

As she began running up the stairs, she heard the person behind her approaching rapidly. She wasn't going to make it to the tenth floor. He—it must be a *he*, mustn't it?—was younger, faster, breathing heavily. She felt a hand touch her shoulder.

What did she do, after taking that course to boost her self-defense abilities and her confidence? She kneeled in a corner of the landing and screamed.

"Miss Prim, are you OK?" The voice belonged to George, the sweet-natured, slightly overweight doorman who'd worked in her building for more than twenty years. He extended his hand and helped Miss Prim to her feet.

"Miss Prim, I'm real sorry, I didn't mean to scare you. Your sister stopped by today and left this package for you." He held out a small box. "I was putting the broom away in the closet when I saw you go into the stairway. I thought I could catch you before you got up to your apartment."

After Miss Prim returned to her apartment, locked the door's three bolts, and placed the safety bar under the door-knob, she sat at her kitchen table and unwrapped Celia's package: low-gluten, low-carb, low-fat, low-cholesterol minicakes from a trendy bakery that had just opened in Celia's West Village neighborhood.

Miss Prim caught a glimpse of herself in the reflective foil in which the minicakes had been wrapped. She didn't recognize the person looking back at her. A haggard, fearful mess had replaced an upbeat, positive, independent woman. And she knew, as deeply as she'd ever known anything, that it was time to leave New York City. To retire. To find a little house in the country where she'd be safe.

As Miss Prim planned the next stage of her life, she wondered: What would Papa (which she pronounced by accenting the second syllable) have recommended? What would Mama (which she also pronounced by accenting the second syllable) have advised?

Papa would have asked, *Do you think, perhaps, that after so many years of living in Manhattan, you are longing for the summers we spent on Nantucket and Martha's Vineyard? You often spoke about how much you loved the house we rented, how free you felt having your own four walls, a yard, and a garden. A house in the country is a wonderful thing; and if you want one, you should have one.*

Mama would have said, *Felicity, this is the twenty-first century. You are free to make your own decisions. There will be risks involved in decamping to the country, yes; but I hope I have taught you to see life's challenges as opportunities for growth and higher levels of wisdom. You have always helped other people; perhaps it is time you did something for yourself. And I know you, dearest; no matter where you go, you will find a way to help people, just as you do now, every day, in Doctor Poe's office.*

Miss Prim smiled as she straightened up the front room of her apartment, reorganizing a bookshelf on which, somehow, the books had gotten out of alphabetical order. The question was, of course, how to combine her parents' sage advice into a cohesive whole. "A house in the country" plus "helping people" equals … what exactly? Certainly the book in her hand—the latest in the long-running series featuring plucky female sleuth Fatima Larroquette, New Orleans native and devoted Wiccan—wouldn't help her make any decisions.

Or would it? Heroes and heroines are found everywhere, not just in big cities, Miss Prim reflected. To be helpful to one's fellow man, one need not save the world from greedy corporations and devious terrorist cells. One could be of service while serving as a criminal outsmarter in a New England village, helping the locals find stolen jewelry, solving missing-persons cases, and uncovering malfeasance in Town Hall. Certainly if Fatima Larroquette, heroine of *When Life Hands You Limes, Make Limeade*, could do it, so could Miss Felicity Prim.

Once Miss Prim decided to undertake a career in criminal outsmarting, she found that such a drastic change in lifestyle could not be accomplished without a good deal of preparation.

First there was the need for additional, specialized education. Yes, she had her degree from Teachers' College, granted so many years ago, and she treasured the liberal arts with all her being. She was not so naïve as to believe, however, that a more-than-passing acquaintance with Spinoza, Chaucer, and Locke would stand her in good stead when engaging with criminal types. No, she would need schooling in certain legal and procedural matters, thus acquainting herself with the limits of what she could do (legally, as a concerned citizen) without falling afoul of the authorities.

As for forensics, ballistics, and those other aspects of modern crime-scene investigation—she dismissed them with a mental wave of her hands. These were, she believed, crutches used by people with little or no imagination, moderate (at best) intelligence, and a tendency to prefer cold, hard facts over the psychological factors involved in crime. How thoroughly weary she'd become of *CSI: Something or Other*, which seemed to proselytize the message that blood spatter, microfibers, and stray hairs could answer all questions. No. As Miss Prim knew from decades of counseling patients at Doctor Poe's office, at the heart of all problems lie relationships and *people*, not strands of DNA.

At the New School, where Miss Prim had signed up for the accelerated course in criminal justice, Miss Prim met with her advisor to discuss the choices available to fledgling criminal outsmarters. Interestingly, Miss Prim noted, these options more or less corresponded to those followed by the fictional protagonists in the books she adored.

Policewoman? her advisor suggested. No, police work would not do, Miss Prim replied. She was not one to gladly take orders from fools above her in the police hierarchy. She knew from reading Ed McBain and Dell Shannon how much time she'd spend knocking on doors and filling out useless paperwork, and she did not want to waste her time (or her talents) cutting through red tape and fending off the advances of oversexed coworkers. For, in fiction at least, there seemed to be at least one *roué* in every police squad, and who had time for *that?*

Private detective? If she'd decided to continue living in New York, perhaps. In such a complicated city, she'd have no difficulty getting work, helping worthy clients find swindlers and cheating spouses. But private detection could too easily lead her into a hardboiled world. And she did not relish the idea of searching through Mafia safe houses for stashes of stolen money or befriending transgendered prostitutes with cruel and merciless pimps who would not have thought twice about bashing Miss Prim's delicate skull. The Underworld might be an interesting place to visit in fiction every now and again, but she did not wish to take up permanent residence there.

Profiler? Certainly a high-interest job, and one to which she felt suited, for don't the most depraved criminals have the most interesting psychology (usually as a result of the poor parenting they received)? To be a profiler, though, she'd probably have to work for the FBI or the CIA. On the positive side, she could live somewhere in the country and report into Quantico or Langley when her services were needed. But, she told her advisor, she didn't want to get involved in the federal bureaucracy, what with all the infighting, incompetence, double agents, and so on.

Forensics? Absolutely not, for the aforementioned reasons.

In the end, she was left with the choice that she'd always known, in her heart, would be right for her: a cozy criminal outsmarter, living in a lovely cottage with a garden, in a town where nothing truly bad happens. And she knew where she might find such a place: in Connecticut.

2

The Supporting Cast

While reading the *New York Times (Sunday) Magazine*, Miss Prim discovered an article fulsomely praising a group of Northwestern Connecticut hamlets. Many of these towns, Miss Prim read, offered not only upscale coffee houses and art-movie houses but also various "townie" bars likely patronized by well-connected people in the community, such as off-duty police officers, local gossips, and bartenders to whom the populace confides its secrets. These quietly prosperous towns, Miss Prim reasoned, would likely provide ample opportunity for a fledgling criminal outsmarter. Why? Because there is always conflict when the haves live alongside the have-nots—when down-at-heel, somewhat underprivileged natives encounter overprivileged yuppies who buy up the land, improve the schools, and raise the property taxes.

Finally, after two months of taking Miss Prim to examine properties that were not quite right for one reason or another, Miss Prim's real-estate agent took her to view a delightful, snug two-bedroom mock-Tudor cottage nestled on an acre of wooded property. Olivia Abernathy explained away the cottage's shocking price by touting the benefits of the Greenfield school system, as well as the cottage's "famous" rose garden and proximity to the town square.

Miss Prim looked at the contract, spread out on Olivia's desk. Once she signed it, there would be no turning back. She'd be leaving behind her sister and her dearest friends.

Gone would be the spontaneous get-togethers, the confidences shared over cups of tea at local coffeehouses, the easy camaraderie of relationships developed over a lifetime. There was the phone, of course, and friends would pay an occasional visit; but everyone knows that the farther from Manhattan you go, the less frequent the visits. No longer would she have the security of the well-compensated job she'd held in Doctor Poe's office for decades, and she'd be sacrificing that rarest and most valuable of New York commodities: a rent-controlled apartment with a million-dollar view. If she ever returned to Manhattan, she would end up living in an airless, windowless shoebox on a noisy avenue rather than in the bright, affordable apartment on the park close to the subway. Among Manhattanites, there is one unbreakable rule: *You never, ever, for any reason, give up a rent-controlled apartment.* Yet she would have to do exactly that to move to Connecticut, because she could not retire from her position at Doctor Poe's office and support two homes on her savings. And her lease prohibited her from subletting her apartment.

But the cottage … on a street of older homes, all lovingly cared for. And the charming town square, with its green, its eateries, its old-fashioned gaslight lampposts. And the cottage itself … so lovely, so bright, so quiet, so safe. And with so much *space*, Manhattan's holy grail! A full acre of property on which to spread out. A barn for storage. An extra bedroom, an eat-in kitchen with miles of cupboards. And nooks and crannies in which to store and display books, books, and more books—those wonderful tales that lived forever in her memory but took up far too much space in her one-bedroom New York apartment. No more harassment from strangers to purchase one of those space-saving "Kindle" or "Nook" devices, which seemed to miss the point of books entirely. Even her parents' books, long held in an expensive storage facility, would finally see the light of day again, as the cottage's attic held ample promise for renovation into a library. Yes, a *real library*, with comfortable chairs, brass reading lamps, and plush carpets into which one might dig one's toes while reading a particularly suspenseful novel.

But first things first. Miss Prim took a deep breath and signed the contract.

Doctor Poe greeted Miss Prim's announcement with shocked silence, and this reaction took her off guard. She had expected moderate to strong protests, appeals to her overall indispensability, even an impassioned entreaty to delay her move a year or two. Instead, the good doctor accepted her resignation stoically. Which was not, she realized, the response she'd been hoping for.

Much more gratifying was the shock that greeted Miss Prim's general announcement in the staff room of Doctor Amos Poe's Park Avenue practice. Norah would be the least sorry to see her go, of course; Miss Prim's departure would mean a staff vacancy that Norah longed to occupy. The agonized regrets of Viveca (the phlebotomist), Zoroastria (the receptionist), and Dolly (Doctor Poe's assistant) were much more sincere, and much more prolonged, than Norah's non-grudging acceptance of Miss Prim's decision to take her life in a different direction. Viveca knocked a cup of coffee onto a manila folder containing x-ray results and burst into tears. "Miss Prim," she said, "you *can't* go. You *cannot.* We can't run this office without you. I just can't let you leave."

Well, Norah can, Miss Prim thought, noting the impatient look on Norah's face. Already Norah appeared to be eyeing Miss Prim's favorite chair, considering how she would adjust the tilt and lumbar support to better suit her ergonomic preferences. *When I am gone*, Miss Prim thought sadly, *Norah will take my place. Soon, it will be Norah, not me, upon whom Doctor Poe relies.*

Meanwhile, Dolly Veerelf stood quietly next to Miss Prim, trying to be supportive of her friend's decision. Miss Prim knew it would be as difficult to leave Dolly as it would be to abandon Doctor Poe, that dear man who'd been a trusted, valued colleague and friend since the early 1970s. In Dolly she saw a young woman whom she would have wished to have as a daughter of her own. For Dolly had little in common with the female patients Doctor Poe saw each day, many of whom suffered from a surfeit of self-confidence and a deficit of humility.

Miss Prim had her consoling words at the ready.

"My dearest friends," Miss Prim said to the gathered staff, "You have all been so wonderful to me during my recovery, and you know you can call on me any time you need my help. *Of course* we shall remain in close touch. I'm moving to Connecticut, not to the end of the world. You all will come up to visit, as often and for as long as you like."

She embraced Dolly, who returned the hug with fervor.

"Dear Dolly," Miss Prim said gently, "you know my home will always be *your* home, too."

That evening, as Miss Prim settled herself into her reading chair, she heard an urgent rapping of knuckles on her apartment door. Odd: The doorman had not called to announce a visitor.

Looking through the peephole, Miss Prim saw Doctor Poe shuffling in the hallway, his hat in his hand. She undid the three locks, removed the safety bar from the floor, and welcomed her employer into her home.

"Doctor Poe," she said warmly as the doctor rushed in. "What an unexpected and delightful surprise. I was just thinking about brewing a cup of tea, perhaps you'll …"

"Miss Prim," the doctor said, "I'm sorry to be peremptory, but we have an emergency on our hands. Or, rather, I do. You see, I've thought about it, and I simply cannot allow you to move to Connecticut. You must discard this notion of criminal outsmarting and stay with us, where you belong."

At last! The words she'd waited to hear. Fortunately, she'd already prepared her response.

"Doctor Poe, I so appreciate your kind words. I cannot tell you how many hours I have spent in coming to my decision. Eventually I had to admit to myself that my life, and my way of viewing the world, have changed. After so many years of living in such a stimulating, rich, and unpredictable environment, I long to hear the crickets and see the stars. I want less stimulation and more predictability. And I believe that once I establish myself and my new career in Greenfield, I shall find a way to make my mark, helping people in small or subtle ways that will be meaningful nonetheless."

"But Miss Prim, you help people now! Every day, at the office. Half of my patients do not come to see me. They come to see *you*."

Miss Prim was touched. "Doctor Poe, to hear such compliments from someone for whom I have the greatest respect is …"

"Is that what you feel for me, Felicity? Respect?"

"Of course, Doctor. But not only respect. Admiration. Affection. These are just a few …"

She was not permitted to finish her sentence. Doctor Poe threw his arms around her and dragged her into his embrace.

"But can't you see, Felicity? Your feelings for me may be those of respect, admiration, and affection. But I love you with all my heart. You must stay with me. Please, say you will stay."

3

A Stranger Comes to Town

Long a person able to handle anything life threw at her, Miss Prim found herself somewhat overwhelmed. The stresses of purchasing a small home were, she was sure, soon to be outweighed by the joys of having four walls of her own, with no rambunctious children or argumentative couples living above, below, or alongside her (an all-too-rare blessing in her years on East 26th Street). For now, though, getting the utilities set up; purchasing comfortable furniture; hiring workmen to paint the place in those difficult-to-find upbeat yet relaxing colors—all these arrangements ate up surprisingly large chunks of time.

The stresses were not lessened by her conflicted feelings regarding Doctor Poe. His admission had come as a surprise, if not a complete shock (since the death of the doctor's wife, Celia had repeatedly insisted that Doctor Poe's affections were Miss Prim's for the asking); and the unresolved nature of their future relationship made for some awkward moments at the office.

"You cannot tell me, honestly, that you have no feelings for me, Felicity," Doctor Poe had said, after she had sputtered unintelligibly following his declaration of love. "We have known each other far too long, and far too well, for me to believe that my affections are unrequited. The time has come for us to be fully honest with each other."

"I will admit, Doctor Poe—"

"Amos. For the love of God, call me Amos."

"Doctor Poe, I cannot deny that I hold great … affection for you. I have always thought that you and I would remain the dearest and closest of friends until … well, shall we say, until the end. I have sometimes marveled at the … comfort … of our relationship. We have known each other for decades, and yet rarely have we disagreed or come into serious conflict. Each day I have looked forward to seeing you, to starting our days with our chats over our tea"—here tears began to spring into her eyes, an awkward situation not improved by Doctor Poe's taking and holding her hand at that moment—"and I have thought, many times, how lucky I am to have such a dear and trusted friend in you."

She had pulled herself together and continued speaking. For Miss Prim was not a repressed woman unable to get in touch with her feelings. No, despite outward appearances and her dedication to her privacy and dignity, she had known passion, and intimate affairs, and dangerous liaisons; and all of these had taught her that long-term decisions regarding lifemates must not be made at moments of peak emotion but rather as a result of intense intellectual reflection on the assets and liabilities of the relationship. For indulging in an *affaire de coeur* is one thing, Miss Prim knew; and marrying (and then living with) someone is quite another.

"But Doctor Poe," she had continued (she could not use his given name, she simply could not!), "it is only a year since your beloved Lavinia passed on. How can we know, at this time, whether your romantic intentions toward me are those on which a future can be built, or whether you are quite understandably missing the companionship and affection of your wife of more than forty years? No, do not protest. Surely a man of your intelligence and wisdom understands that both of us must feel assured of the permanence of our own, and the other's, feelings before we can make life-altering decisions. You married wisely, and I have long been content in my solitary state. Neither of us, I am sure, would wish to rush into … something … without being quite confident that doing so would not jeopardize our current friendship.

"So, allow me to offer a modest proposal. Let us take six months to think on this, to continue as we always have, and to discuss the matter, as we see fit, when we have something to say about it. And then, at the end of that period, we shall decide whether to remain the best of friends or to further our commitment. We shall visit each other over the next six months, and if our relationship progresses to something more intimate, we will then have the joys of sharing an apartment in Manhattan and a home in Connecticut. Does this sound like a reasonable plan?" This arrangement seemed rather appealing to Miss Prim, who could envision returning to work in Doctor Poe's office for, say, three days a week after spending long weekends at Rose Cottage.

"It is not what I hoped for, Felicity," Doctor Poe replied, "but I must respect your wishes. And I suppose six months is not too long to wait, in the big scheme of things. But I make one request. Now that I have declared my intentions, you must use my given name. Amos. No more Doctor Poe."

Miss Prim had thought long and hard. Though she considered herself a forward-thinking woman, she did not hold with modern ideas of instant friendship and rushed intimacies. No. As in all important matters, one must take one's time.

"Let us agree as follows," she had suggested. "The day I begin using your given name is the day I consent to be your wife. Is that acceptable?"

"It is," Doctor Poe had replied, kissing her hand tenderly.

The good-bye party was a sorrowful/joyful affair, filled with kind gifts, loving testimonials, and heartfelt best wishes. Fearing a lack of support from people who might pooh-pooh her aspirations, Miss Prim had confided her plans to become a criminal outsmarter to only three people—Doctor Poe, Dolly, and Celia—so her post-retirement career was not mentioned at the going-away party.

Her last stop before leaving New York City—*leaving*: such a sorrowful word after so many happy years—was at Franklin Motor Works on Eleventh Avenue, where she picked up her sporty new Zap sedan. As a younger woman she'd had a coupé she'd quite loved, but as a burgeoning countrywoman she thought a four-door model would be much more practical in terms of grocery hauling, visits to and from the garden center, and so forth. As she drove along the West Side Highway and merged onto the Henry Hudson Parkway, she couldn't help but notice how slowly everyone else was driving. She was also taken aback by the number of drivers slamming on their brakes, blasting their horns, and displaying their middle fingers to her. When, exactly, had people become so rude? New York was a city perpetually on the move, after all. One would think drivers would be motivated to get to their destinations, instead of crawling along like lazy inchworms.

She thought her fellow drivers might become less pokey when outside city limits but, alas, this prognostication proved untrue even on Interstate 684, where slow-moving cars in the left lane swerved crazily into the center lane as she approached them. She remembered an old saw much repeated by her mother—"Everyone thinks he's a good kisser and a good driver"—and she recognized the wisdom in these words as her spirited little sedan passed monstrous SUVs, 18-wheelers, and foreign sports cars whose drivers didn't seem to understand they were driving on an *expressway*, not a winding country road.

Two hours later she was placing her key into the uncooperative lock on the front door of her new home. She gazed with pleasure at the hand-painted new mailbox (a gift from Dolly) and at the sign above it (a gift from Celia):

Rose Cottage

Celia had bestowed the name on the house after seeing photos of the gardens. Miss Prim smiled; she was enough of an Anglophile to admit to a certain pleasure in owning, and living in, a house with a name instead of an apartment with a number.

Reaching into her handbag and rummaging under the Laser Taser 3000, she pulled out her to-do list. So much to do—where to begin?

1. Do grocery shopping
2. Buy wine and spirits for guests
3. Explore downtown
4. Get to know bank and post office personnel
5. Volunteer somewhere
6. Adopt trusty animal companion

Points 1-5 could wait. Until the refrigerator and freezer were stocked, one could dine at charming local eateries; downtown would still be there tomorrow; volunteer organizations would still need people next week. Point 6 seemed the most urgent. So, after dropping her valise into her sweet, sunny bedroom, she returned to the Zap and drove to the Greenfield Animal Shelter.

Thoughts of an animal companion had occupied her obsessively for a number of weeks. Her new career made adopting a pet an absolute necessity. All the literature made the case for a cat, or cats. Their presence would establish the mood of conviviality and secret-sharing that was essential in her line of work. A couple of cats would allow her, when necessary, to play the role of the dotty older woman who cannot be taken seriously. She knew she would have achieved an important milestone in her career the first time she heard someone, most likely a criminal, whisper at a party, "Oh, that's barmy old Miss Prim! An absolute dear, but quite out of it."

Yet, despite all the factors pushing her towards felines, she could not ignore certain facts. One: She had a long and abiding affection for large dogs, having loved them as a child. Two: Despite the security afforded by the Laser Taser 3000, a trusty canine companion would undoubtedly be better at dissuading, or mauling, intruders than a cat would. In Manhattan she would have had to choose a small dog, one that could live comfortably in an 800-square-foot apartment. In Greenfield, with her acre of property, she had no such constraints.

Miss Prim felt instant affection for the young woman volunteer, whose smile and enthusiasm reminded her of Dolly's.

Phoebe took Miss Prim to see the many healthy, neutered or spayed cats and dogs currently calling the shelter home, and Miss Prim needed to marshal all her strength to prevent herself from adopting every one of them. How she wanted to offer a home to that beautiful Samoyed with the bright but somewhat sad blue eyes; she longed to hug that timid Alsatian to her bosom; she wanted to scoop that little Yorkie into her arms and carry it home in her bag (but only after removing the Laser Taser 3000, as one did not want to risk any accidents). But it was a large muscular brindle Boxer named Bruno who would not let her walk away. There he stood, his rear end shaking with unfettered delight at Miss Prim's attentions, as if daring Miss Prim not to be dazzled by his charms. When Miss Prim's concentration was momentarily distracted by a chocolate Lab trying to get her attention, Bruno let out a small whimper of terrible emotional pain. *You will not walk away from me*, Bruno seemed to be saying, *for you are a person of impeccable taste and judgment, and you know a good thing when you see it.*

And so the decision was made.

Bruno seemed impatient as Miss Prim underwent the third degree and filled out reams of paperwork. First, she assured Phoebe that she had already purchased everything Bruno would need to be comfortable in his new home; she also promised to provide ample exercise opportunities for her new companion. Phoebe provided a list of local veterinarians, recommending Dr. Emerson as her favorite while admitting that she found him to be rather cute.

Phoebe got down on her knees to say goodbye to Bruno. "I'll miss you, B," she said, hugging the Boxer around his neck. "Be a good boy."

Bruno gave Phoebe a big, sloppy lick. But Miss Prim saw the twinkle in his eye. *I'll miss you, Phoebe,* Bruno seemed to be thinking, *but I am out of here. Woo hoo!*

4

The Secret Passage

One of the really lovely things about adopting a mature pet, Miss Prim acknowledged, was the built-in discipline, for Bruno was already fully trained in terms of the correct times and places to do his business. Upon arriving at his new home, Bruno quickly sniffed the perimeter of the rear yard and christened his first tree, gazing excitedly at all the other trees to be conquered. Miss Prim looked wistfully at those same trees and exhaled with pure joy. In Manhattan she'd had to share the trees in Madison Square Park with millions. These trees were *hers*.

"Come, Bruno," she said emphatically—as with children, one must be firm with animal companions in the early days of the acquaintance—and watched with alarm as Bruno sprinted toward her with distressing speed. Oh no, was he about to jump on her? She was not an unsturdy woman, but it would be most indecorous to be knocked to the ground on her first day of residence in the cottage. As Bruno rapidly approached, she stood her ground, pointed a finger, and commanded, "Heel." Bruno stopped dead in his tracks and did as directed.

Miss Prim reached into her handbag, pushed the Laser Taser 3000 aside, and found a few tissues with which to wipe the drool from Bruno's mouth. *A characteristic of the breed*, Phoebe had warned her. Well, Miss Prim had few worries about *that*. She had studied the classic psychological experiments in college and knew a thing or two about behavioral conditioning. If Pavlov could train his dogs to begin salivating at the sound of a bell, surely she could teach Bruno to *stop* drooling by using the same technique.

As Bruno explored the cottage, Miss Prim retrieved her to-do list, scratched out "adopt trusty animal companion" and added *purchase ringable hand bell.* As she was dotting the *i* in *ringable*, the telephone began jangling. When furnishing the cottage, she'd chosen the telephone with care, eschewing the modern plastic electro-boxes for a sturdy, working Ericsson telephone from the 1940s, much like the one that had dominated the desk in Papa's study. The phone's ringing stimulated a quite unexpected level of glee in Miss Prim. Here she was, in *her house*, on *her property*, about to answer *her phone*, in *her parlor*, and it was all just too wonderful for words.

"Hello, Rose Cottage," Miss Prim announced brightly into the receiver, expecting to hear the voice of Celia or Dolly on the other end of the line. But all she heard was dead air.

"Hello?" Miss Prim repeated tentatively, fearing that the connection was not quite as it should be and that a call to the phone company might be in order.

More silence, and then a gentle *click*.

He or she will call back, Miss Prim thought, hanging up the receiver and going in search of Bruno, who was eyeing her bed and the comforts it would undoubtedly provide. "Don't even *think* about it," she said, lightly, while Bruno pretended to have been scoping out the bedroom for burglars.

Several hours later, as Miss Prim napped on her overstuffed couch, Bruno had an opportunity to prove his mettle. The doorbell rang and Bruno leaped to his feet, barking a deep, menacing woof.

Peering out the window to the side of the cottage's front door, Miss Prim spied a moving van in the driveway and a young, burly moving man holding a clipboard. She opened the door, her hand on Bruno's collar. The Boxer continued to growl satisfyingly.

"Hey, I'm Josh," said the mover. Upon close inspection, he looked more like an extremely large 14-year-old boy than a full-grown man. "I got a bunch of boxes for a Miss Felicity Prom. Are you her?"

"Yes, I am Miss Felicity *Prim*," Miss Prim replied, enunciating the last syllable slightly as Josh thrust the clipboard at her. The manifest showed fourteen cartons of books, all shipped from her storage facility in Manhattan. "May I ask—would you mind bringing the boxes up to the attic for me? That would so incredibly helpful, and I will of course offer a gratuity for your services."

Always a planner, Miss Prim had thought this request through. Going through all the boxes would require several weeks, and at the end of the process many more books would end up stored in the attic than displayed on the main floor's built-in bookcases. Thus it seemed sensible to sort the books in the attic and then carry a few of them to the main floor, rather than sort all the books on the first floor and then carry the majority of them to the attic.

"No prob," Josh said, sticking two fingers into his mouth and whistling to capture the attention of the other movers, who all seemed completely absorbed in miniature electronic devices that kept their fingers (especially their thumbs) moving rapidly.

Miss Prim led the way into the attic, clearing a few cobwebs here and there. She hadn't spent much time in the attic yet; too many other tasks had taken precedence as she prepared the cottage for full-time occupancy. The movers galumphed up the stairs behind her, Bruno trailing at their heels to ensure their proper deportment.

"Right along that wall, if you would be so kind," Miss Prim directed. "And not stacked on top of one another, if you please. I would like to minimize the lifting," she added, with a smile.

"I don't blame ya, lady," said one of the movers. "These boxes weigh a ton. Hey, do you want me to move this stuff?"

Miss Prim swept her glance over a few boxes that the previous owner had left behind. She hadn't remembered seeing the boxes during her final walkthrough of the cottage with Olivia Abernathy a couple of months earlier, but no matter. Perhaps they contained materials about the cottage's history or other antiquarian delights.

"Would you mind moving them to the center of the room? Under the light bulb, please. That'll be convenient when I start looking through them."

"You got it," said the young man, and within ten minutes all the boxes had been deposited on her attic floor. After signing the manifest, Miss Prim slipped a $20 bill into Josh's hand. He reminded her of her beloved late brother, Noel, who'd died, far too young, of a disease whose name Miss Prim didn't like to say.

When Miss Prim was a girl, her mother had trained her in the proper methods of managing her time. First you do what you *have* to do, Mrs. Charity Prim had said, and then you do what you *want* to do. Now, fifty years later, Miss Prim *wanted* to look through those fourteen boxes of books that had been in storage for years, but first she *needed* to clear out the materials left behind by the cottage's former owner.

So, after baking a batch of cinnamon rolls, and then brewing a cup of tea and adding a packet of Mrs. Mallowan's Lemon Sugar to it, Miss Prim returned to the attic to begin sorting through the left-behind boxes.

If she had expected the boxes to contain fascinating bits of material culture from times gone by—and she *did* expect just that—she was sorely disappointed. Several boxes contained modern paperbacks and celebrity magazines instead of the old issues of *Look* and *Life* that she'd been hoping for. The paperbacks included installments of long-running mystery series. *Fabulous Fifty-Nine* and *Sensational Sixty-Five* focused on the exploits of an old woman who had been juggling two suitors for the better part of forty years, while *Here Comes a Chopper to Chop Off Your Head* and *She Cut Off Their Tails with a Carving Knife* featured a Washington, DC-based African-American detective who seemed to receive an inordinate amount of attention from serial killers. Flipping through the latter two books, each of which contained 300 pages divided into 500 chapters, she marveled at the modern reader's attention span, or lack thereof, before placing them in a "Donate to Library" pile.

Another box contained jars filled with assorted screws, nails, nuts, and bolts. The previous owner of Rose Cottage must have been a craftsman; the box also contained old tools, including a chisel encrusted with red paint, a ball-peen hammer, a hacksaw with a dull blade, and screwdrivers of the flathead and Phillips-head varieties. Miss Prim had limited experience with such hardware but decided to keep all of it, at least for the time being. One never knew when such items might come in handy.

As she returned the tools to the box, her hand brushed against something she had missed. She reached into the box and pulled out a wooden block in the shape of an eight-pointed star. She turned it over in her hands, wondering why its shape seemed so familiar. Then it hit her: An eight-pointed star was carved into the kitchen wall, just next to a built-in cupboard. She'd found the detail moderately interesting when she'd first visited the cottage, but it had not fully captured her imagination. So, while furnishing her new home, she'd covered up the star-shaped crevice with a clock that had belonged to her great-grandmother Prim.

She carried the star down the stairs and placed it on the kitchen table, then removed the clock from the wall, exposing the star's outline. She inserted the wood carving into the outline and took several steps backwards. Hmmm. There was something to be said for old-world craftsmanship, not to mention the return of the star to its intended location, but the star lacked aesthetic appeal. No, she liked her antique clock much better. She would keep the star, of course, and perhaps use it as a wall ornament somewhere—the history of Rose Cottage must be preserved—but the clock must return to its rightful place next to the cupboard.

She grabbed at the star, which seemed to have become wedged in the depression, with all five fingers of her right hand. In attempting to extricate the star, she lost her balance slightly. In doing so, she pitched forward a bit and applied much of her weight to the star.

She heard a click behind her. As she turned around to determine the source of the noise, she saw a panel of the kitchen wall spring open to reveal a staircase leading downward.

5

The Body in the Basement

This was a most unexpected development. A secret basement? For secret it surely had to be. Olivia Abernathy certainly had not been aware of it; had, in fact, deflected Miss Prim's question about basement space with a precision acquired by only the savviest of real-estate professionals. "No basement space, and thank God! That means no water problems, no mold, no hidden places for termites to set up shop!"

Miss Prim ran her hands along the walls of the staircase and found a light switch. She flipped it up, and a few weak light bulbs illuminated the space below. Dust motes glinted in the dirty light as a musty smell traveled up the stairs and into the kitchen.

Miss Prim did not closely study the staircase itself, and this error was to be the first hard lesson she learned in her new career. For if she'd examined the stairs, she would have noticed recent footprints on the dusty treads, and it might have occurred to her not to disturb them. But, excited about exploring the basement and not feeling the least trepidation about doing so (for this was Greenfield, population 1,400, with a crime rate close to zero), she slowly descended the stairs, holding onto the handrail to ensure a steady footing and partially obliterating key pieces of evidence.

Miss Prim hoped to find old furniture and other household implements (perhaps an ancient spinning wheel, perhaps a long-unused wheelbarrow that could be turned into an outdoor planter) and boxes of less-than-useful flotsam and jetsam, not unlike the contents of the cartons she'd found in the attic. What she did *not* hope to find was a body in the center of the floor.

Miss Prim moved quickly to the body, which was lying face down. The shape of the form seemed to be male, and when she turned the body over, she discovered that her suspicion was correct. She felt for a pulse, but she knew she would find none: The body was cold and stiff. The poor man's intense blue eyes stared at her, in shock and horror, as if the last thing he'd seen before dying had frightened him immensely. His mane of salt-and-pepper hair was wild and unkempt, his beard untrimmed. Dirt was caked under his fingernails. His denim jeans, flannel shirt, and work boots were those of an outdoorsman.

Was the person a tradesman who'd locked himself into the basement accidentally? While working, had he fallen and hit his head? No, these explanations were illogical, for surely the man's truck (or other means of transportation) would have been discovered in the driveway long before now. Olivia Abernathy, or some other real-estate person, would have found the basement door ajar during a house tour and gone downstairs to take a look, thus discovering the injured (or dead) man.

Miss Prim rose from her knees to get a better look at the corpse. She knew not to move it again, as the authorities would want to use tape to outline the body if they suspected foul play. She ran upstairs and retrieved a flashlight from the kitchen, then used it to shine a beam slowly down the length of the body. She caught her breath when the beam alit on the man's abdomen. A dark, crusty material had formed on the shirt. Miss Prim suspected this material was congealed blood.

She let out a small cry and fled up the stairs.

In English novels, police officers use the cup of tea for many purposes. That liquid panacea not only loosens tongues and stimulates cooperative behavior but also calms the nerves. Which, if she thought about it, was a bit counterintuitive, for doesn't tea contain caffeine, and isn't caffeine a stimulant, not a depressant? No matter; Miss Prim was not one to argue with four hundred years of British conventional wisdom. Right now she needed a soothing refreshment, so she put the teapot on while considering the almost fictional quality of her situation. She'd left (some might say *fled*) her home in Manhattan to begin a career in criminal outsmarting in Connecticut; and here, on her first day in her new home, she'd stumbled upon a dead body. In a novel, would readers accept such a coincidence? They might, or they might not. But that was fiction and this was *real life*.

Sipping her tea and trying to stop her hands from trembling, Miss Prim questioned her new career choice for the first time. It was one thing to read about clever murders and brilliant criminal masterminds, but quite another to encounter the victim of a horrible crime. The man lying on the basement floor was a son and grandchild to someone; he was also, most likely, a friend, husband, lover, uncle, colleague, neighbor. And he had such lovely blue eyes: the type of eyes that would look fondly at a child, provide a *frisson* of pleasure to a young lady, gaze indulgently at an elderly aunt or grandmother. Beneath that wild hair was a human being who'd lived and breathed, a man with interests and ruling passions. *Anyone who knew him wouldn't have been intimidated by all that hair*, Miss Prim thought. In the 1970s she'd had a suitor with feral hair and an untamed beard; he'd been a pacifist, a poet, a lover of nature and animals. *Yes*, Miss Prim thought, *such hair is the sign of a free spirit, a kind heart. It is the short-haired, buzz-cut Wall Street types of whom we must be cautious.*

Miss Prim had known that, sooner or later, she would encounter Death in her career as criminal outsmarter, but she hadn't expected to make his acquaintance quite so soon. No, she'd expected that early cases would focus on more mundane matters. Perhaps she'd help a neighbor locate a missing niece, or help the friend of a friend determine who had stolen her prize-winning pumpkin pie recipe. After successfully disposing of those cases, she would have moved up to things like petty theft and perhaps even a robbery or two.

But murder? No, it was much too soon for murder.

Miss Felicity Prim took stock of her situation. Everything she'd planned for her new home—its coziness, its comfort, its safety—had vanished the moment she'd found the man in her basement. A murderer had found his way into her house once. What would stop him from doing so again? The next time, would he slit her throat while she lay sleeping?

Bruno nuzzled supportively against her leg as she lifted the phone receiver and called information to request the phone number of the Greenfield Police.

"Hello," she said, slowly and calmly, when someone at the Greenfield police station answered the phone. "This is Miss Felicity Prim of Rose Cottage. I would like to report a murder." Then, feeling very much a fool, she burst into tears.

6

A Handsome Detective

Miss Prim was waiting at her parlor window when the cars drove up. She had told the police there was no need to send an ambulance—the poor man was quite dead—but they sent one anyway, its bubble screaming as it drove along her quiet street.

So here she was, quiet and retiring Miss Prim, at the center of exactly the type of drama she'd spent her entire life avoiding. She doubted that the day's events would endear her to her neighbors, whom she hadn't met yet, or to the wealthy people who lived in the large homes on the ridge above Undercliff Lane.

The door chime pealed, and Bruno, sensing an onslaught of people from whom he would have to protect Miss Prim, barked menacingly. "Really, Bruno, you can be *quite* convincing," she said, patting his head reassuringly. "No one would say you are not earning your kibble, so stand down, please." Bruno's tail wagged furiously, and he obliged Miss Prim's request by taking his growls down a few notches.

Waiting on the other side of the door was a handsome police officer, a man Mrs. Charity Prim would have called a "tall drink of water," to the delight and scandal of her better-behaved friends. Taking him in with a long sweeping glance from his head to his feet, Miss Prim decided she heartily approved of his physical being, from his salt-and-pepper crew cut, to his large brown eyes, to his strong nose and lips, to his cleft chin and prominent jawline, to his admirably fit physique, to his shoes, which were nicely polished and maintained. One sideburn was slightly longer than the other, and she noticed that his fingernails could have used a good shaping. But all that was to the good; if there was one thing Miss Prim did not like, it was a persnickety male. Besides, the imperfections only made the man more intriguing. "Delight in disorder," Robert Herrick would have said.

"Miss Felicity Prim?" the man asked. When Miss Prim nodded yes, the large man extended his hand. "I'm Detective Ezra Dawes." He stepped aside to introduce the two officers standing behind him. Pointing to a chubby but not very jolly-looking man who was peering into the shrubbery, Dawes said, "That's Officer Martin Reed, and this"—pointing to a woman who was no taller than 4'6" and no heavier than 90 pounds—"is Officer Rebecca Fremlin."

"Hi," said Officer Fremlin in a surprisingly gruff, two-pack-a-day voice. "Not exactly the welcome wagon you were expecting, I bet. I mean, you just get here and bam! There's a dead guy in your house. I hope you didn't kill him, we don't go for that in Greenfield. And don't bother with the Rebecca thing. Call me Spike. Everyone else does. I don't have the time to tell you why right now, but if you really want to know, then stop by Maude's sometime when I'm off duty and —"

"Spike," Detective Dawes interrupted, "maybe you can offer local color and your life story later."

Spike looked at Miss Prim and rolled her eyes heavenward, as if to say "What a bore he is." Miss Prim liked her instantly.

"In the basement, right?" Fremlin asked.

"Yes," Miss Prim responded. "Just go through the parlor and into the kitchen …"

"Hey, no offense, Miss Trimm, but it's hardly a mansion. I'm sure we can find the basement. Come on, Reed. And yes, I smell the cinnamon rolls too, but it would be rude to ask her for one, so don't." Fremlin made eye contact with Miss Prim again, this time giving her a "Men-they're-so-predictable-and-all-the-same" look.

"You'll have to forgive Officer Fremlin," Detective Dawes said. The words tripped off his tongue easily, signaling Miss Prim that he'd made the same request many, many times in the past. "She's forthright, perhaps to a fault."

"Well, there is certainly something to be said for getting straight to the point," Miss Prim replied. She'd spent enough years observing human behavior in Doctor Poe's office to understand the psychology that drives a person as petite as Rebecca "Spike" Fremlin.

"I need to ask you a few questions, Miss Prim. You won't mind, I hope."

Now this is rather dangerous, Miss Prim thought. She'd always had a soft spot for men with lovely manners; and when the men looked like Detective Ezra Dawes, the size of that soft spot tripled or, in this case, quadrupled. This was one of her hidden secrets: She was far from impervious to the charms of a dashing man, as long as she found the man sincere and authentic. As for charmers, schmoozers, and snake-oil salesmen: She could smell them coming from a mile away, and she treated them accordingly. The pharmaceutical salesmen who tried to get past her to Doctor Poe could attest to *that*.

"Of course, Detective Dawes. Would you like a cup of tea? And a cinnamon roll, of course."

"That would be great, Miss Prim. I just want to go downstairs and look around a bit before the techs do their work."

Thirty minutes later, sitting at Miss Prim's small dining room table with a gooey cinnamon roll and strong black tea in front of him—how alarmingly, and attractively, large he looked sitting there!—Detective Dawes took out a notebook and began his questioning.

"Would you go over exactly how you found the body, Miss Prim? Tell me everything, step by step."

So Miss Prim repeated the story she'd told him hastily on the phone: how she'd been rummaging in the attic, how she'd found the wooden star, how she'd sprung the hidden door.

Dawes scribbled in his notebook. "Other than turning the body over, you didn't move it?"

"That's correct. I wanted to see if he was still alive. When I realized he wasn't, I thought I shouldn't contaminate the crime scene."

"Why do you think it's a crime scene?"

"Because the hidden door was closed tight and the light switch was turned off. If he'd gone down there himself, I'd have found the door open and the light bulb on. There's no source of natural light in the basement, so it would have been too dark down there to do anything if he *hadn't* turned on the light. He was nowhere near the staircase, so he couldn't have fallen down the staircase and died. And the wound with the blood … and the expression on the poor man's face … it all seemed to suggest that a crime had been committed, here or elsewhere. But I am assuming elsewhere."

Dawes looked at Miss Prim with curiosity. Miss Prim couldn't quite read his expression. Did it say, "This one's got what it takes to be a criminal outsmarter"? Or did it imply "Great, another one who watches too much TV and fancies herself a forensics specialist"?

"And how did you come to the conclusion that the man died elsewhere, Miss Prim?"

"I ran up the stairs and called you as soon as I realized the man was dead, but while waiting for you, I went back into the basement and looked around with my flashlight. Don't worry, I didn't touch anything I hadn't already touched. But I didn't see a trail of blood. It made me think he might have been killed somewhere else and then dropped in my basement."

"You said earlier you just moved into the house today?"

"I bought the house several months ago, but I've been busy having it painted, repaired, and furnished. I've been here for an occasional day or afternoon since I bought Rose Cottage, but this will be the first night I've spent in Greenfield. Before today, I've always gone back to New York at the end of the day."

"Were you here every time something was delivered, or when work was done on the place?"

"No. In fact, most of the time, I wasn't. I used a local realtor, Olivia Abernathy"—Dawes nodded in recognition—"and she was happy to help with all the arrangements."

"For a fee, of course," Dawes said, knowingly.

Miss Prim nodded. Perhaps Olivia had nickeled and dimed her more than was strictly necessary, but real-estate agents had fallen on tough times during the recent economic woes, and everyone was entitled to make a living. Besides,

Olivia's efforts had saved Miss Prim a great deal of time and effort (if not money), and for that she was grateful.

"So, you don't know who Olivia gave keys to?"

"No, I don't. She assured me that everyone she hired was local and trustworthy. I left detailed instructions regarding what I wanted done and where I wanted the furniture placed, and each time I showed up, everything had been done exactly as I asked."

Dawes scribbled another note. "I'll talk with Olivia and get a list of everyone who's been in the house. After the M.E. examines the body, I may need you to account for your whereabouts over a particular period of time. I don't mean to make your day more stressful, but it's standard procedure, so we should get it out of the way."

"I understand, Detective Dawes," Miss Prim said. "Also, if you need to take my fingerprints, I assure you I shall cooperate."

Dawes threw another inscrutable glance at her.

"Your fingerprints?"

"I assume you will dust the house for prints, and of course you'll need to eliminate mine from consideration. To do that, you need to have a set of them, yes?"

"I must say, Miss Prim, you certainly seem well schooled in these matters. Patricia Cornwell? John Grisham? Michael Connelly?"

"Life, Detective Dawes. Life." *And* Cornwell, Grisham, and Connelly; but far be it from Miss Prim to allow a good-looking man to score quite so many points during a first meeting.

"Last question, and then I'll ask you to come to the station to sign a statement. Do you have any idea who the man might be?"

"None whatsoever. I've never seen him before. I had considered looking through his pockets to see if he had any identification, but I reconsidered. I figured you would do that soon enough."

"That was the right decision, Miss Prim. Has anyone ever told you you'd make a good detective?"

Miss Prim positively beamed.

A moment later, Officers Reed and Fremlin entered the dining room.

"It's all taped off, Boss," Reed said to Dawes.

"Yeah, it's good to go," said Fremlin. "We'll wait here for the M.E. if you want to go back to the station, Ezra. Hey, Miss Limm, I gotta tell you, there sure is a lot of dust down there. I felt like I was gonna get black lung. Listen, it's your house, do what you want, but I'm just saying."

"I do plan on undertaking a thorough cleaning once you are all done here, of course," Miss Prim replied.

"This place is real cute," Fremlin said, surveying her surroundings. "Is it campy on purpose? I mean, come on with the frills. Is that real lace? People still make that stuff? And doilies? What are you, like a hundred or something?"

"Spike," Dawes interrupted, "I think we should have a more *professional* look around, with Miss Prim's approval of course." He glanced at Miss Prim.

"Yes, of course," Miss Prim said. "I'll keep Bruno with me."

While the detective and the two officers nosed around, Miss Prim sat, patiently sipping her tea, thinking about Spike Fremlin's lace and doilies comments. She had always found such furnishings delicate and refined. Were her tastes old-fashioned, outmoded? No, not at all, she decided. A country cottage must have lace and doilies to have credibility. Everyone knows *that.*

"Miss Prim, is there an attic?" Dawes asked. "We should have a look up there, too."

Miss Prim rose and led them to the narrow attic staircase. After they climbed the stairs, she pointed to the boxes that the moving men had placed against the walls. "Those are all boxes of books that just arrived earlier today, so they wouldn't have anything of interest in them. These boxes"—she nudged one of them with her shoe—"were in the attic when I got here. At first I thought the previous owner left them behind, but I don't think that's right, because I don't remember seeing them when I did the final walkthrough with Olivia. So it's a bit of a mystery how they got here. I found the wooden star in this box."

Dawes got down on his knees, snapped on a pair of rubber gloves. As he rummaged through the boxes, Reed and Fremlin wandered around the attic. "More dust," Fremlin muttered. "Someone told me dust is made up of dead bodies. Hey Reed, you think that could be true? That would be freaky, eh? Dead people all over our houses and we don't even know it …"

Dawes held up the chisel that Miss Prim had discovered earlier. He examined it closely. "Oh boy. I think we may have found the murder weapon."

7

Cooperating with the Police

Returning to Rose Cottage after being fingerprinted and signing her statement, Miss Prim unlocked her front door with trepidation, wondering what might await her on the other side. She heard Bruno barking, and that was comforting; it was good to know that her faithful companion of less than 24 hours avidly defended the homestead while she absent, not just when she was present.

Before taking her jacket off, she placed a call to the locksmith, asking him to come over as soon as possible. Two hours later, as the crime scene investigators finished dusting the cottage for prints, the locksmith arrived to replace all the door locks and install locks on all the windows.

It had been thoroughly disconcerting day, and Miss Prim felt quite exhausted and emotionally drained. Still, in keeping with Mama's dictates that one must remain active in managing one's life, she'd formulated a decisive plan of action that she would begin implementing after a good night's sleep. She'd asked Detective Dawes to give her a photo of the murdered man. Spike, who'd been present at the time, had told her she was a ghoul for requesting such a thing. Miss Prim had replied, "Not at all, Officer Fremlin. I shall be meeting many of my neighbors and other townspeople in the coming days, and I thought I might take the opportunity to help you discover the victim's identity. Of course, if anyone recognizes him, I shall ask him or her to contact you immediately."

"I'm not sure about that, Miss Prim," Dawes had responded haltingly. "It's not exactly established procedure …"

"Oh, let her do it, Ez," Spike had ordered. "Creepy McGee took plenty of pics, I'm sure he can find one that isn't too gruesome. The stiff's face is gonna be all over the papers soon enough anyway. Besides, we're gonna need all the help we can get. In case you haven't noticed, we're not exactly overstaffed at the Greenfield PD."

Recognizing the truth in Spike's words, or just unwilling to remain on the receiving end of her harangue, Dawes had used the station's color printer to print a not-very-good copy of one of Creepy McGee's photos. It wasn't much, Miss Prim thought, but it was a start.

After preparing a bowl of kibble for Bruno, Miss Prim kicked off her shoes and lay on the couch, trying to decide how to spend the rest of her evening. As her mind shuffled through the possibilities, the telephone rang. Hoping to hear a friendly voice on the other end of the line, she lifted the receiver.

"Good evening, Rose Cottage."

"Miss Prim? Is that you?"

"Oh, Dolly! How lovely to hear from you! I have just sat down after a somewhat wearying day."

"Do you have time to talk, Miss Prim? You must be busy getting the house ready."

"I always have time for you, Dolly."

"I said to myself, don't bother Miss Prim. Give her some time to enjoy her new house before you start harassing her. But I couldn't help myself. The office is in a complete uproar. The patients just won't accept that you're gone. And poor Doctor Poe, he's so distracted. Norah is trying to be his right-hand woman, but she's being sort of unctuous about it, if you know what I mean. I'm afraid Doctor P doesn't see through it, the way the rest of us do. Already she's talking about computerizing everything, as if computers can solve all of the world's problems."

This was exactly the sort of gossipy conversation Miss Prim needed after a tough day. As Dolly recounted tales from the office grapevine, Miss Prim struggled with the question of whether to regale Dolly with a retelling of the day's events. Her first inclination was *not* to mention finding the dead body in the basement or its aftermath. Both Dolly and Doctor Poe had expressed concerns regarding her new career, and she did not want them to worry. But Miss Prim had made a vow, months earlier, that she would not behave in the stupid manner of so many fictional heroines—those supposedly intelligent women who nonetheless ventured into dangerous neighborhoods alone at night, or followed an armed suspect into a crack house, or found ridiculous excuses to avoid sharing the details of their lives with friends and family. Miss Prim reasoned thus: If you don't share the events of your life, your secrets, your dreams, and your passions with your friends—then they are not your friends at all, and you are nothing more than a character who exists to service a plot. And she was not about to let anyone level that accusation against *her*.

So, amidst Dolly's gasps of shock and disbelief, Miss Prim related the entire story, downplaying the effects of the day's events on her psyche. For she *was* shaken, mostly because she hadn't counted on the emotional after-effects of stumbling onto a real-life crime. Perhaps, up to this point, her mostly optimistic brain had not paid enough attention to the challenges that beset protagonists who undertake careers in criminal outsmarting: alcoholism, broken marriages, estranged children, drug addictions, sexually indiscriminate behavior, lone-wolf syndrome … the list went on and on. These trends in the personal lives of criminal outsmarters did not necessarily mean *she* would succumb to such weaknesses of character. But Miss Prim could sense, after only one day and only one crime, that her new career might carve deep, and not altogether desirable, impressions on her perceptions and belief system. She would have to guard herself against fearfulness, cynicism, paranoia, and a host of other unpleasant possibilities.

"Oh, Miss Prim!" Dolly exclaimed after Miss Prim completed her narrative. "You have to come back to the City tonight. I can't stand the thought of you being there all alone."

Miss Prim did not relish the idea either, but one must get on with it, mustn't one? And perhaps in reassuring Dolly of her safety, she could reassure herself, too. "Now, dearest, there really is nothing to worry about. This murder has nothing to do with me. In fact, the detective in charge of the case agrees with me on that. It would have been obvious to the murderer that Rose Cottage was not occupied and had not been occupied for quite a while. No cars in the driveway, no window treatments on the windows, no lights on at night. The cottage was an ideal place to hide the victim until the body could be disposed of. Now, let's talk no more of this. I want to hear about you. How are things going with Benjamin?"

Benjamin Bannister was a young patient of Doctor Poe's. A quiet graduate student studying magical realism at Columbia University, he'd been suffering from migraine headaches. In the manner of inward-looking graduate students, he had mistakenly self-diagnosed these as the manifestations of a brain tumor. He and Dolly—who, at the statuesque height of 6'2", found the Manhattan dating scene more challenging than most young women—had begun meeting for coffee, then for lunch, and just, in recent weeks, dinner.

"I'm glad you brought him up, Miss Prim. I need your advice. I just don't understand how relationships work and what I'm supposed to do and not do. Or say and not say. We have such a nice time when we're together, but everything is left so … *unstated.* Zoroastria said I should be more forward, invite him to a movie or a concert, cook him a nice meal. So I suggested a play and he seemed … hesitant. I backpedaled immediately, and then it got a little awkward. The next day I stopped at a deli and bought him a little bamboo plant as a peace offering. The doorman called his apartment, but Benjamin wasn't there, so I scribbled a note and left the plant at the front desk. Then I went into the Barnes & Noble across the street, and when I came out I saw Benjamin leaving his building! He was there the whole time, which meant he didn't want to see me. I felt so awful, but when I got home there was a message waiting for me, thanking me for the plant, and he sounded really grateful and sweet. I just don't know what it all means. Or doesn't mean."

How many times over the decades Miss Prim had engaged in variations on this conversation with friends, cousins, siblings, colleagues! Despite technological progress and the advances made by civil society, men and women still had not learned to communicate with each other.

"Dolly, the course of true love never did run smooth, to quote my dear Mama. Magical realism is a difficult taskmaster, and it may be that Benjamin was too engrossed in his studies to hear the doorman's buzzing on the intercom. Or he might have stepped out to the laundry room, or the garbage shoot, when the doorman attempted to make contact. Simply act as if nothing has happened and let nature take its course. Do not overthink; doing so amounts to self-torture."

Dolly sighed. "Miss Prim, you always know the right thing to say."

"Well, not always, dearest, but sometimes. It's one of the benefits of getting older. But Dolly, may I ask a favor? Would you not share my adventures here in Greenfield with Doctor Poe or our friends at the office just yet? The doctor has so much on his mind right now, and I don't wish to add to his worries."

Dolly promised to take Miss Prim's secret to the grave—perhaps not the best metaphor given the circumstances—and the two friends decided that they'd soon find time to meet, whether in Manhattan or Greenfield.

After making sure the cottage's doors were locked, Miss Prim removed the Laser Taser 3000 from her handbag, placed it on her nightstand, climbed into bed, and turned off the light. Five minutes later, her telephone chimed. She climbed out of bed and went to the parlor to answer the ring.

"Rose Cottage," she said, tiredly.

The only response was a quiet *click* as the caller disconnected.

8

Enter the Sidekick

If fiction reflected reality to any significant extent, Miss Prim thought, the media would be hovering at her door, drooling like vultures, early the next morning. Situations like hers were tailor-made for cub reporters who have grown weary of reporting on the activities of the women's club and school board. A mutually beneficial alliance might be forged with these journalists, provided they were not of the sleazy, stab-anyone-and-everyone-in-the-back-for-a-good-story category. Thus Miss Prim looked forward to greeting the pulsing throngs of the Fourth Estate.

But as the morning wore on, she had no visitors, and she grew weary of waiting for them. They would find her soon enough, she thought, so she brewed and sipped a cup of tea as she prepared to leave the cottage to engage in that most pedestrian of activities: grocery shopping.

The doorbell pealed. *It begins!* Miss Prim thought, straightening her skirt and checking her fashionably styled silver-white hair in the hallway mirror.

She opened the front door to find a tall, frail woman a decade or so older than herself. The woman's arms were wrapped around a heavy paper sack overflowing with crackers, dried sausages, and sprigs of fresh herbs.

The woman's appearance was altogether extraordinary, Miss Prim thought. She wore purple striped jeans and a yellow blouse with magenta polka dots. The blouse was dotted with pins featuring the logos of heavy-metal bands: Motorhead, Pantera, AC/DC, Grim Reaper, Apocalyptica, Ethel the Frog, Anthrax. Most surprising was the woman's thick, waist-length black hair. A wig?

"Good morning," Miss Prim said pleasantly.

"Well helllooooooo! You must be Felicity Prim. I'm Lorraine Koslowski, your next-door neighbor. Well, actually, your over-your-head neighbor. I'm in that white elephant on top of the ridge behind your house." She moved her head to indicate the white elephant's general direction. "I heard what happened here yesterday. It must have been awful! Is that tea? I'd love a cup, even though I prefer coffee." Lorraine Koslowski scanned the parlor and dining room. "I see you're going for the twee look. How adorable. My own tastes are more eclectic, perhaps a bit more contemporary, but to each her own."

Lorraine thrust the paper sack into Miss Prim's arms. "Here are some goodies for us to nosh on. Why don't I brew myself a cuppa while you slice the cheese?" With that, Lorraine swept into the cottage and made straight for the teapot.

Miss Prim, familiar with all the tropes, had expected to encounter different neighbor-types as she made the rounds: the nosy neighbor (who might have seen something important without realizing it), the wacky neighbor (who might be prone to unexpected flashes of insight), the uptight neighbor (who would closely monitor property lines and the length of grass blades), the reclusive neighbor (who would reveal him/herself only toward the end of an adventure to provide a vital clue). In Lorraine Koslowski, Miss Prim saw a character who might fit into the nosy and wacky categories simultaneously.

And her name—Lorraine! This was not a name associated with church guilds and garden parties. Every Lorraine of Miss Prim's acquaintance had been quite unconventional, even wild. While the mothers of Miss Prim's friends had strongly discouraged friendships with Lorraines, Mrs. Charity Prim had allowed, even encouraged, these friendships, arguing that such girls were on the vanguard of modern thinking. So to have discovered a Lorraine on her second day in Greenfield—well, this was a delicious treat to be savored and thankful for.

Miss Prim unpacked Poundstone's water crackers, Akbar's Turkish delight, a ring of dried figs, a bag of brightly colored Jordan almonds, a small box of red pistachios, and several cans of dog food from the grocery sack while Bruno sat beside her and drooled.

"How kind of you, Miss Koslowski, to bring so many treats! With the events of the past day or so, my plans to stock the larder have quite gone awry."

"Miss Koslowski? Please, I'm pushing seventy. I haven't been a Miss for fifty years! Not that 'Mrs.' is any better. 'Mrs. Koslowski.' Makes me sound like a high-school gym teacher. As for 'Ms. Koslowski' … well, that would be misleading, don't you think? I'm married, for better or for worse, and disguising it wasn't part of the vows. Anyway, let's dispense with the formalities. Call me Lorraine and I'll call you Felicity."

Mrs. Charity Prim had always said, "When in Rome, do as the Romans do." Having trained in cultural geography, Mama had been an unrelenting advocate of fitting into a new culture rather than attempting to wrestle it to the ground and impose new and unwelcome rules upon it. Greenfield was Lorraine Koslowski's turf, Mrs. Charity Prim would have said; and when on new turf, one plays by the natives' rules.

Miss Prim smiled broadly. "I would like that, Lorraine. It seems natural, as I suspect we may be kindred spirits."

Lorraine looked at Miss Prim skeptically. "Kindred spirits? I'm thinking more yin and yang, or opposites attracting. I mean, look at us. There you are, all well-coiffed and permanent-pressed at this time of the morning. And here's me, my usual slobbo self, busting through your door the day after you find a dead man in your basement. My husband's always telling me I lack manners, but I don't, you know. It's more that I have a childlike enthusiasm for life that sometimes makes me act before I think."

"My mother always taught me," Miss Prim replied, "that the purpose of manners is not to divide people, or to create a hierarchy separating those who know the correct fork to use from those who don't, but rather to make everyone comfortable. And I must say, you have made me feel not only comfortable, but also welcome, in the space of just five minutes. So, while your methods are not necessarily my own, I already appreciate them."

Lorraine looked at Miss Prim with a mixture of respect and disbelief. "Who even talks like you any more? No one, I think. And it's damned nice. I have a feeling we're going to become the best of friends. Who does your hair? I like the color. Dyed or the real thing?"

"It's my own color. I began going silver in my twenties. Rather than hiding it, I decided to embrace it."

"How do you like mine? I'm going for a Crystal Gayle-meets-Morticia Addams-and-Cher look. Crystal has that country sweetness and purity, while Morticia and Cher are all sex. Both sides of womanhood, you know? Lucian—that's my husband—doesn't like it. He wants women to look like they did during Hollywood's Golden Age, with those short, slick hairdos that the film stars wore. *So* not me, at least not right now. That might change, though. I like to mix it up."

"It is most distinctive, Lorraine. I don't know you well yet, but I would think people say, 'That hairstyle is distinctively Lorraine Koslowski.' The young businesspeople seem to talk about *branding* a great deal. I suspect you have managed to create your own brand quite successfully."

"Felicity, you're either extremely perceptive or 100 percent full of beans, but I'm putting my money on *extremely perceptive*. Say, hand over a few of those water crackers, would you? I don't really love them, but when I caught a glimpse of you yesterday, I said to myself, 'She's the water cracker type.' Looks like I was right! Would I also be right in thinking you like madeleines and shortbread but find petit-fours and éclairs somewhat scandalous?"

So accurate was Lorraine's assessment of Miss Prim's taste in cookies and pastries that Miss Prim was momentarily lost for words. As she regained her *sang froid*, it struck her that Lorraine Koslowski might fall into yet a third category of neighbor: the wise, somewhat older woman who serves as both sidekick and foil.

"Quite a handsome Boxer you've got there, Felicity. Come, boy." Lorraine gave the command with a quiet authority, and Bruno did as ordered, his stubby tail wagging bashfully as he submitted to Lorraine's rough affections, which took the form of rubbing his neck and scratching his rump.

"I must ask, Lorraine—You seem very well informed about what's happened here. How did you manage to gather so much information so quickly? I'm at a point in my career, and in my life, where the ability to gather intelligence rapidly will be a valuable asset."

"No secrets in Greenfield, Felicity. Olivia Abernathy was flapping her gums about selling the Saxe-Coburgs' house to this proper New York City lady. I knew about Bruno because I heard him barking, and my own dogs are quite frantic with the anticipation of meeting him. They're big, too, and they like a lot of exercise, but Lucian and I can't run around with them the way we used to, so they're waiting expectantly, I think, to come down here for a romp. I help out at the animal shelter, and yesterday Phoebe told me that some new woman had adopted Bruno, so it was easy enough to put two and two together. As for what happened in your basement, Spike Fremlin came to my house an hour ago to show me a photo of the dead man and to ask if I recognized him. It's not difficult to get information out of Spike. Just let her talk long enough and sooner or later she'll tell you what you want to know, whether you ask her or not. So here I am."

Miss Prim was impressed by Lorraine's connectedness in town, and an idea occurred to her. "Lorraine, I need to run a few errands and make a few inquiries. If you are free, I would love some company. Strictly between you and me, I am helping the police with their inquiry, and I would be most grateful for the assistance of someone who knows the town so well."

"'Helping the police with their inquiry'? Is that shorthand for 'I've got my sights set on Ezra Dawes'? Now, don't blush, Felicity. The man is positively dreamy and everyone knows it. Except Ezra himself, which is exactly what makes him so dreamy. I've been known to make a match or two in my time … and I'm damned good at it, if I do say so myself. Should

I start laying the groundwork for you two? Just say the word. It's about time he found a good woman. His wife died about ten years ago and he hasn't looked at anybody since."

"Oh no, Lorraine. Please no. You see, I am embroiled in the beginning of something in New York. Or maybe I am in the middle of it. I don't quite know yet. My suitor and I have just begun a six-month process of trying to figure it all out."

"All right, Felicity. I'll behave, but don't wait too long to make a decision. We're not getting any younger, you know, and we all need love and passion, no matter how old we get."

"Agreed, Lorraine. Now, let me get my handbag, and I'll give you the details about me and Doctor Poe as we make our rounds. I suspect your insights will be most … unique."

9
Making the Rounds

As Miss Prim, Lorraine, and Bruno strolled along Greenfield's well-kept streets on their short walk to the village green, Miss Prim said, "Lorraine, were you and Lucian friendly with the people who owned Rose Cottage before I bought it? I'd love to know more about the house's history."

"Lucian and I have lived at Ridgemont—that's the name of our house—since the late 1950s. We watched your house being built between our trips to Europe and Asia. That was in the late 70s, I want to say '77 or '78. Honestly, none of the people on the ridge were too happy about the houses going in below us, but we had no power to stop it. 'Progress,' they called it. Ha! Maybe if you're a developer or a realtor. Anyway, Ralph Saxe-Coburg was a doctor with a practice in New York, I think Poughkeepsie or Beacon. He and his wife, Elizabeth, were looking for a weekend country retreat, so they bought the property and built your house. Lucian and I made a few overtures of neighborliness, but the Saxe-Coburgs were private people and they weren't interested. Even when the two of them retired here, things never progressed beyond our waving hello to them and them waving back. Over the years they got more and more cranky. My dogs get out once in a while—I should warn you about that now—but it's only because they like to visit other dogs and people. I mean, it's not like they're drooling and rabid in the town square like that dog in *To Kill a Mockingbird*. Most people just call me up and say, 'Albert's here, come get him when you get a minute,' or 'Henry's paying us a visit—I'm going to give him something to eat and send him home.' But not Elizabeth Saxe-Coburg. No, she preferred to call the police or the animal shelter. It's how Lucian and I became so well acquainted with Ezra, Martin, and Spike. And it's how I started volunteering at the shelter, too. Phoebe said to me, 'You spend so much time here, you might as well *do* something,' and I couldn't argue with that."

"Did the Saxe-Coburgs have children?"

"If they did, they hid them really well. Lucian and I used to joke they were like a couple out of an Edward Gorey cartoon. You know, the type who lock their children in the attic and feed them kidney beans and gruel. But seriously, no kids."

Miss Prim shuddered. To think that her little attic—soon to be transformed into a small but magnificent library—might have been home to such horrors for the nonexistent Saxe-Coburg children!

"Am I right to assume the Saxe-Coburgs are no longer with us?" Miss Prim asked.

"Ralph kicked the bucket four, maybe five, years ago. Nobody even knew for a week, which is pretty remarkable given how fast news spreads in this town. But that was Elizabeth for you, everything was a big secret. She stayed in your house as long as she could, but the big A—Alzheimer's—kicked in, and she couldn't take care of herself any longer. I think one of their nephews is her conservator. He shipped Elizabeth off to a nursing home somewhere around here and put the house on the market. And here you are."

"So you never visited the cottage before today?"

Lorraine nodded. "Can you believe it? Took me more than forty years to penetrate the house's defenses. But it was worth the wait. I know you for only fifteen minutes and I can tell, you're quite a pip." With that, she affectionately linked her arm through Miss Prim's.

"You may be interested to know, Lorraine, that the house does have some secrets. I've already discovered one of them." Miss Prim recounted the tale of finding the wooden star in the attic, unintentionally triggering the secret door in the kitchen, and discovering the body.

"How positively Gothic!" Lorraine exclaimed. "I knew about the body, of course, but I hadn't heard these details. I have visions of catacombs down there as well, and perhaps treasure chests filled with gold doubloons or the Crown Jewels of the Netherlands."

"None of that, sadly," Miss Prim admitted. "Just some old junk and that poor man's body. The police spent several hours collecting evidence and examining the scene, but they didn't uncover any catacombs. I think their main focus is learning the victim's identity, so that they can notify his next of kin." Miss Prim believed this to be the correct ordering of priorities, for, at the end of the day, isn't consideration for human life the mark of a civilized society? Bringing the perpetrator to justice (eventually) was essential, of course, but respecting the murdered man's memory was more important in the big scheme of things.

"I'm sure we'll know who he is soon enough," Lorraine replied. "They'll run everything through those databases of theirs. If they can't find a match in Connecticut, they'll move on to the FBI or the CIA."

Miss Prim huffed. "Lorraine, words cannot express how weary I have become of the modern belief that computers can conduct our criminal investigations for us. Yes, I know the world is now a connected place thanks to these great networks about which one reads in the magazines, but do we really need to search through Interpol's records to discover the identity of a man who was killed in our own town? No. Local murders have local victims, local perpetrators, and local motivations. We must begin with the local, not with the state, nor the national, nor the international."

"If you say so, Felicity. And speaking of local, if that's what you're looking for, here's a good place to start."

They had stopped in front of an ivy-covered red-brick building. A sign in the shape of a potbelly stove dangled over the front door: MAUDE'S TAVERN.

Yes, Miss Prim thought, tying Bruno's leash to a bicycle rack. *This looks like an excellent place to begin.*

Maude's Tavern was everything one could ask for in a local bar/eatery. Lorraine and Miss Prim entered a cozily decorated front room with two dozen or so tables and banquettes. Each table was covered with a red-checkered tablecloth and decorated with a Snapple bottle overflowing with fresh-cut flowers. A fireplace along one of the walls would provide a pleasant background crackling, as well as far too much heat, in the winter months. Bookshelves around the room held a large assortment of books that patrons could borrow, trade, or simply take any time the mood struck.

At the rear of the tavern was a well-stocked bar. Lorraine elbowed her way through the crowd—it was nearing lunch-time—and approached the bar as Miss Prim followed close behind.

A yellow-haired older man sat at the bar, sipping a pint of Guinness and glancing occasionally at the television mounted to the ceiling. Lorraine poked him. "Jedediah Mason, can't you see two ladies need a seat? Be a gentleman and take your fat buttocks elsewhere."

Jedediah Mason turned slowly, revealing a wonderfully craggy face.

"Sweet Mother of Mercy, Lorraine, can't a man sit back and enjoy a pint? If I wanted harassment from women, I'd have stayed at home." But, despite his protests, Jedediah rose and offered his seat to Lorraine. Miss Prim couldn't help but be amused. Contrary to Lorraine's description, Mr. Mason's buttocks were nonexistent, not fat.

"It's not for me, it's for my friend here." Lorraine pointed to Miss Prim. "This is Miss Prim. She's new in town."

Jedediah turned to face Miss Prim. "Welcome, Miss Prim," he said. "Jedediah Mason, Mason."

"Lovely to meet you, Mr. Mason-Mason. I didn't mean to conscript your seat …"

"Just one Mason, Miss. It's my last name and my profession. Here's my card. Feel free to call me if you need any work done." He looked at Lorraine skeptically. "And steer clear of this she-devil. She'll get you into scrapes you don't rightly want to get yourself into."

"Off with you, Jedediah," Lorraine commanded. "Or perhaps I'll have to let Juanita know you're enjoying a pint at an inappropriate time of day."

"Oh, for the Good Lord's sake, Lorraine …"

"Mr. Mason, before you go," Miss Prim said, "would you mind taking a look at a photo? We're trying to discover a man's identity, and I'm asking around to see if anyone recognizes him."

Jedediah took the photo from Miss Prim's hands. "This the guy you found in your basement?"

"Yes, actually. Does he look familiar?"

Jedediah squinted at the photo. "Can't say that he does. I'd check with Maude. If anyone knows who he is, it'll be Maude." Jedediah Mason drained his pint and took his leave.

Miss Prim settled onto her bar stool while Lorraine bullied another man into giving her his seat. Lorraine raised two fingers to call the bartender, a short, barrel-chested man with a great deal of hair on his arms but none on his head. The bartender ambled over, neither smiling nor unsmiling.

"Maude, meet my friend, Miss Felicity Prim. She's new here, so I know you'll make her feel welcome."

"Hi," Maude said.

In her nearly six decades on the planet, Miss Prim had never met a man named Maude. She smiled cordially and complimented him on the tavern's atmosphere.

"Thanks," Maude said.

"Now, Maude, Miss Prim is trying to find someone. Or rather, she's trying to determine somebody's name. We thought you might help. Can you have a look at a photo—Felicity, give it here, please—and tell us if you recognize him?"

Maude looked at the photo.

"Nope."

"Not familiar at all? You've never seen him?"

"Nah."

"You'll let us know if you have any sudden recollections, Maude?"

"Yup."

"Thank you. We'll be grabbing a table and ordering some food. Send over an apple martini for me and a club soda for Miss Prim."

Maude nodded and went to fix the drinks as Miss Prim wondered how, exactly, Lorraine had ascertained that club soda was her decadent non-tea beverage of choice.

"Maude seems to be a man of few words," Miss Prim noted as they took a table recently vacated by two women of indeterminate age with chunky ankles and impressive helmets of salt-and-pepper hair.

"Indeed," Lorraine said, handing Miss Prim the menu, a laminated card folded in two. "But he's a total dear. You just have to know how to talk to him."

While Miss Prim scrutinized the menu, Lorraine showed the photo around the dining room, but with no success. Nobody recognized the man Miss Prim had discovered in her basement. After a very pleasant lunch—Lorraine insisted on paying, explaining that Lucian had more money than God and she was hell-bent on spending it—the two women took their leave and continued their exploration of downtown Greenfield.

Miss Prim stopped to gaze in the windows of the local bookshop, Cambria & Calibri. To the left of the door a dozen mystery novels with brightly colored jackets featured prominently under a sign reading CRAPPY MYSTERIES BY PEOPLE WHO HAVEN'T WRITTEN A GOOD BOOK IN YEARS. In the window to the right of the door was a sign reading REALLY GOOD MYSTERIES BY WRITERS YOU SHOULD READ: WHY AREN'T THESE PEOPLE ON THE BEST-SELLER LIST? Nicely displayed under the sign were books by Wallace Stroby, Karin Fossum, Brian Freeman, Jeff Markowitz, Sandra Carey Cody, C. Solimini, D.J. McIntosh, Robin Spano, and Dennis Tafoya.

I like this bookstore already, Miss Prim thought. "Let's go in here, Lorraine?" she suggested.

"Oh, not right now, Felicity. I have to be in the mood for Valeska, and I'm just *not.* Come along, there are plenty of other things to see."

10

Introducing Some Conflict

Miss Prim had fallen in love with the Greenfield village square upon seeing it for the first time. Now, strolling through it arm in arm with Lorraine, she appreciated it anew as Lorraine described the colorful and sometimes sordid histories of the buildings and businesses surrounding the central green. For instance, The Green Fields Bed and Breakfast, a pricey restaurant-hotel, had at one time functioned as a house of ill repute. The building that housed the Greenfield Post Office on the first floor and the Greenfield Historical Society on the second floor had once been a gathering place for a New England branch of the Mafia. Prothero's supermarket, a town institution, had expanded by taking over the firehouse located next door to it, much to the consternation of the historical society and some of the locals.

The north and east sides of the square were currently the more fashionable, Lorraine pronounced, in a non-ironic manner similar to Lady Bracknell's. "These things go back and forth," Lorraine elaborated, explaining that the Old Timers (a group whose dwindling membership included Lorraine and Lucian) were currently boycotting the south and west sides of the square, where real-estate speculators had managed to erect tasteful but still very much unwanted condominiums for, ahem, New Yorkers looking for a little place in the country. "But we never win these battles," Lorraine said with a sigh. "Give us twenty years and we'll accept the buildings grudgingly, or we'll just die off. In the meantime, some intrepid younger locals have started patronizing the new coffee shop and the bakery. Thus the assimilation begins."

Miss Prim soaked up the town gossip as a sponge soaks up water. "Lorraine, let's walk around the entire square, if doing so will not compromise your standing in town," she suggested. "Since I am one of the new people, I feel I should be open to the other new people. I wouldn't mind stopping at that coffee shop you just mentioned."

"For you, Felicity, I'm willing to risk becoming a pariah. Truth be told, I've had a cup of Joe in Beantown—that's the name of the coffeehouse—once or twice, and it's pretty good, if a bit thick and muddy. That's the preferred style today, the baristas tell me. And you know what happens when one resists current trends. I'm rather a slave to them, myself. One must keep one's edge. Or else."

With this rather ominous statement, Lorraine pushed open Beantown's door as Miss Prim tied Bruno's leash to a lamppost. An overhead chime announced their arrival, and the barista looked up from her book lazily, nodding a greeting without being overly effusive, which was, of course, the New England way. *And a good way to be it is*, Miss Prim thought, for the rest of society seemed to be crashing along on waves of false smiles, fawning insincerity, and plastic surgery.

Lorraine insisted on ordering the refreshments (Earl Gray for Miss Prim, a hazelnut latte for herself), dispatching Miss Prim to find a table among the ill-coiffed and alarmingly unkempt young people intently focused on their portable computers. Really, Miss Prim thought, some of these young men would be quite handsome if they would trim their whiskers, wash their clothes, and doff their woolen caps (why exactly were they wearing them indoors?), but she prevented herself from inwardly railing against youthful fashions. She herself had indulged in them as a younger woman, and while Papa had been driven to distraction, Mama had been quite supportive (and had even helped the young Felicity obtain difficult-to-find fashion items). *Styles come and go*, Miss Prim thought, *but beneath all styles lie people with hearts, souls, dreams, ambitions*. Perhaps that young man, tapping away on his laptop, would become the next Ellery Queen; perhaps that young lady with dreadlocks, scribbling in a journal, would become the next Ruth Rendell or P. D. James.

Miss Prim found a table and squeezed her way into one of the chairs. The tables were set most disconcertingly close to one another, but such were the exigencies forced upon business owners by the notoriously high rents in business districts. She smiled pleasantly at a few coffee and tea sippers, including a man in uniform surrounded by a cup of coffee, a cheese danish, a Boston cream donut, and a chocolate chip muffin.

"Why, Officer Reed! At first I didn't recognize you, sitting there. Any progress to report on our case? I haven't had any luck yet, myself."

Reed sipped from his cup of coffee. "Hi, Miss Prim. Spike and I have been knocking on doors all day. Nobody's identified the guy yet, and working as a team takes too much time. So we split up. I'm covering this side of town, and Spike's covering the east side. All that walking around is tiring. I needed a snack."

At that moment Lorraine arrived carrying two steaming cups and two cinnamon scones.

"Hi, Lorraine," Reed said.

"Good day, Martin," Lorraine responded graciously. "Are you and Felicity conferring on the facts of the case? I must warn you, she has very strong ideas about crime and criminals. Isn't that right, Felicity?"

Reed's walkie-talkie squawked. Miss Prim recognized Spike Fremlin's voice. "Reed, where are you? You'd better not be eating donuts when I'm out here pounding the pavement. God, these shoes are uncomfortable. They call us flatfeet in the movies, right? Now I know why. If I don't sit down for half an hour my arches are going to collapse and that'll be the end of that. But then I won't get drafted, at least. They don't take people with flat feet in the army, right? But I heard …"

Reed switched the radio off. "I should go. I know you got off to a rough start, Miss Prim, but Greenfield is a nice place to live. Try not to let it get to you. We'll figure out who the guy is, somehow. And we'll figure out who killed him, too."

"Of course you will, Martin," Lorraine said. She reached into her purse (Miss Prim thought it looked more like a pillowcase than a handbag) and retrieved a few Ziploc bags. "I'll just pack these goodies up so you can take them with you. I hate to see good food go to waste."

Officer Reed gone, Lorraine steered the conversation away from the investigation.

"We'll continue your official research soon enough, Felicity, but now's as good a time as any to give me all the details of your *amour* back in New York. Is he simply dashing? Totally unsuitable, or so suitable it's boring? Don't hold back on the details, please. My marriage to

Lucian is so devastatingly uninteresting that I must live vicariously through others. If you need to embellish for entertainment value, feel free to do so. I've been known to embellish myself, every now and again. Makes life worth living, yes?" She tapped the side of her nose twice and winked conspiratorially.

Thus Miss Prim found herself talking about her longtime relationship with Doctor Poe and how they seemed to be on the cusp of … something difficult to define. His timing had been quite poor, Miss Prim admitted, what with waiting to declare his affections until after she'd purchased a home quite a distance from New York City.

"Isn't that just like a man?" Lorraine asked in her usual rhetorical way. "They admire us from afar, mooning all over the place like courtly knights in medieval days, but God forbid they ever put themselves out there emotionally. Do you know I had to ask Lucian to marry *me*? I got so tired of all the dithering around, and it wasn't as if I didn't have other suitors who knew a good thing when they saw it. And the smarter they are when it comes to books, the dumber they are when it comes to women. Your doctor sounds like a good egg, but the dead wife thing worries me. When they've been married for so long, they get used to it, you know? And they figure one woman is as good as another. It's being married that they like, not necessarily the woman. That's not meant as a swipe against *you*, Tootsie Pop. We girls have to stick together when it comes to men. Let's face facts: *They* need *us* more than *we* need *them*."

When Lorraine interrupted her own monologue to visit the ladies', Miss Prim took the opportunity to chat with the barista and the patrons of Beantown. All looked closely at the photo of the dead man. All shook their heads; sorry, they did not recognize him, though the barista thought him "ruggedly handsome" and asked if he was single.

Miss Prim encountered her first piece of luck when she approached the young woman writing in her journal. Miss Dreadlocks looked at the photo, pursed her lips, and said quietly, "Hmm. I can't say that I *know* him, but somehow he looks familiar. I can't place him, but I'd say I've seen him around town, or at least someone who *looks* like him. I think it's the beard that's throwing me off."

"Any idea where you might have encountered him?" Miss Prim asked hopefully.

The woman shook her locks. "Maybe the library? Or the post office? I just don't know, but the bone structure—it's nice—I would remember a face like that, and something's telling me I've seen him before."

Not much specific information, Miss Prim thought, *but it's a start.* Clearly the victim hadn't lived in town. If he had, someone would have recognized him by now. But maybe he was related to somebody who lived in Greenfield? That might explain the resemblance.

Miss Prim belatedly introduced herself.

"Pleased to meet you," said the young lady. "I'm Faye Cotillard."

Their next stop was Prothero's market. As Miss Prim found a basket, Lorraine promptly disappeared down one of the aisles.

Because she had not brought her much-loved wheeliecart to Prothero's, Miss Prim added just the necessities to her basket: vegetables—bread—eggs—Milk Bones—even, yes, a small and overpriced dinner bell that she would use to train Bruno not to drool upon seeing or smelling food. As she strolled the aisles, she saw Prothero's concessions to modernity: a gourmet-foods section at the rear, where busy professionals could purchase prepared foods; an overpriced salad bar with many epicurean goodies, such as bleu cheese crumbles and five-bean salad; even a gifts section, a boon for husbands and children who remember (or are reminded of) birthdays at the last minute.

Deciding that she had selected the maximum weight and bulk that she and Lorraine could carry to Rose Cottage without a loss of gravitas, Miss Prim began walking to the front of the market. Behind one cash register stood a patrician-looking woman with stiff silver hair. She wore a pearl necklace and pearl earrings. Copious rings called attention to her well-manicured fingernails.

Miss Prim began unloading her groceries onto the belt and—could she be imagining this?—felt the cashier's withering stare stabbing ice picks into her. Miss Prim glanced up to read the woman's name tag: Hi! My name is MISS LAVELLE and I've been serving you for 42 year(s)!

Pay dirt, Miss Prim thought. *Here is someone who will recognize the man in the photo.* She would have smiled if she had not continued to sense the hatred emanating from Miss Lavelle's pores.

Miss Lavelle began ringing up Miss Prim's groceries, handling them much more roughly than a cashier should. Loaves of bread were squashed between Miss Lavelle's beringed fingers; eggs in their styrofoam containers were crushed against the aluminum sides of the bagging area; produce was weighed and then tossed like yesterday's garbage down the belt.

After giving Miss Lavelle the benefit of the doubt for half the order, Miss Prim decided to speak up.

"Excuse me? May I ask you to be a bit more … gentle … with the goods?"

Miss Lavelle's eyes became Satanic slits.

"*So* sorry," said the queen of Prothero's market in a tone indicating she was not sorry in the least. "I apologize if we aren't up to your New York City standards."

Miss Prim took a breath, remembering the shibboleths Mama had drilled into her head. *A stitch in time saves nine*: Yes. *Don't lose the forest for the trees:* Yes. *A stranger is just a friend you haven't met:* Yes, until this very moment.

Miss Prim was preparing her response when Lorraine materialized, as if out of thin air.

"Knock it off, Gladys. If I'd seen your broom parked outside, I would have warned Felicity about you. Felicity, for the record, Miss Lavelle here has been sleeping with Ethan Prothero for the last 41 years, but he has yet to marry her. The fact that he's already married is probably what's standing in their way. As you can see, the wait has made her irritable."

"I'll tell you what's making me irritable, Lorraine. You. And Miss Prissy here, thinking she's going to sweep Greenfield off its feet with her charms." Miss Gladys Lavelle eyed Miss Prim again. "You're a nosy little thing, aren't you? Running yourself all over the place with a photo and acting like you're a member of the police department that my taxes pay for. You think you're going to be everyone's best friend and confidante? Well, you got another thing coming. That job's already taken. By me. *So back off.*"

The patent untruthfulness of this assertion—could this harridan really be friend and confidante to the entire populace of Greenfield?—caused Miss Prim to lose the words that had been on the tip of her tongue.

Lorraine was not cowed. "Miss Prim *can* and *will* do whatever she likes, and you'll stay out of her way, Gladys Lavelle, or I'll have a good long conversation with Ethan. And with Mrs. Prothero. So I'll thank you to do your job, shut up, and mind your own business."

"Why don't you do the same, Lorraine Koslowski? I have half a mind to …"

Lorraine reached into her pillowcase and removed her cell phone. She ran down her list of contacts, "Miriam Lockwood. June Milutich. Perry Norbert. Here she is, Amanda Prothero …"

Ethel, another Prothero's cashier who'd been watching and listening to the histrionics with interest, interceded. "Gladys, I'd shut my trap if I were you. You know Lorraine isn't one to bluff."

Perhaps sensing defeat, Miss Lavelle furiously began bagging Miss Prim's purchases. She completed the transaction without another word.

On the walk back to Rose Cottage, still trying to cope with the embarrassment that goes with being made into a public spectacle against one's will, Miss Prim admitted to Lorraine that the Miss Lavelle incident had left her a bit shaken.

"Don't mind her, Felicity," Lorraine said, kindly. "I should have warned you. As you've probably figured out, Gladys Lavelle is easily threatened. Her parents were muckety-mucks in town, and back in the day everyone thought Gladys would marry some robber baron and live in a mansion in Boston. But it never happened, and her family's money has run out, and … well, you can see what it's done to her. She was less of a harpy forty years ago. But look on the bright side. You're experiencing everything that a New England village has to offer. It's not quite what you expected, is it?"

Miss Prim nodded in agreement.

As they strolled past the Cambria & Calibri bookstore, the proprietress stuck her head out the door.

"You!" she called to Miss Prim. "You're new to Greenfield, right? Stop in soon, please. And don't let me hear that you're buying books on the Internet."

Thoroughly exhausted by her altercation with Miss Lavelle, Miss Prim could only nod, wave, and keep walking.

"Now you see why Martin Reed loves his sweets," Lorraine said.

"I'm afraid I don't understand," Miss Prim replied.

"That was Valeska Reed. His wife."

11

A Feisty Teenager

The following morning, Miss Prim was up and about early, watering the roses, waiting for journalists who never arrived, and taking Bruno for a brisk walk.

Miss Prim smiled in greeting as she passed Jedediah Mason, who touched his cap in a delightfully old-fashioned manner, and she pretended to window-shop when, from the corner of her eye, she caught Miss Gladys Lavelle striding purposefully toward Prothero's, her name tag glinting aggressively in the sun.

Miss Prim arrived at the Greenfield Police Department, on the fashionable east side of the village green, and tied Bruno's leash to a lamppost. The PD was empty save for Detective Dawes, who sat at his desk peering at a document through half-moon glasses. As Miss Prim entered, Dawes glanced up and quickly removed his spectacles.

"Hello, Miss Prim. Sorry I haven't called you back yet. I'm *assuming* it was you, at least. Spike left a note saying that Miss Trimm called."

"Yes, it was I who called. I hope I am not disturbing you? I understand how valuable a detective's time is. But I think we both know that challenging cases are quite often solved by a professional and an amateur working together. Yes, the professional is sometimes resentful of the amateur's meddling; and yes, the amateur is sometimes frustrated by the draconian rules imposed by the professional. But they come to realize that two heads are better than one, and they end up with a profound respect for each other."

Dawes smiled, a lightning flash that was like an arrow to Miss Prim's secretly passionate heart. "Well, Miss Prim, perhaps the scenario you describe is common in books and on television, but it would be a new phenomenon in Greenfield. I've been here more than twenty years and I haven't yet forged any alliances with amateur detectives. And you're absolutely correct, there are rules against such things. But who knows? There's a first time for everything, and like Spike said, we're not exactly overstaffed here at the Greenfield PD." He sighed. "We haven't had a murder in decades, and everyone in the department is rusty. I think I've become complacent writing the occasional traffic ticket and calming down rowdy sports fans at Maude's once in a while."

"Has any new information come to light?"

"Not yet. Spike and Reed are still asking questions around town, but nobody knows who the guy is. Olivia swore on a stack of Bibles that she knew nothing about the hidden basement. Which ticks her off, because she thinks she could have gotten you to pay more for the cottage if she *had* known. Extra square footage, you know. And your house was on the multiple-listing service. That means that any real-estate agent in Connecticut could have shown it to a prospective buyer while it was empty. The agents usually leave their business cards behind, and Olivia had collected them, but she threw them out when you closed on the house. So we have no record of who went there, or which realtor showed it to which client. That's next on my list, actually—calling other real-estate agents in Litchfield County. The locks are old and could have been easily picked"—Miss Prim did not mention that she'd since had the locks replaced—"so anyone could have gotten in. I've talked to everyone worked on your house before you moved in, too. All dead ends."

"I see." Miss Prim was not surprised by any of this. Her reading experiences had prepared her for the likelihood that discovering the man's identity would prove challenging.

Dawes continued. "The M.E.'s been backed up—we share him with four other towns—and he hasn't even done the autopsy yet. Once that's out of the way, I'll start with Doc Frasier, the only dentist we have in Greenfield, but it'll probably be a waste of time. If our victim lived in or near town, we'd already know who he is."

"I may be able to help with that, Detective. The reason I called you last night is this: I met a young woman at Beantown, Faye Cotillard."

"I know Faye. She inherited a house in Greenfield and lives in it with her brother. She's often in Beantown until it closes, writing in her journal."

"She told me she didn't recognize the man *per se*, but that he bore a resemblance to someone she's seen around town. She couldn't be any more specific than that. I think the man's facial hair was skewing her perceptions. So I started thinking, maybe we could ask your police artist to do a sketch of the man *without* the beard and moustache, and then show that around? It might ring some bells."

"Police artist? Miss Prim, this isn't the FBI. We can barely afford electricity, much less Identi-Kits and full-time artists. But we do have Photoshop, and I know a little about it."

"Photoshop?"

"It's a computer program that allows you to manipulate photos. For example, let's say you want to change your hair color. I'm not saying you should, because it's very nice as it is"—it took every ounce of self-control in Miss Prim's body to prevent an embarrassing blush from spreading across her face—"but if you wanted to see what your hair looks like with a different color, I could feed a photo of you into Photoshop and we could fiddle around with colors until you find one you like."

Oh, dear. Only two days on the case, and already the police were calling on technology, that smoke-and-mirrors game that reduces the complexities of a crime to pixels on a computer screen while ignoring its psychological and relational underpinnings. But, Miss Prim supposed, the professional criminal outsmarter must use all the tools at her disposal, whether she approves of them or not.

"Shall we give it a try?" Miss Prim asked.

Dawes pulled up a chair and patted it, indicating that Miss Prim should sit next to him. As she sat, Miss Prim was disconcerted to find herself becoming slightly shaky at the woody scent emanating from Ezra Dawes. Was it the man's natural scent, or a cologne or deodorant? Either way, it made Miss Prim's toes tingle. Fortunately, those toes were encased in sensible shoes and thus did not betray her.

Dawes opened the file containing the photo Miss Prim had been showing around. With several clicks (not all of them well-chosen, for at various times Dawes managed to eliminate the man's eyes, nose, and chin) he was able to remove the facial hair.

Miss Prim examined the image closely. "Does he look like anyone you know?"

Dawes squinted at the screen. "Not really. I mean, he's just an average-looking guy, looks like a million other people."

Oh, how Miss Prim disagreed! The victim's blue eyes were soulful and hinted, perhaps, at artistic avocations, such as poetry or lute playing. His jawline was strong and solid, and the crow's feet at the corners of his eyes added character and a touch of mischief.

Miss Prim made a request. "Would you mind printing a copy of this doctored photo for me, Detective? I'll go back to Beantown and see if I can find Miss Cotillard. If she's there, I'll ask her if she recognizes the face."

Dawes clicked the mouse and the printer behind him spit out a low-quality printout. Miss Prim took the sheet of paper, folded it in half, and placed it in her handbag, promising the detective she'd been in touch immediately if she uncovered any helpful information.

Outside the police station, she saw an ill-kempt teenage boy petting Bruno's head. Bruno's stubby tail was moving so fast she fully expected it to soar off his rump and fly through the air like a propeller.

The boy noticed her and nodded. "Great dog, lady. What's his name?"

"He's Bruno, and I'm Miss Prim. And you would be … ?"

"Kit. You're new here, right? I heard you and Miss Lavelle went at it in Prothero's."

"It's nice to meet you, Kit, and you're right, I am new in Greenfield. But it would be an exaggeration to say that Miss Lavelle and I 'went at it.' I suspect she was having a stressful day, and I was just in the wrong place at the wrong time."

Kit looked unconvinced.

"Miss Prim, no offense, but I really doubt that. Miss Lavelle is a pit bull and she's always looking for Chihuahuas to eat."

Miss Prim had to smile at this most apt of metaphors. Still, one should not encourage teenagers to speak ill of adults. She gently changed the subject.

"Are you a dog lover, Kit?"

"Yeah, definitely. But my sister, who I live with, isn't. We have cats and she says a dog would throw off the balance. So I have to play with other people's dogs. It's not exactly fair."

A delightful idea struck Miss Prim. "Kit, I'm devoted to giving Bruno as much exercise as he needs, but I am going to be quite busy over the next several weeks. Maybe we could work out a business arrangement, you and I, where you come to my house to put Bruno through his paces?"

Miss Prim recalled her teenage years well enough to remember that most teenagers frown upon appearing excited, but she could see the enthusiasm in Kit's eyes.

"Sure, Miss Prim, that would be great. I'll stop by tomorrow."

"Lovely! My address is …"

"I know, Rose Cottage, over there on Undercliff Lane. You're the lady who found the dead guy in her basement. You're not planning to kill me, too, are you?"

Seeing Miss Prim's shocked and horrified expression, Kit rushed to undo the damage. "Just kidding, Miss Prim! Bad joke. Sorry about that. Faye is always telling me I don't know when to keep my mouth shut."

"Faye?"

"My sister."

"Faye Cotillard?"

"Yeah, the one with the crazy hair. I have to tell you, it smells bad, but she thinks she looks cool with it."

"Coincidentally, I met Faye yesterday. Why don't you bring her along when you come to play with Bruno?"

"Well, she's not super-social, but I'll ask. I bet she'd like your cinnamon rolls."

Miss Prim wondered, *Is there no detail of my life that has not spread like wildfire through Greenfield?*

"How do you know about my cinnamon rolls?" she asked. "Of course, to say they are heaven on a plate would be immodest, but I can truthfully say that most people like them a great deal."

"Are you kidding? That's all Officer Reed has been talking about. Apparently he wanted one when he was at your house, but Spike Fremlin shamed him out of asking, and now he's feeling all deprived. Miss Lavelle isn't happy about it because she makes cinnamon rolls too, but they're kind of hard and chewy. *She* thinks they're good, though."

Ah, an explanation, Miss Prim thought. No woman likes to watch her prize recipe get knocked out of the top slot.

"I shall see you tomorrow, then, Kit."

"I shall see you, too, Miss Prim," Kit responded. Was he mocking her, or had she managed, in just one brief conversation, to convey the importance of correct grammar to this unformed youth?

She chose the latter explanation, untied Bruno, and began her walk back to Rose Cottage.

12

The Hidden Diaries

During her many years living on the island of Manhattan, Miss Prim's free time had been precious to her, simply because there had been so little of it. Now, having decamped from the big city and embarked on a new career, she found she could do *what* she wanted, *when* she wanted. And what she wanted was to spend more time with her books.

Now, finally, she could waste hours poring through the books that had long been exiled to a storage locker. Criminally, she hadn't read all the Josephine Tey books in her collection; that oversight must be corrected as soon as possible. She'd always wanted to read more of Daphne du Maurier beyond *Rebecca*; *Jamaica Inn* and *My Cousin Rachel* awaited her in those boxes in the attic, as did a large number of Victoria Holts and Phyllis A. Whitneys, books that she knew (in her head) had set the women's movement back by decades, but (for her heart) provided lovely romances and vicarious thrills.

And who knew what fond memories she'd uncover in the boxes of her father's books, which she and Celia had tearfully packed up after Papa's death, when they'd undertaken the heartbreaking task of cleaning out his apartment? Papa, God rest his soul, had been a man's man and had insisted on reading the manly books of such rugged types as Dashiell Hammett, Mickey Spillane, Rex Stout, Raymond Chandler, Henry Holt, Leslie Charteris, and Ross MacDonald. Mama had teased him about it, occasionally sneaking an Elisabeth Sanxay Holding or Charlotte Armstrong onto his bookshelves. "Charity, you know the only woman novelist I can bear to read is Margaret Millar," Cornelius Prim had once said offhandedly. Miss Prim smiled at the memory of Mama's gritted teeth as Mrs. Charity Prim inquired, furiously, whether Cornelius had stopped to think about the effects of such a statement on his two impressionable daughters, who had been drawing silhouettes of each other as their parents engaged in this discussion. The next evening, Miss Prim had noticed a Mary Stewart novel on her father's nightstand.

Miss Prim changed into a pair of comfortable slacks and sneakers, then carried a kerosene lamp up the attic stairs, expecting that the single bulb hanging from the ceiling might not provide enough light to prevent eye strain. Bruno settled himself beside her as she lugged one of the boxes to the center of the room and began pulling the books out of it one at a time.

This box contained Papa's biological collection; he'd always been quite interested in anatomy and botany. She would keep his copy of Gray's, of course; this was an indispensable reference work that any serious collection must include. And here were the Audubon books which, she remembered, had cost Papa a pretty penny, still worth the investment so many years later. But a textbook on elementary biochemistry need not be kept; surely advances in the field rendered it obsolete. She placed it off to the side, into a pile to be donated to visitors, the library, or anyone else who might want it. Because, if there was one thing Miss Prim was certain of, it was this: There is a reader for every book. It is simply a matter of matching the two.

She spent several pleasurable hours going through the boxes and dwelling on pleasant memories, a welcome change of pace from the upsetting events of the past two days. The sixth box she opened was filled with leather-covered journals. Miss Prim remembered Papa tracking his investments in these journals in his careful, legible handwriting. The box held dozens of them, dated from the late 1930s through the late 1990s.

Miss Prim wanted to keep all of them, but pragmatism won the day. If she was not cautious about using her space wisely, the library would become full much too quickly. So she decided to look through each journal and choose the five that preserved her father's memory best. She would start with the most recent and work her way backwards.

The journals from the 1990s contained mostly to-do lists and medication schedules, along with notes and reminders from Papa to himself: "Look into the idea that practicing Theravada Buddhism can cure insomnia." "Purchase four black buttons, or five brown ones." "Attempt to fold sheet of paper in half more than four times."

An entry dated 2 February 1996 was puzzling:

> *Saw Providence briefly today for her 10th birthday—just a glimpse, which is all that A. would permit. Oh, how P. resembles my beloved girls, with her sunny disposition and her air of engagement with, and interest in, the world! She would melt anyone's heart, much less her own father's. I must again try to talk with A. about the situation. It is weighing too heavily on me, and I begin to regret my concession to A.'s and O.'s wishes. Oh, how I wish Providence to have the full serving of love that can be provided by not one, but two, loving parents as well as siblings who will watch over her! But A. has never welcomed me, and*

the situation remains unchanged … I must respect her, for she has loved and cared for Providence, even as I have been forced to spectate from the sidelines. But how do I ensure that P. continues to be cared for? I must force A. to have this conversation, to do what is right, for everyone's sake.

Alarmed by the implications of what she'd just read, Miss Prim hurriedly searched through the earlier journals. She found one dated 1 June 1985—14 November 1986 and scurried through the pages. The entry marked 5 February 1986 was written in a more emotional hand than was her father's wont.

I have just returned from visiting O. in the maternity ward. She is as beautiful a mother as she is a woman. And the baby—my baby—is as beautiful as my Celia and my Felicity! And yet, with Noel's strong chin and clear eyes. Since O. told me of her delicate situation, a secret part of me had hoped for a boy. No one could ever take Noel's place in my heart, but to have a strong boy—it had been my fondest wish. But now! To see this angel in O.'s arms is to know that she is as perfect as anyone could have wished. We discussed the name, and O. likes Providence, feeling as she does, as we both do, that the child is a gift, and one whom we shall acknowledge as ours as soon as we determine the correct course of action.

No more entries until February 14, Valentine's Day.

O. is not doing well, post-partum. While the child is healthy and happy, the Mother has contracted a virus that is causing high fevers and delirium. Doctors reassure me but I worry. O.

> *has lost too much weight since the birth of Providence, and she is slow to respond to treatment. I hold the baby as much as I can, to provide her the warmth and care that an infant needs, and to show her my love … I must give her the love of two parents, because one is too ill to do so. More later.*

Then a devastating entry from February 20:

> *O. has not survived. I am overcome with grief. The hospital staff have asked A. to make the funeral plans and burial arrangements. I must be the one to care for P., not an aunt, though of course A. will always be welcome in our home. I am old, but not elderly, and I shall hire help.*

Miss Prim closed her eyes. A baby sister, of whose identity she had been completely ignorant these last twenty-five years! How could Papa have kept this information from her and Celia? Charity Prim had died, too young, more than ten years before Providence's birth, so Papa need not have hidden his love for another woman; of course Felicity and Celia would have embraced a stepmother who loved their father. The Prims had always been close, mutually supportive, loving. Why would Cornelius have hidden Providence's existence from his family? Did he see his daughters as closed-minded, selfish, unfeeling?

Bruno at her side, Miss Prim rushed to the main floor, picked up the telephone receiver, and dialed a 212 number. Celia answered on the first ring.

"Hello, Sister," Miss Prim said, her voice shaking a little. "I have quite a lot to tell you. You must come to Connecticut as soon as possible. No, it cannot wait. Tomorrow, shall we say? … Yes, I shall pick you up at the train station. I am looking at the schedule now. A noon departure gets you to Greenfield at 4:04 PM. Until then, dearest."

13

A Locked-Room Mystery!

Miss Prim had stayed awake much later than her usual bedtime, and arisen much earlier the next morning, to prepare Rose Cottage for her first set of invited guests. Of course, the police and Lorraine Koslowski had been welcome, but they had not exactly been *invited*. When guests drop by unexpectedly, they expect to find an item out of place here and there, a dish or two in the sink, a blanket thrown over the couch cushions: in short, all the indicators that a house is lived in and loved. But invited guests require a higher standard. Miss Prim had quite taken to Kit and wanted him to feel comfortable and welcome, and she thought the proper atmosphere (including the smell of baking cinnamon rolls, known for their ability to win friends and influence people) might encourage the somewhat shy Faye to confide in her. As for Celia, Miss Prim loved and adored her sister, but Celia was the older, and Felicity the younger; and, try as she might, Miss Prim had never quite succeeded in quashing her need for her sister's approval.

Even Bruno seemed aware that visitors were expected. He paced around the cottage happily and expectantly, his tail wagging in anticipation. Not that it took much to get that little stub shaking like a seismometer: a smile, a word, any attention paid whatsoever. *Who ever would have let such an animal out for adoption?* Miss Prim asked herself. But she counted her blessings. *Their loss is my wonderful gain.*

As she mixed the cinnamon roll batter, she noticed Bruno off to her side, sitting on his haunches, watching her pathetically, knowing better than to beg for whatever it was that smelled so succulent. But the drool! Here was an opportunity to make use of Pavlov's conditioning techniques. She did not want to reinforce negative behavior, so she distracted Bruno by tossing his ball a few times and then engaging in a spirited tug of war with him for his chew toy. Among the exertions, he stopped drooling. Miss Prim grabbed the hand bell she'd purchased at Prothero's and rang it twice. Bruno's ears pricked up, and for some reason he sat. *Now* was the time for the proper reinforcement. She reached into her pocket and offered him one of the Milk Bones she'd purchased at the market. Bruno took it like a gentleman, swallowed it in one gulp, and sat again, hoping to coax another treat from her pocket. Miss Prim knew better than to be such a soft touch, so she patted his head and returned to the kitchen to continue working on the buns. When Bruno began drooling again, she repeated her training method. Her second attempt was as successful as her first.

The completed buns had been sitting just long enough for the icing to melt perfectly when the doorbell rang. Bruno barked once to make the visitors aware of his presence, but he piped down quickly. Could he know who was waiting on the other side of the door? He seemed quite intuitive that way, Miss Prim thought.

Wiping her hands on a towel and removing her apron, she strode to the front door and asked "Who is there, please?" After all, a murderer was running loose in Greenfield, and while it was not *likely* that he would be so audacious as to attack her in broad daylight, it was *possible* that he resented her interference. And that resentment could lead to …

"It's us, Miss Prim," Kit Cotillard said. "Kit and Faye."

Miss Prim unlocked the door and welcomed her guests.

"Hey, Miss Prim," Kit said, as Bruno bounded up to him. "Bruno! Hey boy! I brought you a bone! Miss Prim, is it OK if I give him a bone?"

"I'm not sure that's a good idea, Kit. Bones can be bad for dogs."

"This one should be OK. I went to the butcher and specifically asked for a bone that a dog could play with. He gave me this one"—he lifted a brown paper sack that he carried in his right hand—"and he said it won't splinter up and it'll last a long time."

"Kit, that was exceedingly thoughtful of you. Do you want to play with Bruno in the backyard for ten minutes while I brew the tea, and then while we're having refreshments, Bruno can enjoy his bone? Outdoors, of course."

"Sounds good, Miss Prim. Come on, Bruno!" Bruno, so well behaved around and protective of Miss Prim, saw the opportunity to partake in some much-needed roughhousing with a fellow male who would enjoy it just as much, and he took off like a shot after Kit, jumping on him and nearly knocking him over. *Boys are boys regardless of species*, Miss Prim reflected.

"Your brother is a sweet boy," Miss Prim said to Faye as a way of breaking the ice. She knew from experience that a compliment about one's siblings is like a compliment to oneself. Her own brother, Noel, had sometimes driven her to distraction during his adolescent years, but he'd become a fine man before dying much too young.

Faye was skeptical. "Well, maybe. But rough around the edges, to say the least."

"But they all are, dear, at that age. Too much testosterone, and they don't know what to do with it. It's a biological thing. I worked in a doctor's office for many years, so I know about these matters. As women, we must love them while also maintaining a somewhat gruff exterior with them, lest they take advantage of us. For they know how to do that, don't they? The same way they know how to manipulate their mothers, they know how to manipulate their sisters. I am convinced it is an ability they developed as a survival skill during evolution."

Faye took a seat on the couch while Miss Prim settled into one of the overstuffed chairs.

"Your house is cute, Miss Prim. It would work for a film set in an English village in Suffolk. Or Norfolk."

This was the highest of compliments for Miss Prim, and she acknowledged it with great satisfaction.

"Do you enjoy films, Faye? I admit, I do not see as many of them as I would like to. I used to live in New York City, not far from a cinema, and I always had such good intentions of going to see the latest inscrutable French films. But free time was so rare, and by the time I finally made it to theatre, the films were usually gone. I understand there are new technologies that will allow me to rent films to watch here on my telly, and I may look into that possibility once I'm settled in."

Faye perked up. "I'd love to give you some recommendations, Miss Prim. I see a lot of films, and I keep a list of them in my journal." She patted the backpack she carried with her—the younger generation's answer to the purse or handbag, and not a style that Miss Prim really approved of, but to each her own. Faye added, confidentially, "I keep my ideas for films I want to write in my journal, too."

"Oh, so you are an aspiring filmmaker, Faye? How exciting! What talent it must take to put a film together. I imagine that everyone, from the actors to the makeup people to the costumers, must be quite wonderful. So much creativity in one place. What a rewarding way to make your mark on the world!"

Faye blossomed like a rose. This had always been Miss Prim's gift: She spoke with such sincerity, and with such unabashed enthusiasm for others' dreams and plans, that most people, from family members to complete strangers, were instantly drawn to her. Her father had often remarked on this quality, with a sort of awed affection; meanwhile, her mother had worried a bit about her daughter's propensity toward naïveté.

"Are your parents in the creative industry?" Miss Prim asked. "I would venture to guess they are not. Are they perhaps accountants, or something dreadfully uncreative? Often, I have found, children seek to differentiate themselves from their parents by going a completely different route. It's just human nature. My father was a businessman and spent all day behind a desk. I wanted to work with people, to help them in some way, which is how I ended up working in a doctor's office. My mother was very active in women's rights and was forever going to meetings or organizing rallies. But that life was too public for me. I wanted something on a smaller scale, working with individuals. We are fortunate that the world is large enough to need both types of people."

"Our parents are gone, Miss Prim. They were international journalists, covering wars and things. Our aunt took care of us while they traveled, which was most of the time. But they died about fifteen years ago, just after Kit was born. Terrorists bombed the hotel they were staying in. I can hardly remember them now."

"Dear, I am so sorry to hear that. But your aunt is lucky to have you."

"Actually, I think she was happy to see us go."

"You don't live with her?"

"God no. She's up in New Hampshire. When I turned 21, I got my inheritance, which included the house in Greenfield, so we packed up and here we are."

"You and Kit live on your own?"

"Yes, we've been here about a year. I know, everyone says how young I am to have my own house and to take care of Kit. But it works and we're pretty happy here. Our parents made some really good investments, so money isn't a problem for us."

"So your parents used Greenfield as a sort of home base between their travels?"

"You could say that. They bought the house when they first got married, long before they had us, but they were rarely here. When they died, the house went to me and Kit. Aunt Victoria rented it out until we were old enough, and then we moved in."

Miss Prim was thoroughly impressed. What strength of character it took for Faye Cotillard, at the tender age of 21, to move to another state, set up a home, and care for her teenaged brother.

The teakettle began to whistle.

"Faye, would you fetch Kit? The tea will be ready in just a couple of minutes."

Faye retrieved Kit while Miss Prim dished out the cinnamon rolls.

"I think Bruno likes his bone, Miss Prim," Kit said, tucking into the cinnamon roll with gusto, ignoring the knife and fork and using his fingers instead. Miss Prim and Faye exchanged a knowing and indulgent glance.

"While you're here, Faye," Miss Prim said, "I wonder if you would mind taking a look at another photo. Do you remember yesterday, you said the man in the photo might look like someone, if he didn't have all that facial hair? Well, the police have used some technology to create a simulacrum of what he might look like if he were clean-shaven." She handed the photo to Faye, and Kit got up from his chair to stand behind Faye so he could examine it too.

"Does the face ring any bells?" Miss Prim asked, hopefully.

Faye bit her lip. "I don't know, Miss Prim. I feel like I did yesterday, like I've seen him before. But I still can't place him. I mean, it could have been here, or it could have been back in New Hampshire. Maybe just someone I saw in a store or something. I have this thing for faces because I'm always looking at people and trying to figure out what kind of role they'd play in a film. There's something nice about his face. It's strong; I like that. Not super-handsome in a leading-man kind of way, but a good supporting actor who might upstage the star and walk off with the Oscar. Or at least, that's probably what would have flashed through my mind the first time I saw him. But I think that about a lot of guys."

"What about you, Kit?" Miss Prim asked. "Do you recognize him?"

"Not really," Kit replied. "He just looks like a guy."

"If for any reason either of you has an epiphany, would you let me know? It could greatly help the police with their inquiries."

"Sure, Miss Prim," Faye said, continuing to squint at the photo, while Kit's eyes seemed to silently ask the question *What's an epiphany?*

Miss Prim retrieved her handbag, removed a $10 bill from her wallet, and tried to give it to Kit.

"What's this for?" Kit asked.

"For exercising Bruno, of course. All young men should have jobs, and I'd like 'exerciser of Bruno' to be yours. I'm hoping you'll come perhaps two or three times a week to frolic with Bruno a bit. I can pay you each time, or weekly if you prefer."

Kit refused to take the proffered cash. "No, Miss Prim. We don't need the money. Me and Faye have plenty of it. I'll do it for free. And maybe for some good food once in a while. Faye cooks gross things. I bet *you* cook good things, though."

"I believe I do, Kit, though perhaps you will be the better judge of that. So, I believe we have a deal, as long as the arrangement meets with Faye's approval." Faye shrugged her shoulders, as if to say "Whatever."

"Next time you visit," Miss Prim continued, "kindly bring a list of your favorite meals, and I shall see what I can whip up. I must warn you, though, that I will balk at preparing anything too unhealthy or too fat- or cholesterol-laden. Ingesting such meals habitually is simply deadly."

"I accept your conditions, Miss Prim," Kit negotiated, "but you have to agree that the food has to *taste* good. Otherwise I can just eat what Faye cooks."

"The right spices work wonders, Kit," Miss Prim said. She was about to expound on the merits of oregano and coriander when the doorbell rang. From the rear yard, she heard Bruno woofing halfheartedly, too involved with his bone to pay much attention.

Miss Prim opened the door to find Detective Dawes standing on her doorstep. "Detective!" she exclaimed. "Do come in. Cinnamon roll for you?"

"Don't mind if I do."

"Hi, Detective Dawes," Faye and Kit said simultaneously. Kit added, "Did you figure out who the dead guy is?"

"Not yet, Kit."

As Faye and Kit gathered their belongings to take their leave, Faye said to Miss Prim, "I heard about what happened at Prothero's. Miss Lavelle's a woman of moods, if you know what I mean. Her bark is worse than her bite. Don't worry, she'll come around."

"Granted, it might take twenty years," Dawes acknowledged, "but she'll come around. Perhaps."

"So, what brings you to Rose Cottage, Detective?" Miss Prim asked, as Dawes settled his appealing bulk into her rather small chair. Why, oh why, did she keep noticing his form? And why was she *permitting* herself to notice it when she had the loveliest of men, Doctor Poe, waiting for her to accept his proposal?

And, speaking of Doctor Poe, why hadn't she called him since her arrival in Greenfield? Today was only her fourth day of residence, and she'd been quite busy, given the discovery of the body and other events; besides, the rules of modern romance permitted each partner a good deal of independence. Still, she was beginning to feel a bit guilty, and she resolved to call the doctor before day's end.

"Well, Miss Prim, I know you like mysteries, so I have a new one for you. The lab techs got done analyzing all the SOC—that stands for 'scene of crime,' but you probably know that—photos. The stairs leading to your basement were very dusty, I'm supposing from years of not being used. We were able to identify eight sets of footprints going up and down that staircase: yours, mine, Reed's, Fremlin's, Bruno's, and the three SOC guys. But there was a ninth set of footprints, too. They went *up* the stairs but not *down* the stairs."

Miss Prim took in this information. "I see what you are getting at, Detective," she said. "We've been assuming that the murderer dumped the body in the basement. If the killer carried the victim downstairs, there should have been a set of footprints going both up *and* down. If the murderer surprised the victim in the basement, there should have been *two* unidentified sets of footprints going down the staircase, as well as one set of those footprints going back *up* the staircase."

"Exactly," Dawes said. "Which means, Miss Prim, that we have a locked-room mystery on our hands."

14
A Beloved Sister

After Dawes's departure, Miss Prim made up the bed in the guest room with the lavender-scented sheets that Celia found so relaxing. Then she cut roses from the bushes—really, there were so many blooms, she could have roses every day, all summer long—and arranged them in a small vase that her mother had purchased on a trip to Sri Lanka (known as Ceylon in those days). She placed the vase on the nightstand in the guest room, retrieved the Laser Taser 3000 from her bedroom nightstand, and patted Bruno's head, admonishing him to be good while she was away. For a moment, Miss Prim wondered if she'd hurt his feelings, for the look on his face very clearly said *You know I shall be good while you are not here, and I am insulted that you would imply otherwise.*

The Greenfield train depot was located not in Greenfield but rather in the neighboring town of Two Oaks, Connecticut. As she navigated the Zap through downtown Greenfield to access the feeder road to Two Oaks, Miss Prim could not help but notice the behavior of the other motorists. If they chose to drive so excruciatingly slowly—almost at a snail's pace, really—why not just walk instead? Still, one could not fault the politeness of the New England driver: Several cars rather abruptly swerved to the right or left to accommodate her. Miss Prim waved in thanks and could not understand why some people responded by shaking their fists at her. Was this perhaps a Connecticut-specific greeting, a regionalism she would come to appreciate? Perhaps, but in the meantime she had a sister to retrieve.

In the train station's small lot, Miss Prim easily found a parking slot for the Zap. As she awaited her sister's arrival on the 4:04 from New York, Miss Prim entered the ticketing station, where a refreshment stand sold beverages and snacks. She ordered a fresh-squeezed lemonade, a confection for which she and Celia had developed an inordinate fondness during their teenage summers on Nantucket and Martha's Vineyard. She asked the girl at the stand, who could not have been more than 15 or 16 years old, if she would mind adding a sprig of mint to the lemonade. The girl did so, her eyes registering distrust, for who would add mint to lemonade?

"You must try lemonade with mint sometime," Miss Prim volunteered. "My sister and I discovered this recipe when we were about your age. On Martha's Vineyard in those days, in summertime, our parents enjoyed sitting on the veranda and sipping mint juleps. Of course, we were much too young for the juleps, so Mama would pour large glasses of sweet tea or lemonade for us instead. But in true teenage fashion, Celia (my sister) and I always felt as if we were missing out on something by being restricted from the juleps. One day, Mama had the brainstorm of making our beverages taste more like theirs by adding mint to our lemonade. Well! It made all the difference in the world. We felt so sophisticated, and then we introduced the recipe to our friends, and we became quite popular. Of course, we didn't bother to mention that the recipe had been Mama's idea." She winked at the girl conspiratorially. "Anyway, my sister is coming for a visit today, and I can think of no better way to welcome her."

"If you say so," the girl said. "*My* sister's kind of a pain in the neck."

Miss Prim instantly became crestfallen. "Oh, you must never think of your sister that way! Perhaps you do not understand this just yet, but a sister is the greatest gift the world can give you. Trust me, my dear, others come and go with the ebbs and flows of life. But a sister—well, a sister is forever. Promise me you will cherish yours! You are at an age where the two of you are bound to have conflicts. These are quite normal. See them for formative experiences they are, and you will develop quite another perspective."

The girl continued to look skeptical. "Maybe. What's a mint tulip by the way?"

"It's actually called a *julep*, not a tulip. It's an alcoholic drink favored by women in the South. Now, here is the secret of mint juleps. They are really quite awful. Mint lemonade, and sweet tea with mint, are much, much better." She opened her handbag to retrieve her wallet, pushing the Laser Taser 3000 off to the side and hoping the girl did not see it and get the wrong idea. After paying for the lemonade and providing a generous tip, Miss Prim once again rummaged in her handbag, retrieving the Ziploc bag in which she stored her emergency supply of Mrs. Mallowan's Lemon Sugar. She handed the girl four of the precious packets. "Take these, please. When you get home, mix up a batch of lemonade and add two packets to the pitcher. They will give the lemonade a certain *je ne sais quoi*. Then, crush a few mint leaves and stir them in. Serve the lemonade over ice, then add a few more whole mint leaves. If you are feeling particularly decadent, you might sugar the rims of the glasses, but make that only an occasional indulgence, my dear, because—well, I don't have to tell you about the dangers of too much sugar."

"All right, why not," the girl said, taking the packets and sticking them in the pocket of her apron. "You do make this Junusakey lemonade sound pretty good."

At that moment a whistle announced the train's arrival. Miss Prim took the plastic tumbler filled with lemonade and turned to go. As she exited the station house, she heard the girl say, "Thank you, by the way." More evidence, Miss Prim thought, to support her theory that surly, truculent teenagers are simply teenagers who have not been spoken to as if they are real people, with valid feelings, going through a difficult transitional period.

As the passengers disembarked from the train, Miss Prim craned her neck to look for Celia. Miss Prim expected her sister to be the last passenger to leave the train, and in this expectation she was not disappointed. Celia sometimes lacked organizational skills; she was forever leaving something behind, or getting involved in puzzling conversations with handsome men, or reading tarot cards for strangers who always ended up wondering how, exactly, Celia knew what she knew. "It is the cards that know, not I," Celia would respond. "I am merely their vessel for passing along that knowledge, along with, perhaps, some advice."

Sure enough, five minutes after the last passenger appeared to have left the train, Celia exited, carrying her usual assortment of ragged carpetbags. She was chatting with someone behind her, and Miss Prim was not surprised to see the (male) conductor following Celia down the stairs, looking quite infatuated to boot.

Upon seeing Miss Prim, Celia dropped her carpetbags (Celia had always had a penchant for turning movie scenes into reality) and ran to her sister. The two embraced fervently, as if they had not seen each other in a decade.

Miss Prim knew that Celia had up-ended her life to help her recover after the mugging, though Celia herself would never have admitted it. Celia was the more free-spirited of the Prim sisters. While Miss Prim had maintained the most stable of lives, Celia had always been more prone to flights of fancy, becoming a private, live-in chef for this person (despite having no talent in the kitchen); flying off to take part in a dig in Iraq with that person (despite having no interest in archaeology and being intolerant of heat); taking part in a month-long regatta with yet another person (despite a tendency to become quite seasick). Of course, these various persons were all of the male variety. Celia's appreciation of the opposite sex had driven Mama and Papa to distraction, but Miss Prim admired her sister's willingness to follow her heart, despite its tendency to lead her into sometimes unwise decisions.

"Sister, let me look at you!" Celia exclaimed, breaking the embrace and holding Miss Prim at arm's distance. "How marvelous you look! So svelte! And with such a glow! It must be this New England air. And it goes without saying that nothing helps a woman's complexion like knowing a suitor will simply *die* if she rejects him." Of course Miss Prim and her sister had spoken about Doctor Poe's recent admissions, and Celia, being Celia, had urged her sister to accept the doctor's proposal immediately and worry about the consequences later.

"For you, Sister." Miss Prim extended the mint lemonade—or, as the girl had called it, the Junusakey lemonade. Celia squealed with pleasure.

As Miss Prim began retrieving her sister's dropped carpetbags, the conductor, who had returned to the train, watched them wistfully through a window.

"Have you conquered another heart?" Miss Prim asked, motioning with her eyes to the conductor.

"*Such* a lovely man, Sister, I cannot even tell you. I must say, life on the railroad seems quite fascinating. Paul has invited me to travel the full length of the train system with him, as he often does what he calls the 'transcontinental run.' Wouldn't it be fascinating to see the heart of our country, as well as the hinterland? The only issue is that I become quite ill from the rattling of a train, but I suppose there are ways to overcome that with a strong mind and the proper diet."

The two sisters walked to the Zap, Miss Prim struggling with the bags while her sister sipped the lemonade. Miss Prim's task was not made any easier by Celia's insistence on walking arm in arm with her, but, so delighted was Miss Prim at seeing her sister, she found all reason to be joyful and no reason to complain.

As they drove back to Greenfield, Miss Prim noticed the death grip with which Celia held onto the dashboard. Celia had gone quite white in the face, her pupils turned to pinpricks with terror. Might Celia have developed a fear of automobiles, or was she simply unaccustomed to traveling in them? *This too shall pass*, Miss Prim thought, for Celia had a long history of developing inexplicable maladies that departed as quickly as they had arrived.

Back at the cottage, Celia stumbled out of the car and took a minute or so to find her legs. Then she straightened up and took in the view: the pleasant cottage with its quasi-Tudor façade, the well-tended shrubberies and rose bushes, the barn, the ridge above and the woods behind.

"What can I say, Sister?" Celia asked with wonder. "It is everything I expected it to be from the photos, and more. As always, your taste is simply flawless." Miss Prim unlocked the door and Bruno bounded out, stopping respectfully at Celia's feet, where he sat and promptly began licking her hand. The two became friends instantly.

As Celia settled into the guest room—after providing many compliments on the cottage's décor and ambience, a food that Miss Prim found altogether nourishing—Miss Prim began preparing the leek-and-onion quiche that had long been one of Celia's favorite dishes. Celia emerged and began to set the table, knowing instinctively where Miss Prim stored the dishes and cutlery.

Miss Prim had not yet told Celia about their father's love child, their missing half-sister. Nor had she broken the news about the dead man in her basement. Some news was just too delicate, too personal, to deliver over the telephone. Rather, she wanted to reveal her secrets over a good meal, for the sisters had a long history of sharing intimacies while dining together.

"Sister, I've determined what exactly makes the energy in this cottage so *right*," Celia declared as she began uncorking the wine. "I know you are not trained in such matters, but you have the *feng shui* exactly correct. The site of the cottage is ideal, and the windows and doors are positioned to allow the natural spirits proper ingress and egress. Really, I think nothing bad could ever happen in this house. Now, make me wait no longer. Tell me all your secrets, and I shall tell you mine."

Miss Prim began.

"Well, Sister, it has been a most eventful few days. Take this wooden star. You see that star-shaped impression next to the cupboard door? Fit the star in there properly and push. That's exactly what I did, and you'll never believe what I discovered ..."

Well, Sister," Celia said, after Miss Prim had completed her narrative, "you certainly know how to make an impression when relocating! What I find most difficult to fathom is the ... *appropriateness* of it all. Of course I am not suggesting that the poor man *deserved* to be murdered. But given your new career plans"—of which Miss Prim had spoken with her sister many times—"it does all seem rather ... fortuitous. What I am trying to say, I suppose, is this: If the man *had* to be murdered and *had* to be dumped in somebody's house, it is probably best that it was *your* house. I know you will not rest until you have brought the perpetrator to justice."

"But Sister," Miss Prim continued, "believe it or not, the body in the basement is not the only secret that this cottage has revealed. This next secret is very personal, and it is of the utmost importance to both you and me. It is the reason I asked you quite urgently to pay a visit ..."

Miss Prim related the tale of discovering her father's journals again after they had been in storage for so many years. She ended her narrative (throughout which Celia remained mostly, and uncharacteristically, silent) with, "So, you see, we have a task ahead of us. We must find Providence."

Celia was resolute. "Of course I shall put everything else aside until we can locate her. What a gift this is for us, Sister. I am quite overwhelmed."

"I could not agree with you more," Miss Prim replied. "But I am left with so many questions. Why would Papa not have shared this blessed event with us? Why would he have orphaned Providence or allowed her to live without knowing the joys of our family and traditions? Can it be he was ashamed of his behavior? Or that he was ashamed of us, his own daughters? What could we have said or done to make him behave thus?" So strong were the emotions engendered by these questions that Miss Prim found her voice becoming quite wobbly. "Oh, Sister, there is a part of me that feels so betrayed by Papa! Since his death, I have treasured my memories of him, and our family, and everything we shared. But now I almost feel as though I never knew him."

"You must not think this!" Celia replied vehemently. "If there is *one thing* of which you and I can be sure in this life, it is our parents' love. Papa had nothing to be ashamed of. As the journals make clear, Mama had been long departed when he found himself involved in the *amour* that led to the birth of our sister."

"Do you think he did not tell us for fear we would reject O.? That we would not embrace her because of our devotion to Mama?"

"That is not it, Sister. Of that I am sure. I distinctly remember conversing with him on this topic after Mama's death. Several years after her passing, as I saw him looking lonely, I sat him down and assured him that he must not condemn himself to isolation. I know, Sister, you would not have had such a direct conversation with him, but I felt I must, so I took the proverbial bull by the horns. I told him, in no uncertain terms, that no man had better judgment, or better taste, in women. I also assured him that, should he find the right partner for his later years, you and I would welcome her as the dearest of friends. The poor main fairly wept with gratitude. So, no, I cannot, I *will not*, believe he would have kept our sister from us unless he had very good reasons for doing so. The journal refers to 'A.'s and O.'s wishes.' I can only assume that these people asked for Papa's discretion. And Papa, being the man he was, respected their wishes, despite his misgivings."

"Do you have any idea who A. and O. might be?" Miss Prim asked. "I have been racking my brain to no avail. Of course, I shall go through all of the journals, line by line, to find hints. But given the number of journals, that may take some time."

Celia Prim pursed her lips. "I cannot think of any likely candidates right now," she admitted. "But I shall begin my research as soon as I return to the City. I exchange holiday cards with the children of some of Papa's business associates, and I know that some of their parents are still with us. Why, Nathaniel Branson lives only a few blocks from me, and I believe Miss Spry"—Papa's longtime secretary—"is living quite happily in Westchester with the man she married in her seventies. Of course, this means I shall not be able to accept Paul's kind offer—at least not yet—but the railroads have been with us for centuries. They can wait. A sister cannot."

Thus in this, as in all important matters, the sisters were in agreement, and a plan was made.

"Now," said Celia, as Miss Prim poured the tea and retrieved cinnamon rolls from the refrigerator, "we must conclude the evening with some fun. This meal has been rather more intense than usual. Let us see what guidance the cards give us."

Celia retrieved her well-worn tarot deck (which she'd bought in Lily Dale, New York, in the 1960s) from one of her bags. She asked Miss Prim to shuffle the cards and then laid them out in front of her sister, making small noises as she revealed each card. When the layout was complete, Celia took a sip of her tea and decreed, "There are many puzzling situations here, but also many prospects for happiness. Missing people everywhere! I see not one or two, but perhaps even three or four, missing children. And yet the presence of the Sun indicates that all will be found, with happy endings for almost all concerned. I fear that at least one of these children bears a heavy weight, but I think it is not our sister … no, as the Page of Cups suggests, our sister is quite a strong, independent woman on her way to great success in life. She is closer than we think, Sister! And what have we here? Well, if it is not a love triangle—with *you* at its center. I see you still have some untold secrets, Sister. Well, you will tell me about this mysterious suitor in your own time. He is the King of Swords, I see—a man with dark hair and light eyes. Oh yes, a deadly combination in the right man. He is a man of authority, with a strong but understated personality. It cannot be your Doctor Poe, whom I recognize here in the King of Pentacles. I see quite a challenge for you in resolving this, but the cards indicate that you will make the right choice."

Celia paused a moment. "Just one thing, Sister. There is a somewhat worrisome aspect. Almost, but not quite, a bit of danger lurking near you. It is most likely emotional danger, but it could conceivably be physical danger. Please, dearest, do take the proper precautions. "

To calm Celia's fears, Miss Prim told her sister about the protections afforded by the Laser Taser 3000.

It had been a long and somewhat tiring day, but there was still one task left to accomplish. Miss Prim had vowed she would call Doctor Poe before the day ended. So, while Celia engaged in her nightly beauty ritual, Miss Prim brewed another cup of tea and prepared to place a call to the doctor.

She had just made herself comfortable on the couch when the phone rang.

"Good evening, Rose Cottage," Miss Prim said cheerily.

"Miss Prim, is that you? Amos Poe here."

Miss Prim had long appreciated Doctor Poe's old-fashioned and formal way of introducing himself. As Mama had always said, formal too long is infinitely preferable to informal too quickly.

"Yes, Doctor, it is I. I think our connection may not be the best. You sound somewhat crackly."

The doctor made a sound of frustration. "It is this new-fangled 'smart phone' that Norah made me purchase. It seems to be good for everything except actually having a conversation. And now she wants us to purchase computers for the office, too."

"I have been thinking about all of you, Doctor. How are Dolly, Zoroastria, Viveca? Has Mrs. Higgenbottom finally accepted the necessity of taking her medication?"

Thus followed a lively conversation, in which the doctor brought Miss Prim up to date on office events. In return, she regaled him with selected details of Celia's visit. She did not, however, mention the body in the basement (she did not wish him to worry) or the secrets revealed by her father's journals (information best conveyed in person, not on the phone).

As the conversation drew to its natural conclusion, a silence settled on the line. Then, abruptly, Doctor Poe said, "Miss Prim, may I be so bold as to ask a question? Have you missed us at all? Or, more importantly, have you missed *me*? I must admit, I am finding your absence to be quite painful."

Miss Prim was touched by the doctor's openness. "Oh, yes, Doctor Poe. I miss you all. Particularly Dolly and … you. I've been quite wrapped up in events here, but I have found my thoughts returning to you, which I take to be a sign of … something I have not yet been able to define, or to clarify in my own head."

"Very well, Miss Prim. I shall not push my agenda too hard, I promise; but nor shall I allow you to forget me. As we bid each other good evening, know that I am counting the minutes until you use my given name."

By the time Miss Prim disconnected from the call with Doctor Poe, Celia had completed her ritual, and it was Miss Prim's turn to apply her nightly unguents. Afterwards, she joined Celia in the guest room, where the two of them happily chatted in their bedclothes about men, life, and personal philosophies.

Around 11 PM, Celia announced she was quite exhausted, and Miss Prim returned to her own bedroom to turn down the bed. The night had become a bit nippy, so she walked across the room to close the window. As she pulled down the sash and prepared to engage the lock, she noticed a movement from the corner of her eye. Was that a dark-clad figure running through the far reaches of her backyard? Or just a deer, or perhaps even a bear?

It was *most certainly* a deer or some other form of local fauna.

Miss Prim locked the window, placed the Laser Taser 3000 on her nightstand, turned off the lamp, and shut her eyes, trying to ignore her rapidly beating heart.

15

Lunch at Maude's

The following morning, the Prim sisters rose late. Celia declared that the lavender sheets combined with the bracing country air had given her the best night's sleep she'd had in months.

After the morning tea had been sipped and the morning muffins baked and enjoyed, Celia expressed the desire to see all that Greenfield had to offer. She also requested the privilege of holding Bruno's leash as they strolled to the green.

Locals stopped to pat Bruno's head as the sisters sat in the town square, intensely discussing their plans for locating their half-sister. So deeply immersed in conversation was Miss Prim that she failed to notice the large shadow looming over her.

"Miss Prim?"

Miss Prim turned her head and recognized Josh, the foreman of the moving crew that had hauled the cartons of books into her attic.

"Good morning, Josh. How nice to see you again. May I introduce my sister, Miss Celia Prim."

"Hey, what's up?" Josh said, extending a paw that completely enveloped Celia's. "Yo, Miss Prim, the other day, I forgot to tell you. I do handyman work around town and a lot of old—I mean, a lot of ladies call me when they need furniture moved, et cetera. So, feel free to give me a call.

Here's my card. My prices are good and I live right on Harrington Street."

"I shall certainly do that, Josh," Miss Prim said, slipping the card into her handbag.

"Cool. OK, later, Miss Prim." Then, to Celia, "And welcome to Greenfield, Miss Prim the Second. Miss Lavelle down at Prothero's was having a meltdown about you coming. She thinks one Miss Prim is enough."

And off he loped.

Celia raised her eyebrows. "Prothero's? Miss Lavelle?"

"Well, Sister, all I can say is this: Word travels at an alarming rate here in Greenfield." Miss Prim then recounted the details of her donnybrook with Miss Lavelle as Celia gasped in shock, horror, and disbelief.

It was nearing noon and Celia suggested that they enjoy lunch in town, the better to soak up the local color. Though Greenfield offered several pleasant-looking eateries, Miss Prim decided that for the truest taste of the village, Maude's was the obvious choice.

Miss Prim waved to Maude as they entered and felt like quite a beloved and longtime tavern patron when Maude waved back, a single movement of his out-turned palm from left to right. The sisters sat at a table in the center of the dining room, with Celia facing the front door so that she could observe the comings and goings of the townspeople and thereby draw conclusions.

As Celia grabbed a folded, laminated menu, Miss Prim looked at the table tent. One side listed the day's specials: chicken in a basket, lobster roll, New England clam chowder. She turned the table tent around to read the other side:

TRY OUR DELICIOUS
JUNUSAKEY LEMONADE
With just a hint of mint
$2.00
WITH A KICK! $3.50

Miss Prim came close to sputtering but did not wish to disconcert Celia, who was viewing the menu with delectation and engaging in a running monologue on the merits and demerits of each item.

"Hello again, Maude," Miss Prim said pleasantly as Maude arrived to take their order. "How are you this lovely day?"

"Good."

"May I introduce my sister Celia, who's here for a visit. She wanted to enjoy a meal at a fashionable Greenfield eatery, so of course I suggested your tavern."

Maude turned to Celia. "Hi."

Was that a blush spreading over Celia's face as she batted her eyelashes? "Simply delighted to meet you," Celia said. "I bet this tavern has a rich history, Maude. I'd love to hear about it sometime."

"K."

The women placed their orders. Miss Prim selected a Mediterranean salad, which she would soon discover was simply lettuce, tomato, and onions with a dash of vinegar and olive oil. Celia ordered the haddock while flagellating herself for choosing fried food. Maude didn't write down either order; he simply nodded as each woman rattled off her request.

"Maude, before you go, may I ask you a question?" Miss Prim said. "This Junusakey lemonade that you're offering today … I was wondering, from whom did you get the recipe?"

"Deb."

"Is she the young lady who works at the Two Oaks railroad depot?"

"Yup."

"Do you know her parents or someone else in her family?"

"Sis."

"What is her sister's name?"

"Peg."

"Is that Peg over there?" Miss Prim gestured toward a young woman mixing drinks at the bar.

"Yeah."

"Well, please add two glasses of the lemonade to our order. Just the basic version. By the way, what gives the other version its 'kick'?"

"Rum."

"Whose idea was that?"

"Mine."

What a relief, Miss Prim thought. She'd heard stories of the younger generation's fixation on alcohol, as well as their insistence on drinking spirits before the law permitted them to do so. But it seemed that Miss Prim's young friend at the Two Oaks train station had indeed shared the lemonade recipe with her sister. Had the two of them bonded over a glass of that loveliest of concoctions? Miss Prim was disposed to believe that they had.

"Well, Sister," Celia was saying with admiration, "I must say, you have developed quite a knack for speaking with the locals. I am not surprised in the least. You have always been quite adaptable."

"I cannot take the credit, Sister. I've made a new friend here, Lorraine Koslowski. She's been invaluable in terms of acquiring insight into the personalities and quirks of the townsfolk."

"Does she have her sights set on Maude?"

"Oh, no. She is quite happily married to a man named Lucian, whom I have yet to meet. Tell me, do you ask that question for any specific reason?"

"You will call me crazy, Sister, but I cannot deny the vibrations of synchronicity that Maude and I experienced as he stood there. Such intense vibrations are difficult to come by; and, I have learned, one ignores them at one's peril."

What could Miss Prim say? Asking Celia not to pursue a man who had captured her interest would be like asking the sun not to rise, the tide to remain permanently high, the planet to stop spinning.

Celia continued rhapsodizing about the intricacies of the male-female syzygy while Miss Prim nodded, not fully understanding her sister's theories but finding them fascinating nonetheless. Several parallels to her situation with Doctor Poe briefly entered her mind but eluded her grasp, which was a frustrating and yet somewhat satisfying experience, for a relationship too easily categorized likely lacked the depth required to sustain it.

As the sisters enjoyed their lunch, the tavern filled. Men jostled for spots at the bar while women stood patiently (or not) on the outskirts, waiting for a table to become available. The bell over the door jangled—Miss Prim was becoming accustomed to the sound—and Olivia Abernathy walked into Maude's, the feathers on her colorful hat almost poking out the eyes of several of the establishment's patrons. Olivia slithered through the throngs to greet Miss Prim.

"Well, *hello*, Miss Prim," she said with the smile Miss Prim had never successfully deciphered. Olivia flashed the same toothy smile at Celia. "And whom do we have here?"

"Miss Celia Prim," Celia responded. "I am Felicity's older sister."

"Visiting? Or are you so charmed by our little town that you've decided to find yourself a lovely cottage here, too?"

"A visit only. I'm rather committed to the urban lifestyle, as frustrating as I sometimes find it. That means, I'm afraid, that I shall remain on West 16th Street for the foreseeable future."

Was it Miss Prim's imagination, or did Olivia's smile become somewhat less bright, her eyes somewhat less twinkly?

"Would you like to join us, Olivia?" Miss Prim asked, using Mrs. Abernathy's first name. Olivia had insisted upon this, the better to create the agent-client bond.

"Oh no, that's quite impossible. I'm meeting Gladys Lavelle for lunch. She'll be here any minute, and I fear our friendship would never recover if she saw me sitting at your table. How did you two manage to get off to such an awful start, anyway?"

Miss Prim was about to protest her innocence—for hadn't Miss Lavelle swooped down upon her, as an owl swoops down on a helpless rodent?—but remembered one of Mrs. Charity Prim's cardinal rules: *If you can't say something nice ...*

Miss Prim changed the topic. "I understand Detective Dawes has spoken with you about the cottage's hidden basement." Olivia nodded. "And you knew nothing about it?"

"That's right, Miss Prim. I would love to see it sometime. Hidden basements aren't that uncommon around here, actually. In a lot of the older houses, they were used to shelter hidden slaves escaping to the far north via the Underground Railroad. A lot of those basements were used to hide hooch during Prohibition, as well."

"But the cottage isn't old enough for either of those scenarios," Miss Prim pointed out. "Lorraine Koslowski told me it was built in the late 1970s."

"That can't be right. There are plenty of other houses in town that look like yours, and most of them were built in the 1950s and 60s. Gil Fellowes at the historical society will likely have more information, if you're looking to dig into these matters. Somehow he manages to get copies of all the property records. Which is a blessing, because we share our tax assessor with four other towns and she's never here. But you can take my word for it. I am a real-estate agent, you know. I am paid to know these things."

"I wonder if I might talk with Elizabeth Saxe-Coburg also. Lorraine tells me she is still living in the area."

Olivia pursed her lips disapprovingly. "You can *try*, Miss Prim, but the dear old thing is quite senile. Still, she might not mind the company. I think that the nephew who stuck her in that home doesn't visit much."

"Do you know which retirement community she lives in?"

"Heavenly Pastures in Two Oaks."

Miss Prim made a mental note of the information as Olivia Abernathy turned to greet Miss Lavelle, who had just entered the tavern.

"I must go," Olivia said, slipping away guiltily.

Celia watched Olivia depart and noticed Miss Lavelle staring daggers back at her.

"Her," Celia said to Miss Prim, pointing directly at Gladys Lavelle and refusing to break eye contact with Prothero's longtime head cashier. "She's the murderer. You mark my words, Sister. When all is said and done, she will be involved somehow. The last time I have encountered energy so dark was in the tomb of Amenhotep the Fourth."

The sisters finished their meal and Miss Prim paid, leaving cash on the table, steadfastly blocking Celia's numerous attempts to pick up the check. As they made their way to the front door, Miss Prim literally bumped into Detective Dawes, who explained that he sometimes indulged a hankering for Maude's chili dogs.

"My sister, Miss Celia Prim," Miss Prim said, gesturing to Celia by way of introduction. "Tell me, Detective, has there been progress on any front?"

"Nothing since we spoke at your cottage yesterday. But I'll keep you posted. You'll do the same for me, yes?"

"Of course, Detective. Would you excuse us? Celia would like to see more of Greenfield before she leaves for home, so we have limited time."

As Miss Prim untied Bruno's leash from the bike rack, Celia folded her arms and peered down at her sister, a knowing smile on her lips. "'Nothing since we spoke *at your cottage* yesterday'? Well, Sister, I think we now know the identity of the third party in your love triangle. And do not deny it, dearest, for I know you *too well*."

16

Cambria & Calibri

As the sisters strolled along the east side of the square, Miss Prim noticed a bookshelf displayed outside Cambria & Calibri. She squinted (her vision wasn't *quite* what it used to be) and read the hand-lettered sign over the display:

<u>HALF PRICE</u>
BEAUTIFUL BOOKS ON ARCANE SUBJECTS
OF LIMITED INTEREST

"Let's visit the bookshop," Miss Prim suggested to Celia. "I haven't been inside yet." As Celia nodded enthusiastic assent, Miss Prim added, "I must warn you, the shopkeeper may be a bit of a termagant."

"This town seems to have more than its share of them," Celia noted, perhaps an allusion to the dark vibrations emanating from Miss Lavelle. "But fear not, Sister. If we can brave the bookshops of New York City, the two of us can certainly take on"—she looked at the sign over the bookshop's window—"Cambria & Calibri."

As they approached C & C, Miss Prim pondered her sister's point. As a young woman, Miss Prim had ventured into the City's wonderful old bookstores—so many of them now gone—expecting to meet a society of kindred spirits. *Here*, she'd thought, *I shall find my niche, those burgeoning and established intellectuals who love learning, who yearn for witty discussion about the great books as well as the current best sellers, who spend their money on books first and on life's other necessities second.*

Her disappointment had been extreme. Employees, it seemed, did not wish to help but rather to condescend. She once asked a clerk for a copy of Thomas Nashe's *The Unfortunate Traveller*, which had been assigned in her Birth of the Novel class. The clerk had responded peremptorily, "The book's title is *Jack Wilton*," walking away without a further word and without helping her find the book. Her efforts to engage other shoppers in conversation had met with little success, with the book browsers either giving clipped responses or ignoring her completely.

Mama had provided soothing words of guidance. "Felicity, you must not become upset over these matters. As you know, ours is a city of great thinkers, and great thinkers often live in a world of their own construction. It is not that they are spurning you. Rather, they are what the Jungians call *introverts*, or those who tend to be more comfortable in their own company than with crowds or strangers. I urge you not to cease your attempts to know your fellow humans, for through these efforts you will meet lifelong companions and friends. As for that wretched clerk, his snobbery bespeaks a sense of insecurity about himself, and his rudeness bespeaks a misguided upbringing. For the record, you are absolutely correct. Mr. Nashe did title his book *The Unfortunate Traveller*; the subtitle is *The Life of Jack Wilton*. Leave the clerk to his ignorance, my dear, and let us enjoy a cup of tea together."

Miss Prim remembered these words as she entered Cambria & Calibri, wondering what to expect from her second encounter with Mrs. Valeska Reed, proprietress. Still holding Bruno's leash, Celia paused to view the half-price books on display, which looked to be lavishly illustrated treatises on—well, arcane subjects, as the sign had promised. There was one book on the art of *scherenschnitte*, another on matchboxes from 1940s China, another on the various varieties of kangaroo rat, genus *Dipodomys*. But it was an extensive catalog of the *ushabti* in the British Museum that caused Celia to exclaim with delight. Bruno, recognizing the opportunity for a nap, stretched out at Celia's feet, yawned, and promptly fell asleep.

Miss Prim caught her breath as she entered the store. Her first impression of the interior caused her to wonder if her soul mate had designed Cambria & Calibri. Bookshelves stretched to the ceiling, and a circular staircase wound its way to a second floor. Every book was properly and lovingly shelved, and in some cases merchandised to display its cover. A sunken area at the bookstore's center provided two small couches and three stuffed reading chairs, along with two desks with reading lamps and sturdy wooden seats. A small sign on one of the desks read:

COFFEE AND TEA AVAILABLE AT BEANTOWN
FRESH-BAKED SNACKS AVAILABLE AT SWEETCAKES BAKERY

In a corner of the sign, large red stars on a map of the town square marked the locations of Beantown and the bakery.

The store seemed quite deserted, with the owner nowhere to be seen, and Miss Prim began to formulate an exploration plan. Bookstores, she had always thought, were much like museums. When visiting any particular museum, Mrs. Charity Prim had declared, one must choose one or two galleries to explore in detail, rather than running frantically past too many masterworks in an effort to see all of them in too condensed a period of time. A museum was a project for a lifetime, not for a day, Mama had believed, and Miss Prim felt much the same way about bookstores. She need not visit all of Cambria & Calibri's shelves at once. The center of the store would suffice for today. She could explore the books lining the walls, as well as the second floor, on later expeditions.

From her decades of bookstore browsing, she had expected the shelves to be labeled with the usual signage: nonfiction, science fiction, mystery, home and garden, psychology. But Mrs. Reed had chosen nontraditional—to the say the least—labels for the shelves at the store's center:

New York Times Best-Sellers That Nobody Reads

The Latest Dreck from Writers Who Phone It In

Ponderous Literary Prose with No Plot and Snotty Characters

Urban Musings by Self-Involved Authors Who Don't Take Showers

Ongoing Sagas/Series That Lost Their Edge 4-5 Books Ago

Books by Ivy League Graduates That Got Glowing Reviews in Prestigious, Low-Circulation Magazines Edited by Other Ivy League Graduates

In all her years, Miss Prim had never encountered such a daring, one might even say *cynical*, method of cataloging books. In a way it was quite wonderful, as the categories must have represented the personality of the owner, and shouldn't a bookstore be *personal*, not corporate or canned? As she scanned the "Latest Dreck," she was distressed to see the latest installment in the Fatima Larroquette series, *When Life Hands You Oranges, Make Orange Juice,* adorning the shelf. Clearly, Mrs. Reed did not appreciate Fatima's adventures as much as Miss Prim did.

Miss Prim flipped to the first page of *Oranges* and was reading the first sentence—"I knew it was going to be a bad day when my cat, Fluffy, peed in my shoes"—when she heard activity emanating from the far corner of the store. She looked up and saw Valeska Reed approaching her.

"Well, Miss Prim, it's about time. I've heard about those boxes of books that Josh and his crew moved into your house. Time for out with the old, in with the new, yes? Valeska Reed." She extended her hand and shook Miss Prim's hand firmly—and, Miss Prim was shocked to find, warmly and affectionately. No, this was not a cold businesswoman's handshake. It was the clasp of a longtime friend, or that of a person genuinely delighted to make one's acquaintance.

"I'm so sorry, Mrs. Reed," Miss Prim sputtered. "You see, my intentions have been all the best, but I have encountered a most unexpected series of events since taking up residence in Greenfield, and ..."

Valeska waved her hand. "Yes, I know all about it. There are no secrets in Greenfield." She took Miss Prim's wrist and twisted it gently to reveal the title of the book in Miss Prim's hand. "Oh, *her*. She was in here once to do a book signing for

When Life Hands You Apples, Make Apple Cider. She was so drunk she could barely stand up. Mary Frances McCarthy brought in some of her older books and asked her to sign them, which Miss Snippy Authoress refused to do, complaining that the girl hadn't bought them that day, or in hardback. Needless to say, Fatima Larroquette's creator will not be invited to Cambria & Calibri again. The books sell all right, though. I recommend them to vapid-looking tourists who've had a lot of plastic surgery."

Miss Prim eyed the shelves. "To whom do you recommend the titles you've categorized under Urban Musings?" she asked, wondering about the target demographic.

"Those books tend to be favored by youngish men with bad facial hair wearing woolen caps to disguise, or perhaps call attention to, the messy, unwashed hair on their head. And, of course, by the women who find that type of male charming, and who think they can beat a path to his heart by reading books written by pretentious hipsters living in Brooklyn and working for Internet start-ups. As you and I both know, Miss Prim, these women are barking up the wrong tree. These self-absorbed males are not looking for wives, or even lovers, but rather admirers."

"I see," Miss Prim said, trying to determine whether Mrs. Reed was the most perceptive of women or the most jaded. "But do your customers"—she searched for the proper word—"*appreciate* having their favorite books labeled in this manner?"

Valeska looked at Miss Prim incredulously. "Now, Miss Prim, don't be disingenuous. People fall into two categories, as you very well know. There are people like you and me, who understand these labels and know to avoid these books.

For those people, I have the shelves lining the walls, as well as the second floor. Then there are the people who don't quite understand my shelf labels or who don't bother to read them at all. The books here in the center of the store are for them. The system works quite well."

"Your reading nook is most welcoming. I am surprised that you don't sell refreshments. That seems rather countertrend."

Miss Prim had hit a sore spot. "One must specialize in what one does best. I am a bookstore owner, not a confectioner and not a barista," Valeska replied. "This is a small town, and there are other businesses within walking distance that sell snacks and beverages. Greenfield has a vested interest in the success of all these businesses. I don't wish to compete with other proprietors, which is why I am so enraged with Maude for offering those shelves with free books. You and I both know the value of a book, Miss Prim, but many people do not. Why should shoppers visit Cambria & Calibri to purchase a book when Maude is giving them away for free? Maude understands the drinker and the eater, but he does not understand the reader. For that, you must come here."

"Have you tried talking with Maude about this?"

Valeska nearly spat. "Ha! Have *you* ever tried talking with Maude? The man is an automaton incapable of human communication."

Miss Prim came to Maude's defense. "True, Maude is not the most loquacious of men. But how could someone run such a successful business in a small town if he did not have the kindest of hearts? As Lorraine Koslowski pointed out to me, it is just a matter of knowing how to talk with him. If you'd like, I could try broaching the subject with him."

"He shouldn't have to be *told* about this sort of thing, which requires only the smallest amount of respect for one's fellow merchants. But if you think you can make inroads, feel free."

Miss Prim thought it prudent to change the subject. "I haven't been to the Sweetcakes Bakery yet. Do I dare? You see, I recently began a new dietary regimen, and I have quite liked the results. One does not want to lead oneself into *too* much temptation, especially when the bakery is walking distance from one's home."

"Their specialty is German. You know, sacher tortes, linzer tortes, et cetera. All quite scrumptious, and their apricot biscotti—well, if you should become addicted, you cannot say you were not warned. I speak from experience. I have been trying to wean Martin off it for months now. Without much success, I am sorry to report."

Indeed. The last time Miss Prim had seen Officer Martin Reed, he'd had calorie-laden confections laid out in front of him. Of course she would not reveal his secret (or, as Zoroastria would have termed it, "narc'ed him out"). She sensed this was a sensitive subject between husband and wife, so she took the conversation in a different direction.

"Speaking of the police, Mrs. Reed—"

"Valeska."

"Speaking of the police, I wonder if I could ask you to look at a photo?" She reached into her handbag, pushing the Laser Taser 3000 out of the way (it seemed to share certain chemical properties with air, forever bubbling to the top) and handed the Photoshopped photo to Valeska.

"I was talking with Faye Cotillard," Miss Prim continued, "and she mentioned that this man—the unfortunate person whom I found in my basement—looked like someone she had seen before. Do you recognize him?"

"I certainly do," Valeska replied. "I've seen him looking in my windows once or twice, late at night, when the shop is about to close. But he never comes in."

Finally! A solid lead.

"Do you know his identity?"

"No. I do not try to entice customers into Cambria & Calibri. I am not a shill."

This last statement did not quite accord with Miss Prim's initial experience with Valeska Reed, but she chose not to contradict the imposing bookstore owner.

"Have you told the police about recognizing the man, Mrs.—Valeska?"

"No."

"But why ever not? You are married to one of the investigating officers. Surely he showed you this photo?"

"Nobody showed it to me and nobody asked me. And nobody can say Valeska Reed doesn't mind her own business."

This is a marriage, Miss Prim thought, *that suffers from serious communication problems*.

"Well, thank you, Mrs.—Valeska. If you don't mind, I shall share your information with Detective Dawes." Valeska Reed nodded her assent as Miss Prim checked her watch. "This was such a lovely conversation. But I'm afraid I must be taking my leave. My sister is visiting from New York, and I need to deliver her to the train station."

"You're not leaving without buying a book, Miss Prim?" It was phrased as a question, stated as a command.

"Of course not. I'd like to purchase the *ushabti* catalog for my sister."

"That one's not bad, if you go for that sort of thing. Cover price $39.95, half price $20.00, and I'll give you another 15% discount, so let's say $17 and an occasional visit from you, in which we can talk more about books and less about this tiresome murder."

"That sounds both fair and delightful," Miss Prim said, handing Valeska $17, including one dollar's worth of pennies that she'd been trying to get rid of.

"One other thing," Valeska added. "There was a man in here yesterday asking about you."

"A man?"

"Yes. One of that new type of man who is rather too concerned with his appearance and looking youthful."

"Did he give a name?"

"He did not. He asked if I knew you, and I said no, because we hadn't been properly introduced yet."

This is really most odd, and perhaps even worrisome, Miss Prim thought, exiting the bookshop. Who could be seeking her in Greenfield? Her heart accelerated when she remembered the creature she'd seen in her backyard the previous night. Without realizing she was doing so, she touched the bulge in her handbag to reassure herself that the Laser Taser 3000 was still there.

Celia exclaimed delightedly at Miss Prim's gift, then began worrying about where she would store the book in her tiny apartment. "Never you mind about that, Sister," Miss Prim counseled, "for we both know you will *make* the room. That is what one does for the books one must have."

17
Problems with the Opposite Sex

Though Miss Prim had suggested that Celia extend her visit a few more days, Celia had been unable to comply. Work awaited her in Manhattan; she was busy indexing a book on the politics of Antarctica for a man who had not yet declared his intentions.

"But Sister," Miss Prim had asked, "since when do you have expertise as an indexer? Does the job not require the most perfected of"—here she had to tread lightly, for fear of giving offense—"organizational skills?"

"That is one approach to the job," Celia had conceded. "But I also believe one can be *inspired* to prepare an index. When that inspiration comes, everything will fall into place."

"Are you hoping that an index is the way to a man's heart? Or at least to this particular man's heart?"

"Oh, if it were only that simple! You recall Barbara Pym from Mama's bookshelves? In *Excellent Women*, Miss Pym made it very clear that indexing is the expected task of a helpmeet, though she also implies that indexing becomes an obligation only when one has accepted the inevitability of the relationship. I would not say I am at that point, just yet, as there always seem to be so many options. Still and all, it would not be a bad thing to add indexing to my résumé, as I am sure the skill is very much in demand."

Thus, after their visit to the bookshop, the sisters returned to the cottage, where Miss Prim did a bit of straightening while Celia packed up her carpetbags. In short order Bruno's ears pricked up, and a moment later Miss Prim heard a knock at the door. Bruno charged forth, tail wagging like a metronome keeping the beat for a frantic disco song, and Miss Prim followed.

"Hi, Miss Prim," Kit said, fending off Bruno's tongue bath. "I'm here to get Bruno. I was going to come earlier, but I heard you were at Maude's with your sister. Here's the list of foods I like. Please, nothing with watercress. Faye lives on it but it's disgusting."

Miss Prim nodded, trading Bruno's leash for Kit's list. Boy and dog ran off.

In the meantime, Celia had emerged from the guest room, two bags in each hand. "I wonder, Sister," Celia began tentatively, "if you would allow me to drive to the train depot. It's been a while since I've been behind the wheel, and one does not wish to become too rusty with regard to essential skills."

"Of course, Sister," Miss Prim replied. "The Zap is really quite pleasant to drive, though its performance leaves something to be desired. When you step on the gas pedal, you will see that the acceleration is quite poor. You will feel as if you are poking along on a nag from the Old West."

"That may not be such a bad thing," Celia declared. "You may have noticed that people drive altogether too impatiently these days."

"Actually, I have noticed the exact opposite," Miss Prim replied. "But you will see for yourself." She handed Celia the keys.

When the trunk was loaded with Celia's carpetbags, Celia got behind the wheel and fastened her seatbelt. Miss Prim took the passenger seat and did the same, then walked her sister through the process of starting the car and engaging the automatic transmission.

"I don't know about this," Celia said, doubtfully. "I have always thought these automatic transmissions are a fad that cannot last."

"You will quite get used to it, Sister. It is rather freeing, in a way, to have one hand free to adjust the radio and one leg free to tap one's toes to the beat. Those manual transmissions, like the one in Papa's old Packard, did make the driver feel rather like a marionette, with all limbs in action all the time. And you know what Mama always said, Sister: We must not fight modernity. It has its benefits."

Miss Prim provided block-by-block directions as Celia navigated the narrow roads and comparatively congested streets of downtown Greenfield. *Really, so much traffic!* Miss Prim thought as she glanced out the Zap's rear window. How had so many cars ended up behind them, and why had they begun honking their horns? Why did the gentleman driving that German car directly behind them appear on the verge of apoplexy, his face red as a beet? And for heaven's sake, why was he driving so close to them, fairly crawling onto the Zap's bumper? Why, whenever they stopped at a red light, did the drivers behind them gun their engines and then pass them aggressively?

"So, our plan is settled," Miss Prim summarized as Celia pulled into the parking lot of the Two Oaks train station. "You will contact Papa's business associates to try to discover O.'s identity, as well as check the New York Public Records Office, just in case Providence's last name is listed as Prim, or if Papa is listed as her father on the birth certificate."

The previous evening, Celia had called directory assistance in Manhattan looking for Providence Prim, and the operator (who sounded as if she were in India, not in New York City—but perhaps Celia had been imagining things) had informed her that no such person was listed. This did not discourage Miss Prim and Celia, however; Providence Prim might have an unlisted number, or she might have married and now be Mrs. Providence Something-or-Other. "In the meantime, I shall pore through the remainder of Papa's journals to see if I can find any further hints as to O.'s identity and whereabouts."

The sisters embraced just before Celia boarded the train, promising to be in touch as soon as either had information to report.

"In the meantime," Celia added, ostensibly as an afterthought, "do mention me to Maude every so often and report back to me on his reaction. For there is something *there*, Sister; I am quite convinced of it. Do, please, inquire as to his marital status and other matters. As you know, I prefer *not* to traipse down paths that may lead to ruin."

By the time Miss Prim returned to the cottage (for some reason, the trip home seemed to be much, much quicker than the trip to the train station) Bruno had been returned. He was lying in the yard, tied to his tether, chewing on the bone that Kit had brought him. He rose instantly upon seeing his mistress and with his eyes requested permission to accompany her indoors. Miss Prim granted his wish.

As she entered the cottage, she found a note from Lorraine lying on the floor of the entryway.

> FP—
>
> Feel free to drop by sometime in the afternoon, if you are available. I wouldn't mind some company. Bring Bruno, of course. Or just give me a call: 860-555-8989.
>
> —LK

Miss Prim was filling Bruno's water dish when her phone began ringing.

"Good afternoon, Rose Cottage."

"Miss Prim! I'm so glad you're there."

Miss Prim was delighted to hear Dolly's voice. She kicked off her shoes, tucked her legs under herself on the couch, and settled in for a chat.

Miss Prim explained that Celia had just departed, forbearing to mention anything about her lost half-sister. This was first and foremost a family matter, and what would happen if, for some reason, Providence did not wish to acknowledge their familial bonds? Though she longed for a genuine, mutually loving relationship with her new sibling, Miss Prim would have to respect her half-sister's wishes, which might include the desire for confidentiality.

"But you're calling during the day, dearest?" Miss Prim asked. "Has the office hit a lull?" Lulls were rare indeed in Doctor Poe's office, primarily because the good doctor, being of the old-fashioned variety, liked to spend time with each patient—all very well for the patient who was with the doctor, but not particularly functional when the waiting room was full of "impatients" (as they were dubbed by the office staff) tapping their feet nervously.

"Zoroastria is handling the hordes, Miss Prim. I hate to keep calling you for advice, but really, everyone comes to my problems with their own agendas! Zoroastria has that *Sex and the City* approach to men, which may work for her but doesn't work for me. And Viveca just wants me to marry someone, so her advice isn't much help, either."

It was true, Miss Prim thought, that Zoroastria's methods worked for the socially in-demand receptionist. It was a rare evening when a heavily tattooed gentleman did not show up at closing time to take Zoroastria to hear live music somewhere on the Bowery. Yet Viveca's approach had also been successful, permitting her to marry her teenage sweetheart and have six children with him while successfully training him to remember her birthday and their anniversary. Clearly, different approaches work with different kinds of men, Miss Prim thought; it is just a matter of using the correct technique on the man in question.

"I am all ears," Miss Prim said.

"Things seem to be getting stranger with Benjamin, Miss Prim. After you and I talked last time, he called me and was his usual charming self, so I took your advice and went with the flow. He asked me to dinner last night, and I said yes, of course. Zoroastria got on my case about that because she says you *never* accept an invitation unless you have 48 hours notice. Well, whatever! He picked me up and we went to a cute little place in the Village. The waiter had just brought the appetizer when the bartender came over and asked to speak with Benjamin privately. So Benjamin went over to the bar, and the two of them talked, and it looked like they were both pretty agitated. I asked Benjamin what it was all about. He said they were in one of the same classes and were talking about their professor.

"I had no reason not to believe him, so we picked up where we left off, but a few minutes later he excused himself to go to the men's room. Well, there's an emergency exit off the corridor that the restrooms are in, and when he thought I wasn't looking, he slipped out the exit. And no alarm went off. I sat there by myself for about ten minutes not knowing what to do. Then I saw the bartender walk down the corridor to the emergency exit and open the door, and that's when Benjamin slipped back in! He went into the men's room, and a minute later he came back to the table like nothing had happened."

Miss Prim bit her lip. She didn't like the sound of this, not one bit. "I suppose he acted as if he'd been in the men's room all the while?"

"Not only that, but he actively lied about it. I jokingly said, 'I thought you left!' and he laughed sort of uncomfortably and said, 'Sorry about that, there was a wait.' I would have believed him if I hadn't seen him slip out with my own eyes. But then things got even *stranger*."

"Go on, dearest."

"He was on edge for the rest of the evening and barely touched his food. We had talked about maybe going out for dessert, but he said he had a lot of reading to do for his seminar on Gabriel García Márquez, so he wanted to call it a night. He walked me back to my apartment and gave me a quick peck on the cheek, and then he was gone.

"I tried not to think too much about it, but then this morning when I was getting ready to leave for the office, he called me and asked me to hold one of his books in my apartment. He said he'd stop by within an hour, but he never showed up. I waited two hours, and I tried calling him a few times, but he didn't answer. I went home at lunchtime and the doorman said Benjamin hadn't been there and hadn't left any package. In the meantime, I've left him a couple of messages asking if he's OK, but he hasn't called me back. Am I right to be worried? Or am I being crazy?"

It was all very cloak-and-dagger, Miss Prim thought. Perhaps the argument with the bartender could be explained by competing claims on the book apparently in Benjamin's possession? The explanation seemed to stretch the imagination, however. Miss Prim could not quite picture a young graduate student slipping out of a restaurant into a dark alley in order to purchase (or sell) a book of interest only to those who study magical realism.

No, the more likely scenario was a problem too often experienced by a generation facing horrific pressures regarding housing, career advancement, and their prospects for the future: drugs. She'd seen what narcotics could do to even the most mild-mannered of women who'd come to over-rely on their oxycodone or lorazepam. And these were relatively civilized pharmaceuticals. Miss Prim could only imagine the challenges of getting involved with street drugs or with the people who sell them.

"I think, Dolly," Miss Prim said, cautiously, "that you are quite right to be concerned. Something is happening with Benjamin that he doesn't wish you to know about. It may be innocent, or it may be not so innocent. I think it is in your best interests *not* to hold any parcel for him, either on your person or in your home. I fear that doing so may put you in danger, though this is only a hunch. But in my new profession, we are trained not to ignore our hunches. Quite often they are based on unconscious observations and are therefore valid."

Dolly lowered her voice. "Do you really think I'm in danger, Miss Prim? That freaks me out a little."

"I think you are probably not in any real danger, Dolly. But discretion is the better part of valor, and you must *not* risk putting yourself in harm's way if Benjamin has become embroiled in a situation he cannot control. Perhaps staying with a friend might be a good idea?"

"I could stay at Zoroastria's for a few nights …"

"Then please do so, Dolly." Miss Prim had a sudden brainstorm. "And why not come up to pay me a visit, sooner rather than later? The weekend begins in just a few days. Greenfield will be a good place for you to forget your cares."

"I'd love that, Miss Prim! But am I being a bad person for leaving Benjamin stranded if he's in trouble?"

"The best you can do is offer guidance if he asks for it, dearest. If you hear from him and you suspect something is seriously wrong, I beg you to advise him to go to the police. This is not one of those situations that a rank amateur"—she did not add *such as myself*—"is qualified to handle. Do you promise?"

"I promise, Miss Prim. I could take the train after work on Friday. I bet it would get me to you by about seven o'clock."

"Lovely. I shall bake some cinnamon rolls and we shall have a nice chat before bed. Then on Saturday we can enjoy what Greenfield has to offer."

"That would be wonderful! I'll call you back after I check the train schedule."

"Oh, Dolly—would you kindly let Doctor Poe that I send my affection?"

"Of course. I'll be sure to say it in front of Norah so that I can watch her go pale with jealousy." Dolly chortled, and Miss Prim indulged in a titter of her own.

Checking her watch, Miss Prim saw that the afternoon was getting on. As she was putting on her shoes to begin her walk to Lorraine's, the phone rang again. Had Dolly forgotten something?

"Good afternoon, Rose Cottage."

But there was no response, just the sound of a connection being broken.

18

A Derelict Mansion, Inhabited by Eccentrics

Miss Prim was excited by the prospect of a walk to Lorraine's house on the ridge. Of course Olivia Abernathy had driven Miss Prim along the ridge during one of her early visits to Greenfield, perhaps to give her a sense of Rose Cottage's proximity to greatness.

As Miss Prim remembered Ridge Road, it was a quiet street with a characteristic that would have surprised nobody in the real-estate business. All of the houses faced the view, with the result that one could see the fronts of the houses only from below. When one approached them in an automobile, one saw only gated driveways and backyards. Most of the houses, Miss Prim had noticed, seemed to fit into Lorraine's "white elephant" category, with bits and pieces in various states of disrepair: a crumbling chimney here, a dilapidated porch there. Such observations, gleaned in a car, would be confirmed or contradicted by a leisurely stroll that would permit closer inspection.

Miss Prim attached Bruno's leash to his collar, then retrieved the dinner bell from the credenza and placed it in her handbag. Lorraine might offer treats to the canines, or Bruno might inappropriately beg for any tea snacks Lorraine might offer, and Miss Prim did not want to miss any opportunity to continue the Boxer's anti-drool training.

Walking up to the ridge on a road that seemed much steeper on foot than it had in an automobile, Miss Prim was thankful for the exercise regimen that had helped unlock her newer, nimbler self. Within minutes she had arrived at the rear gates of Ridgemont.

Although Ridgemont's property was fenced, Miss Prim could see a series of holes dug around the perimeter. An explanatory factor in the Koslowskis' dogs' tendency to wander the neighborhood?

When Miss Prim called Lorraine to say she and Bruno would soon arrive, Lorraine had told her to enter through the rear gate, then follow the path along the right side of the house to the front door. Miss Prim attempted to proceed as directed, wishing she had brought a machete to chop through the overgrowth. Staying close to the house to avoid the face-shredding brambles encroaching on the pathway, Miss Prim could swear she felt the house vibrating. The closer she got to Ridgemont's front door, the louder the booming became. Even more disconcerting was this: Miss Prim was sure she heard a man screaming at the top of his lungs, raving like a homicidal lunatic. Oh, dear; was this to be her first experience of Lucian Koslowski?

Lorraine was waiting at the door. At least Miss Prim *thought* it was Lorraine. Gone were the long, squaw-like tresses; today Lorraine sported a bouffanty blonde wig that appeared to be made of cotton candy, and she wore a tight, revealing red minidress.

"Lorraine, is that you?" Miss Prim asked.

"In the flesh!" Lorraine replied. "How do you like the new look? Marilyn Monroe meets Courtney Love. Being blonde is back, you know. All of the Hollywood starlets are doing it, even the men. Psychological research shows that blondes really *do* have more fun, you know."

"Lorraine, is Lucian all right?" Miss Prim asked tentatively. The screaming in the background had not abated and had perhaps become even louder and more psychotic.

"Yes, he's fine. He's wandering around the house looking for his reading primers from first grade. He's convinced that the U.S. government used Dick and Jane books as the keys for messages encrypted during World War II, and he wants to crack the code once and for all. By the time he finds the books, he'll forget why he was looking for them in the first pace, and I'll have had an afternoon of blissful peace."

"No, I mean … well, Lorraine, he appears to be screaming his head off."

Lorraine laughed heartily. "Felicity, that isn't Lucian. That's Ozzy Osbourne."

"Ozzy Osbourne?"

"One of the great voices in rock and roll. I have the iPod on shuffle, so I have no idea who's coming up next. Could be Judas Priest, could be Alice Cooper, could be Faith No More."

Judith Priest? Alice Cooper? Faith Nomore? Who were these women? Miss Prim had no idea; and as far as dance steps went, she was well acquainted with the Alley Cat and the Winchester Cathedral but had never heard of the Eyepod Shuffle.

"I see," Miss Prim said doubtfully. "I'm having just the tiniest bit of difficulty hearing you, Lorraine," she added, not untruthfully, for anyone would have difficulty hearing over the furious rantings of a singer who sounded as if he'd just gulped down a large swig of Drano. "Do you suppose we might listen to some Vivaldi or Chopin instead?"

"I never listen to that stuff. So boring! I mean, where are the words? You know what, let me just turn it off for now. Come on in, I'll send the dogs out to say hello. Make yourself comfortable, Felicity. We don't stand on formality here at Ridgemont. By the way, use the house's name a few times in conversation with Lucian, please. It'll tickle him and get you two off on the right foot."

Miss Prim entered as Lorraine strode purposefully down the hallway toward the source of the enraged demonic manifestations. Lorraine whistled—a very loud whistle, one that Miss Prim could hear quite distinctly over the din—and two large dogs, one Alsatian and one Doberman, came barreling down the staircase, running straight at Miss Prim and Bruno with alarming speed.

Her self-defense course had covered situations like this one. Miss Prim stood her ground and let the dogs charge, one at Bruno, one at her. Bruno could take care of himself; indeed, his tail was already wagging, for even the most inexperienced of animal lovers could see that the dogs were charging joyfully, not aggressively. Still, it would not do to be knocked over, so she stood still until the Alsatian sprang. At that instant, she calmly stepped to the side. The dog flew out the front door with a whimper of puzzlement, then returned a moment later, eyeing Miss Prim with stunned admiration. Perhaps to save his mistress any further effort, Bruno chased the animal out the front door while the Doberman brought up the rear.

The noise emanating from the rear of the house came to an abrupt halt, and Miss Prim felt as if she had been set free from a mental asylum. She was about to chase after the dogs (she did not want to be responsible for allowing them to get loose, or for one of the town harpies, such as Miss Lavelle, calling the pound), but Lorraine shouted from the other end of the hallway, "Don't worry about the dogs. They'll be fine. Come on down. We'll have tea and coffee in the breakfast nook."

Having saved herself from canine onslaught and having been resolved of responsibility for the dogs, Miss Prim took a moment to look around her. Ahead of her was a large, wide, almost impassable staircase. Bric-a-brac of all types (the kind person's way of saying *junk*) sat on the stairs: candlesticks, newspapers and magazines, unfolded clothing, hockey sticks and baseball bats, mason jars, light bulbs, dolls with missing limbs or no heads, cardboard tubes around which paper towels and toilet paper had once been wrapped, hair curlers, brassieres, large ceramic platters. To get up or down the staircase one would need to very carefully place one's feet on tiny sections of exposed stair, and a false step might prove to be one's last.

The hallway was marginally less cluttered. Miss Prim recognized wallpaper of the type that had been fashionable when her parents had redecorated their Fifth Avenue apartment in the late 1950s. Photos, or other framed items, had once adorned the walls, but the framed items had been removed, leaving dusty rectangles surrounding comparatively brighter patches of the wall covering.

Entering the kitchen, which overlooked Ridgemont's rear yard, Miss Prim ducked to avoid being blinded by a riot of herbs hanging from the ceiling. The kitchen's planar surfaces were filled with hundreds of coffee mugs, some full to the top with cold coffee, some with just a few dregs left in them, and every level in between. Four pots boiled alarmingly on the stove, as they would have done in a mad scientist's laboratory.

Miss Prim took a seat in the nook and watched Bruno cavorting with Henry and Albert. Bruno and the Doberman were taking turns holding each other in a viselike headlock that looked quite dangerous but was probably all in good fun. Or so Miss Prim hoped.

Lorraine placed a cup of weak-looking tea in front of Miss Prim, then poured a cup of coffee for herself. Watching the three dogs playing fetch with no human aid, Lorraine said wistfully, "Almost makes me wish I'd had children. But everyone knows that dogs are much better behaved, and much more grateful, than kids. Plus, the dogs sleep 22 hours a day. You're lucky if kids sleep six."

"Oh, you and Lucian have no children?"

"The idea was there in the back of our heads for a while, but we never quite got it together. We were busy traveling, and Lucian had his business, and we kept putting it off. Then the day came when I said to myself, It's too late. I think if we'd really wanted children we would have made the time, so I tell myself we made the decision by not making it. Plus, can you imagine raising kids in this house? They'd get lost in the junk and I'd never see them again."

"I'm sure it isn't junk, Lorraine," Miss Prim said, touched by Lorraine's willingness to share confidences. "When I meet someone whose home is filled with intriguing objects, I always think of that person as an inveterate collector, as someone with big ideas who has every intention of doing something with all those items when the opportunity presents itself."

Lorraine whacked herself on the thigh with her palm. "Felicity Prim, you're a hoot and a half. You know very well I'm a slob. *Everyone* knows that, which is why nobody visits.

They can't stand the mess, and I don't blame them. But I have to say—the phrase *inveterate collector* is a heck of a lot nicer than *sloven*, so I accept the new title and embrace it. From now on you can call me Lorraine Koslowski, Inveterate Collector."

Miss Prim liked the sound of that. The title tripped off the tongue easily and would work quite well as the second half of an inseparable duo. Felicity Prim, Criminal Outsmarter and Lorraine Koslowski, Inveterate Collector.

Lorraine sipped long and deep from her coffee cup. "Nectar of the gods," she said. "I don't know how you drink that stuff," Lorraine added, nodding her head in the direction of Miss Prim's teacup. "Tastes like dirty socks to me."

Miss Prim scanned the kitchen and noticed that no two of the hundreds of coffee mugs adorning the countertops seemed to match. Lorraine, who'd followed Miss Prim's eyes, explained.

"I know what you're thinking: She may be a slob, but can't she at least wash a coffee mug once in a while? I do it strictly to keep the peace, Felicity. Lucian is forever pouring himself a cuppa and then getting distracted. He leaves the cup wherever he's standing and then forgets about it. For years I tried dumping them out and putting them in the sink, with the goal of washing them eventually, but every time I did that, he'd come in looking for the coffee he'd just poured, and then we'd get into an argument. So I stopped and now we don't argue." Lorraine made a sweeping motion with her arm. "We bought almost all of these mugs on our travels. The truth is, I kind of like looking at them because each one reminds me of a different place. The one I'm holding now—I bought it in a souvenir shop in the ass-end of Paris in the 60s after Lucian and I attended a concert by a young singer named Bob Dylan."

Miss Prim stared blankly. Bob Dylan?

Lorraine sighed. "I see that our musical tastes will never coincide, Felicity. But different strokes, right? My yin to your yang, and all that. But on to more interesting topics. Are you staying out of Gladys Lavelle's way? Any luck in discovering the dead man's identity? Or any other exciting news?"

"Actually, yes. My older sister Celia was here for a visit ..."

"The woman you had lunch with at Maude's?"

"Yes, that was Celia."

"You two are *sisters*? Who would have guessed? She's so Greenwich Village kooky, you're so New England tweed. Rose Red to your Snow White. Shirley MacLaine to your Helen Mirren."

"Well, yes, you are not the first to remark on our differences, but despite our different approaches to wardrobe and other matters of personal style, Celia and I are the dearest of friends."

Lorraine's expression was skeptical. "I have sisters myself, though saying we're the best of friends would be a stretch. Lorna was a hardheaded, obstinate mule, and Loretta is so emotionally manipulative she would have sent Mother Teresa scrambling for an Uzi."

"But surely you all love one another, yes?"

Lorraine considered this question. "Yes, I suppose so. Loretta isn't a bad sort once you get past her passive-aggressiveness and her tendency to lapse into child-speak around attractive men. Lorna's a different story. Lucian couldn't stand her, so she and I didn't spend much time together after I married, and I can't say that I truly missed her. How do you miss someone who makes an art of complaining about *everything* and feeling sorry for herself no matter how good she has it?"

After successfully initiating a bonding session between Deb (the girl at the Two Oaks train station) and her sister Peg (who worked at Maude's), Miss Prim felt quite bullish about her ability to inject sisterly love into Lorraine's life. "It is never too late, Lorraine. Of course Celia and I had our disagreements when we were younger, but I now see how her quirks have allowed her to lead a rich, full, and happy life. Perhaps you might invite your sisters to Ridgemont for a weekend and see what happens?"

"I don't know about that, Felicity," Lorraine said, not sounding at all convinced. "Besides, Lorna's not with us any longer. She had an aneurysm more than a decade ago. Which wasn't surprising, given how mad she always was about everything. Last time I checked, Loretta was somewhere in Europe, chasing some count around the continent. She always thought she should be European royalty and she's dead set on making it happen before she dies. As if she could become European royalty with a name like Loretta Lipshitz."

"Do make the attempt, Lorraine," Miss Prim responded, resting her hand gently on Lorraine's arm. "And if all else fails, well—you always have me."

Lorraine, touched and momentarily lost for words, cocked her head, as if listening for a distant train whistle. "There's Lucian. Let me retrieve him and introduce the two of you." She skipped away as Miss Prim gazed out the window. The dogs had decided to take a nap and were lying curled around one another.

A few seconds later Lorraine led Lucian into the room. He was a tall, thin, stooped man with a head of wild white hair, almost as tall as Papa had been but without Papa's excellent posture. Miss Prim thought he looked a bit like Albert Einstein, and the naughty side of her was tempted to ask him to stick his tongue out, in order to complete the Einsteinian effect. He was carrying a box filled with large balls of colored twine.

"Lucian, I want you to meet a friend of mine," Lorraine said, taking the box of twine from her husband's arms and trying to distract his attention from the coffee mugs. "This is Miss Felicity Prim. She just moved to Greenfield."

Miss Prim rose and extended her hand. "Delighted, Mr. Koslowski. I was so thankful to be invited to Ridgemont. I had seen Ridgemont the first time I visited town, and I thought, 'What a lovely home Ridgemont is.' It is wonderful to be here in Ridgemont with the two denizens of Ridgemont."

Lucian turned to Lorraine. "What?"

Lorraine raised her voice. "SHE SAYS, SHE LOVES RIDGEMONT."

"Of course she does," Lucian said with a huff, as if Miss Prim were not standing directly in front of him. "Only fools do not love Ridgemont."

Then he took Miss Prim's hand and raised it to his lips. "Welcome to Ridgemont, Miss Tenacity. I am Lucian Koslowski, homeowner. And may I present my wife, Mrs. Lorna Koslowski."

"Lorraine, dear," Lorraine said.

"What?"

"LORRAINE. I am LORRAINE. You hate Lorna, remember?"

"Lorna? A horrible woman! Please, we must not speak of her."

"Then don't bring her up, Lucian," Lorraine said.

"What?"

Lorraine, perhaps weary of repeating herself, raised her voice a couple of decibels. "LUCIAN, GET YOUR COLLECTION OF SILVER MERCURY DIMES TO SHOW FELICITY."

Lucian smiled widely. "Yes, I'd be delighted to. It is quite a collection, quite a collection. Will you excuse me a moment, Miss Duplicity?" And out he went.

"That should buy us a few hours," Lorraine said. "He doesn't *have* a collection of silver Mercury dimes."

Miss Prim chuckled.

"Now, you were saying," Lorraine continued, once they had settled themselves at the table again. "Catch me up on the latest details of your life, if you please."

Miss Prim debated whether to share the information Detective Dawes had given her regarding the locked-room mystery in her basement. She decided she had best not do so. That sort of information, if publicly disseminated, might give the killer an advantage. She opted for homier news. "When Celia and I had lunch at Maude's, we ran into Olivia Abernathy. She confirmed what you said about Elizabeth Saxe-Coburg living in a retirement home, and it turns out the home is in Two Oaks. I shall pay Mrs. Saxe-Coburg a visit tomorrow. It is not likely that she will remember anything—she is apparently quite senile—but talking to her may yield some insights."

Lorraine pursed her lips. "I'd go into it with low expectations, Felicity. Remember, she wasn't a communicative woman even when she had all her marbles."

"Still, I can't see that it would hurt to try. At the very least, she'll have some company. And who can say no to homemade cinnamon rolls? Along with a cup of tea, they have been known to invoke a stroll down memory lane."

"Your cinnamon rolls can do that? Can they also create world peace, impose democracy, and cure all diseases?" Seeing Miss Prim's look of distress, Lorraine added, "I'm joking, Felicity. Cooking was never one of my talents, and I felt it keenly for many years, mostly because Lucian loves to eat. I long envied cooks their talent, and I suppose a bit of that envy lingers. But listen to me, admitting my faults. That's something I try not to do, since most people think I don't have them. Seriously, I hope you enjoy your visit with Elizabeth. I'd ask you to say hello from me, but since she never said a word to me while we were neighbors, I doubt she'd want to hear anything about me now. And do take what she says with a few grains of salt, even if she seems to be making sense. I'd hate to see you going off half-cocked because crazy old Elizabeth Saxe-Coburg sent you on a wild goose chase."

"Never fear, Lorraine. I always double check my information. That is standard procedure."

Lorraine gave her a puzzled look, and Miss Prim realized that she hadn't yet talked with Lorraine about her burgeoning career in criminal outsmarting. Might this be a good time to broach the subject? Perhaps not. It might be better to cement her relationship with Lorraine first, especially because it seemed inevitable that Lorraine would become her sidekick in future adventures. Why, Miss Prim could even see a highly talented novelist writing about her exploits. The book jacket would feature a slim, attractive woman in her rose garden. Under the title, the words "A Mystery Introducing Miss Felicity Prim" would appear, thus positioning her tale as the first in a wildly successful, long-running series. But no—Miss Prim was getting carried away. All of that was fiction, and this was the real world.

Lorraine rose from her chair and opened the rear door. Placing two fingers in her mouth, she whistled shrilly. The three dogs, which had been fast asleep, rose instantly and ran for the door: Albert and Henry first (Miss Prim still wasn't sure which was which), followed by Bruno. As they entered the house, Lorraine reached for a jar of treats and Miss Prim unzipped her handbag to grab the bell in case Bruno began drooling.

Bruno took Lorraine's proffered treat with alacrity (and without drooling), the Doberman borderline rudely. The Alsatian turned aside snobbishly, as if disdaining the biscuit.

"Oh, for God's sake, Henry," Lorraine huffed. "Here, Felicity. You give it to him." She handed the treat to Miss Prim, who in turn offered it to the animal. Henry the elderly Alsatian (she could see the gray in his muzzle and around his eyes) padded over to her and gently accepted the treat, sitting at Miss Prim's side and allowing her to scratch his ruff.

"You lucked out with Bruno," Lorraine said. "Believe me, you haven't been insulted until a dog has snubbed you."

"Perhaps he's just having an off day," Miss Prim offered. But she had to admit to herself that Henry wasn't *looking* off. His tail was wagging enthusiastically as he submitted to Miss Prim's affections.

"No, he's Lucian's dog, always has been. Never mind that I feed him and groom him and force the heartworm pills down his gullet. He just never took to me. Fortunately, I have my Albert."

Upon hearing his name, Albert jumped up gently and placed his paws on Lorraine's shoulders. Then he gave her a lick to demonstrate his undying love.

"It's the craziest thing, Felicity," Lorraine said, lowering her voice to confide her next secret. "All my life, I've never cared whether people liked me or not. And they usually do. I want Henry to like me, but he just doesn't. I can't tell you how much time I've spent kissing up to him, but he just isn't interested. Don't let anyone tell you animals aren't as stubborn as people, Felicity, because they are. They are."

19

In Search of a Sister

Cornelius Prim's journal had placed Providence's tenth birthday on February 2, 1996, which meant Providence had been born on February 2, 1986. Miss Prim tried to think through the details.

Until her discovery of the journal, Miss Prim would have sworn on her life that Papa had no secrets from her. The loveliest of men, he was also the most predictable. She knew what time he arose in the morning (5:45, weekdays and weekends), his favorite bourbon, the clothiers he favored, the writers he would purchase immediately upon publication (and those for which he'd wait for the reviews).

Cornelius Prim was a man who'd believed in standards and proper time frames. Today it is acceptable to think about dating again one year after a spouse's death, but even before her discussion with Celia, Miss Prim was certain that Papa had delayed much longer than that. She'd spent a good deal of time with her father in the years following her mother's death, often stopping at his apartment to offer baked treats, to help with the housework, or to provide companionable good cheer. She searched her memory for any hints Cornelius Prim may have dropped regarding another woman in his life. She could think of none at all. The first five years after his wife's death, Papa had expressed no interest in pursuing a romantic life.

Then, in the sixth year, he'd gradually entered society again, accepting old friends' invitations to join them for a drink or a game of darts at the gentleman's club on Gramercy Park. Not wishing to stand in his way, and not wishing to make him feel that he must stay at home for her sake, Miss Prim had gradually begun decreasing the frequency of her visits. Ultimately she and Papa had established a tradition of enjoying a Sunday meal together (sometimes with Celia, sometimes without) after a busy week with limited contact between them.

Miss Prim climbed the stairs to her attic and hunted for the journals dated between 1981 and 1986. She found dozens of journals from this sequence of years. She carried them in batches to the parlor, where she arranged them chronologically on the coffee table. Then she brewed herself a cup of tea and began reading them.

The first few journals were concerned almost exclusively with Papa's business dealings. Miss Prim tried to read them page by page, but the experience was like reading an accounting textbook, and ultimately she began skimming and scanning. Once she adopted this new approach, the pages began to fly by. Not quite the same experience as reading one of the wonderful fast-paced thrillers by, say, David Baldacci, Joseph Finder, or Iris Johansen, but not quite as bad as plowing through the latest long-winded tome by …

Little by little, the tone of Papa's journals changed. First he began to make notes about having met this friend or that associate for a meal; then he began to ruminate on life, reminisce about his late wife, and make notes for short stories he hoped to write. His to-do list was composed of typical Corneliusisms—"Write to mayor with suggestion for improving service on the #1 train"—but Miss Prim began to notice a bit more levity as Mr. Cornelius Prim began to enjoy life again after his period of mourning. One of Miss Prim's favorite entries was this:

Encountered many annoying children today. Surely my children never behaved thus; or did they? Noel, almost certainly; Celia, quite probably; Felicity, absolutely not.

In one of the 1984 journals, Miss Prim encountered a seemingly innocuous entry that took on greater meaning in light of future events:

Dinner with William Barlowe and that insufferable partner of his. How do two men of such widely differing levels of business acumen, and so far apart on the IQ scale, manage to start a business and work together? Barlowe remains the brain, the operations man, the visionary. Foster McGinniss remains nothing more than the snake-oil salesman I have always known him to be. But the man does have a remarkable talent for cultivating clients of the female gender; and the new secretary he has hired, Miss Ophelia LeFevre, could certainly stop the heart of any man with a pulse.

Another entry was dated two weeks later:

I had the distinct pleasure of conversing with Miss O.L.F. via the phone today. What an intelligent woman; she quite reminded me of Charity, RIP my sweetest. I asked her how she enjoyed working with McGinniss and she replied coyly, "I am sure that you and I enjoy working with him equally." Clever response, and I chuckled despite myself.

And then another, two weeks after that:

I happened to be walking past the offices of Barlowe & McGinniss (perhaps a coincidence, perhaps not?) when I decided to stop in for a brief chat with Barlowe. It was lunchtime, when Barlowe is usually out and about, but I thought it could not hurt to pop in. Miss O.L.F. greeted me with a warm smile and confirmed that B. was indeed lunching with a client. Somehow I found myself asking her to lunch. To my surprise I found her willing to accept my invitation, while stating that she could not possibly leave the office deserted while her employers were elsewhere. I suggested that dinner might be a reasonable alternative, and she accepted for two evenings hence. I cannot help but remember that Charity employed a similar strategy. And I cannot help but think, too, that O.'s acceptance of my invitation has made me feel almost as light-hearted as Charity's first acceptance.

Miss Prim felt a tear sliding down her cheek. She continued flipping through the journals, looking for further references to O.

6 March 1985
Cornelius, you are behaving like an old fool. To think that O. would consider you as a suitor—and to think that you should suggest such a thing! And yet, she promises to entertain my suggestion, declaring that she has become very fond of me in just two months' time. Her words: "very fond." Did not the Old

English use the words "fond" and "foolish" interchangeably? For I do feel quite foolish, seeking the affections of a woman more than three decades my junior, yet I cannot deny that I have not felt quite so happy in years.

26 April 1985

O. and I continue to spend time together. How young she makes me feel, with her gentle laugh and kind heart. She is the intellectual superior of McGinniss and even of Barlowe; and I know Charity would have heartily approved of her. But how do I tell my daughters of this involvement? Their devotion to their mother is passionate, and rightly so. Yet Charity told me I must not live as a hermit after her death, and I know in my heart she would approve of this match. Still, I find myself quite unable to talk with Celia and Felicity on this matter, and I think I shall wait a bit longer until O. and I have sorted out our intentions.

10 May 1985

A small bump in the road, but I knew I would encounter challenges. O.'s great aunt, with whom she lives, has expressed disapproval of the "older man" with whom O. has chosen to keep company. My first meeting with Aunt A. did not go well; I felt disapproval emanating from her every pore. Perhaps I shall have to ask McGinniss how to charm the woman. I did not require such coaching in the past! For O., however, I am willing to court her Aunt A.

14 June 1985

Progress with Aunt A. is damnably slow. I asked O. why she is so tied to this particular aunt, for when O. consents to become my wife, I shall care for her, and she need not worry about retaining the affections of that old crone. Oh, how Charity would admonish me for describing a woman in such terms; but really, there are no other to describe Aunt A., who leads a life of bitterness, anger, and resentment. I believe she is urging O. to break off her relationship with me, though O. denies this. And yet I know O. loves me, as I love her; we have made this declaration, and I know her to be true. Why, then, will she not accept my offer to become my wife? I confess this situation is driving me nearly to distraction.

3 August 1986

How have you gotten yourself into such a situation, Cornelius Prim? You, who were always so proud of your caution and prudence? O. has confided in me that she is with child. How do I know I love her? Because I greeted the news with ecstasy. But O. is not so assured. She worries about her status as a single woman, and what Society (and her Aunt A.) will say. Why, then, will she not marry me? She tells me she must think about my offer and I must not press her. I simply do not know how to behave. I wish to make O. my wife and be a father to the child. What more can I do but continue pleading with her to accept?

11 December 1986

I now understand. We shall cope with the situation to the best of our abilities. In the meantime, as O. enters her seventh month, we must endeavor to remain calm, to keep O. and the child healthy. I have promised not to press my proposal again, until O. is ready to speak of it.

Poor Papa, Miss Prim thought, her heart in tatters as she closed the last of the journals. But the tale had a happy ending. The child had lived, even if the mother had not. Providence was somewhere out there.

Miss Prim picked up the phone receiver and dialed Manhattan.

"Sister," she began without prelude, "I have information of the utmost importance to share. I have discovered O.'s identity. Her name was Ophelia LeFevre."

20

Heavenly Pastures

Miss Prim was up and about early the following morning. Bruno needed his morning walk, and it would take several hours to bake and cool the cinnamon rolls. On a whim, Miss Prim also whipped up a batch of Junusakey lemonade and poured it into an empty milk bottle. Mrs. Saxe-Coburg's peregrinations might be limited to the grounds of Heavenly Pastures, but that did not mean she should not partake in the beverage sensation sweeping Connecticut.

The previous day Miss Prim had called the nursing home and requested an appointment with Elizabeth Saxe-Coburg. The receptionist had slightly reprimanded/upbraided her, saying that Heavenly Pastures was a residential community, not a prison or a hospital that limited visitors to particular days or hours.

Miss Prim packed the cinnamon rolls into a roomy Tupperware container, patted Bruno's head, and reminded him that Kit would be along later for a walk and a romp. She locked the door and left the spare key under a rock in the backyard—the hiding place to which she'd agreed when she'd phoned Kit the previous evening, after returning from Lorraine and Lucian's. Then she loaded herself, the cinnamon rolls, and the Junusakey lemonade into the Zap.

It was a sunny, somewhat humid morning (when, and how, had the weather become so muggy?—It had not been thus, when she was younger), and traffic was light, so Miss Prim did not encounter the usual slowpokes as she navigated the Zap through town. Fortunately, Miss Prim noted with approval, pedestrians understood the health benefits of walking briskly, crossing streets and avenues with urgency as she approached.

As she pulled inside the gates of Heavenly Pastures, two elderly gentlemen who'd been walking alongside the road picked up their pace suddenly, fairly darting onto the property's grassy paths. *Never let it be said that the elderly are not spry*, Miss Prim thought, and she nodded in greeting even as one of the gentlemen began screaming and the other threw his cane at the Zap in an inexplicable fit of rage.

At the visitor center, she signed in and was directed to Mrs. Saxe-Coburg's efficiency apartment, Unit A of Sunflower Lodge. As Miss Prim followed the crudely drawn map, she noticed that all of the buildings were named for flowers or birds. She passed Daisy Cottage, Tulip Village, Nightingale Forest, Starling Manse. Each building was two stories high, and the ground-floor units offered pleasant sitting areas and small gardens.

Arriving at Sunflower Lodge (which, curiously, had no sunflowers anywhere near it) Miss Prim located Unit A and pressed the doorbell. A young, cornrowed black woman answered.

"Good day, I am Miss Felicity Prim," Miss Prim said amiably. "I have come to visit Mrs. Saxe-Coburg. I wonder if she is available?"

The woman eyed her doubtfully. "She doesn't get many visitors." Miss Prim recognized an island lilt. Nevis? St. Kitts? Turks and Caicos? St. Vincent and the Grenadines? "I'm Jacqueline Duvalier, her Assistant. That's what they call us here: Assistants. No nurses or doctors at Heavenly

Pastures, just Assistants, Health Coaches, Life Maximizers, and Activity Consultants." She rolled her eyes to indicate her opinion of these euphemisms. "Let me tell her you're here, and then I'll give you two some private time. We're not supposed to stay with them for more than an hour at a time anyway. Supposedly it makes them feel feeble. Mrs. S-C's pretty easygoing that way, though. Give me just a minute, please. "

Jacqueline Duvalier left the door open a smidge and returned a moment later.

"You're in luck. She's pretending she knows who you are. Come on in." As Miss Prim entered, Jacqueline pointed to a series of large red buttons spaced at even intervals along the apartment walls. "If you get into any scrapes, press one of those buttons and someone'll come running. I'll be deep in hiding somewhere having a cigarette. If they catch me, I'll get fired. 'Staff must set the correct example,' they say. No smoking or drinking at Heavenly Pastures. Ha! If they only knew."

Jacqueline breezed out and Miss Prim moved tentatively down the corridor into a large, sunny room. Elizabeth Saxe-Coburg sat knitting on a richly embroidered couch. The apartment was immaculately clean and decorated in the best of taste.

"Felicity! How wonderful to see you!" Mrs. Saxe-Coburg exclaimed, rising to greet her. "Come in, come in. It's been much too long. Let me look at you! You've lost weight, haven't you? And you still have that gorgeous complexion. Well, you were always a looker. I used to say that to Ralph all the time, you know. 'That Felicity Prim is a looker.' And here you are, still looking like the cat's pajamas after all these years."

Given Lorraine's warnings about Mrs. Saxe-Coburg's lack of agreeableness and general unfriendliness, Miss Prim was pleasantly surprised by this greeting.

Miss Prim did not consider herself an opportunist, but she also knew the rules of criminal outsmarting. When you have a loquacious character on your hands, you must allow her to talk, and talk, and talk, until she says something interesting or relevant. Miss Prim briefly considered the ethical dimensions of winkling information out of an elderly person, but she dismissed her cavil. The police seemed no closer to identifying the man whose body she had found in her basement, and the unfortunate man's family must be frantic by now.

"Elizabeth!" Miss Prim exclaimed, flying into Mrs. Saxe-Coburg's arms. "You always were one for compliments; and now, as then, I simply eat them up. But reserve some accolades for yourself, too. I see you are as trim as ever, with those piercing blue eyes that caused many a man's mind to wander. Of course, Ralph knew you turned heads, and he was simultaneously proud and quite mad with jealousy, wasn't he?"

Mrs. Saxe-Coburg blushed and reluctantly admitted that yes, it was true, it was all true; at her age, why waste time with false modesty?

"I've brought some cinnamon rolls and lemonade for us," Miss Prim continued.

Mrs. Saxe-Coburg's eyes lit up. "You remembered, Felicity! I am not surprised. You were always the most kind-hearted of women. It's so good of you to visit an old friend."

"You say it like it is an obligation, Elizabeth," Miss Prim responded, "when you know it is simply a pleasure. Now, why don't you sit back and catch me up on things while I brew us up some tea? I'll place the lemonade in the refrigerator so that you can enjoy it later."

"You always did love your tea, Felicity! You know I prefer coffee, but I shall indulge you this time, my dear. My Life Maximizer tells me that I must cut back on my coffee intake, anyway. Is Earl Gray still your favorite?"

"Yes, of course." Miss Prim wondered how Elizabeth Saxe-Coburg could know so much about her. Did Miss Prim look like a woman who loves her Earl Gray? Perhaps, perhaps.

As Miss Prim rattled around the galley kitchen searching for a teapot and teacups, Elizabeth engaged in a running monologue regarding the events of her life. She was embroidering new antimacassars for the chairs—she continued to watch Ed Sullivan nightly—she thought President Kennedy was doing a wonderful job in office, and that he was quite handsome to boot—she had just watched the moon landing on the telly and had found it awe-inspiring—she thought this hula-hoop craze to be a fad that would not last long.

Miss Prim nodded her agreement to all of Mrs. Saxe-Coburg's pronouncements, then served up the tea and cinnamon rolls. The two women sat at a small table overlooking the unit's tiny garden with its profusion of gladioli and ageratum.

"Enough about me, Felicity, I feel I have been quite monopolizing the conversation! But you know me long enough to know that I do go on sometimes. Tell me about you, dear. Do you still have your pet kangaroo—oh, what was his name? It escapes me."

"I am sorry to say Punchy is no longer with us, Elizabeth. It was a sad day, but he had lived a very full life, and I am sure he is in a better place."

"How very sad," Mrs. Saxe-Coburg said, wiping a tear from her eye. "I always thought his mastery of Shakespeare was remarkable. I was quite overtaken by his portrayal of Caliban."

Miss Prim nodded in agreement. "I am so impressed with your home, Elizabeth. As always, you have taken a space and made it your own. It is not only bright and cheerful, but also comfortably elegant. Tell me, do you think much about the old house on Undercliff Lane?"

"I do miss it, Felicity," Mrs. Saxe-Coburg admitted. "It was dear, wasn't it? Not very large, but it was home for so many years. Except for, you know, that brief spell. Do you think the townspeople talked very much about it?"

Miss Prim thought it best to tread lightly. "You know Greenfield, Elizabeth. News travels quickly, but I can honestly say I never heard any talk of it."

"I must say, that is a relief. Ralph was of course furious, but I believe our marriage became stronger as a result of it. Which is not to say that we didn't have some rocky years, of course. But those are the ebbs and flows of all marriages, I suppose. Tell me, are Liz Taylor and Richard Burton still married, or have they divorced again?"

"I'm afraid their second marriage has not lasted, either. By all reports, their second outing was as tempestuous as their first." Miss Prim tried to steer the conversation back to Elizabeth's *brief spell.* "Now, remind me, Elizabeth, when you left Greenfield, where exactly did you go? I knew once, and it is on the tip of my tongue now, but I cannot quite access the information."

"Oh, Felicity! Let's not speak of it. Even now, it is much too painful to think about." Elizabeth seemed quite shaken, even on the verge of tears, so Miss Prim changed the subject.

"Of course, Elizabeth, it is much more pleasant to speak of home and hearth. And I do have such fond memories of the house on Undercliff Lane. It had a secret door to the basement, if I recall correctly? One accessed the door by pressing a wooden star into a recessed area in the wall, correct?"

"Yes, that was indeed our kitchen. The hidden basement was a bit of whimsy on the builder's part. He was rather a paranoid type, worried about the Cold War and such, just as so many of us were in the 1950s. I stored my preserves in that basement, and Ralph used it as a root cellar."

"Did you and Ralph keep the basement a secret from the larger world? Outside our immediate circle, that is? If it had been my house, I might have done that, just for the fun of it all."

"Oh, no. Everyone knew about it. But so many of our old friends have moved on, and I suppose it's possible that nobody left in Greenfield remembers life the way it was."

"I sometimes long for the old days, Elizabeth. Is there anyone from Greenfield whose company you particularly miss, or do you still prefer your own company? I remember that you seemed very content to stay in the house, tending to your garden, rather than flitting about and hosting parties."

Elizabeth Saxe-Coburg looked sharply at Miss Prim. "Whatever are you talking about, Felicity? You know that Ralph and I were great entertainers. Every Saturday evening we hosted informal debates, where the gentlemen would hold forth on the matters of the day and the ladies would ask questions and add their own opinions. Oh, the alcohol that flowed in those days, and the number of cigarettes smoked! But it was all quite harmless, and we had many laughs as well as many insightful discussions."

Miss Prim frowned. Elizabeth Saxe-Coburg's view of her life differed rather substantially from Lorraine's memories of the reclusive Saxe-Coburgs. And Elizabeth had just confirmed Olivia Abernathy's assertion that Rose Cottage had been built much earlier than Lorraine had remembered.

An idea struck Miss Prim. Nothing ventured, nothing gained, so … "Wasn't Lucian Koslowski quite vociferous in his debating style? And Lorraine as well. I can remember her holding forth at length on the merits of withdrawing the U.S. troops from Vietnam."

Elizabeth smiled indulgently. "Felicity, is it possible that you are experiencing a senior moment? Of course you are correct about Lucian. As for Lorraine, was there ever a greater shrinking violet? She was quite understated and soft-spoken, but her devotion to Lucian could not be denied. I don't think she ever knew, and that is for the best."

Elizabeth stood and walked to a large armoire. She opened the doors, pulled open a drawer, and removed a photo album. She carried it to the table, sat next to Miss Prim, and began flipping through the photos. In every photo, Miss Prim saw Elizabeth Saxe-Coburg as a younger woman: petite, vital, attractive, with a broad genuine smile. The dark-haired, handsome man on her arm must have been Ralph.

Elizabeth stopped at a black-and-white photo of two happy couples taken in a night club. She recognized Elizabeth and Ralph immediately. With a shock, she realized the identity of the other couple: Lucian and Lorraine Koslowski. As a younger man, Lucian had been hale and robust, with a full head of dark hair and prominent cheekbones, while Lorraine had been quite demure, with mousy brown hair and a shy, tentative grin.

With a jolt, Miss Prim's brain made a connection. The resemblance between the younger Lucian Koslowski and the retouched photo of the man in her basement was unmistakable.

A moment later Jacqueline Duvalier returned. Miss Prim removed the remaining cinnamon rolls from the Tupperware container—it is a woman's obligation to never, ever leave her Tupperware behind—and wrapped them in aluminum foil to keep them fresh. Promising Elizabeth that she would return soon for another visit, she took her leave, thinking she might bring Bruno with her next time. It was well documented, was it not, that animal companions have many positive effects on the health and well-being of the elderly and infirm.

In the space of her brief visit, Miss Prim had developed quite an affection for Elizabeth Saxe-Coburg. Miss Prim's promise to visit again was not an idle one; she never made a promise she did not intend to keep.

She walked to the visitors' center to return her badge and bade the receptionist a good day. As she turned to exit the building, she looked up and saw Miss Gladys Lavelle striding aggressively toward her.

"Well, if it isn't Miss Goody-Two-Shoes," Miss Lavelle said, her voice dripping with sarcasm. "What are *you* doing here?"

Miss Prim was caught off guard, and she responded quite as she would have to a rational person.

"Oh, hello, Miss Lavelle. I have come to …"

"I know what you've come to do, Missy. It's not enough for you to ride into Greenfield on your horse and become everyone's best friend overnight. Now you want to conquer Two Oaks and Heavenly Pastures, too. Just Miss Prim and her warm, sticky cinnamon rolls worming their way into everyone's hearts. Well, I've got your number, sister. *I'm* the goodwill volunteer here, not you. Go spread your sunshine down in New York City, or some other place that doesn't see you for exactly what you are: an attention-seeking little drama queen. And stay out of my way, and off my turf, or you'll regret it." With that, Miss Lavelle stalked off, leaving Miss Prim standing with her mouth agape in a manner that Mrs. Charity Prim would have heartily disapproved of.

21
Harmless Meddling

The day was still young after Miss Prim's visit to Heavenly Pastures, and workaday tasks needed her attention. During her first trip to Prothero's she hadn't purchased everything she needed because she and Lorraine had been on foot, and her shopping list had expanded as a result of her promise to cook delicious, edible meals for Kit. Realizing that Miss Lavelle could not be simultaneously visiting Heavenly Pastures and womanning one of Prothero's cash registers, Miss Prim pulled the Zap into the market's parking lot. As she pushed her cart through the aisles, she stopped to introduce herself to other shoppers, retrieving the murder victim's photo from her handbag and asking if anyone recognized him. Nobody did.

Examining the overwhelming selection of breakfast cereals, she looked up from the overpriced granolas and noticed a headful of dreadlocks across the aisle. Faye Cotillard was deep in conversation with a tall, thin, harried-looking man with a profusion of wrinkles and thinning fair hair.

Faye caught her eye. "Miss Prim! Hi!"

Miss Prim squeezed Faye's arm in greeting. "Faye, how are you, dear?"

"I need a job, Miss Prim. Everyone else my age is out working, and I just sit around, writing in my journal and drinking too much coffee. Do you know Mr. Prothero? I'm trying to convince him to hire me."

"I haven't had the pleasure," Miss Prim said, extending her hand to Mr. Prothero. "I am Miss Felicity Prim. I just moved into the Saxe-Coburgs' house on Undercliff Lane."

Mr. Prothero shook Miss Prim's hand. His own was rather sweaty and slippery.

"Ethan Prothero. Welcome to Greenfield, Miss Prim. I'm sorry for that, um, encounter with Miss Lavelle. She has a wonderful heart, but she sometimes lacks patience and other, um, social graces."

Mrs. Charity Prim's training kicked in immediately. Isn't it the mark of the well-bred person to help others feel comfortable and at ease, especially in tense situations? "No need to apologize, Mr. Prothero. I'm afraid I come on rather strong sometimes. My mother always said I was much too aggressive in social situations, and I am starting to think that may be the case." The second half of that statement was true, the first half patently false. "Perhaps I have been trying too hard to become a part of the Greenfield social fabric. These things take time and cannot be accomplished overnight. And I do think my relationship with Miss Lavelle is improving ever so slightly. We saw each other not an hour ago and engaged in a not wholly unpleasant exchange." Some might argue that Miss Prim was prevaricating; but her words, if carefully parsed, could be corroborated, for the equation went something like this:

  Miss Lavelle's vicious attack
\+ Miss Prim's attempt to be polite
= A not wholly unpleasant exchange

"I've seen her in action a million times and she *can* be one tough cookie," Faye put in. "She's never been anything but nice to me and Kit, though. I figure, why look a gift horse in the mouth?" She turned to the store's proprietor. "So, what do you say, Mr. Prothero?"

"I do need another cashier, now that Hazel has retired," Ethan Prothero said, his unease evident. "And I suppose if Gladys would accept *anyone* new at the front end, it would be you. Come to my office and let's fill out the paperwork."

"Thanks, Mr. P! I owe you, I really do. Miss Prim, can we catch up later?"

"Of course, dear. Faye, before I forget, are you available this weekend? A close friend, who is much closer to your age than to mine, will be visiting. Perhaps you and Kit might join us for tea and parlor games? I know you and Dolly would get along famously."

"Sure, I've got nothing but time, Miss Prim. As long as I'm not working! Right, Mr. P?"

Mr. Prothero looked over his shoulder helplessly at Miss Prim as Faye herded him down the aisle. *Young womanhood at its finest*, Miss Prim thought. For was this not woman's lot in life, to perpetually be keeping after the male species, ensuring that they do what needs to be done rather than thinking about sports all day long?

Miss Prim loaded her groceries into the Zap and decided to complete one last errand before returning to Rose Cottage. She locked the Zap's doors and cut across the town square to Maude's Tavern. The lunch crowd had dispersed and the after-work crowd had not yet gathered, which meant that Miss Prim was able to walk unimpeded to the bar. Maude stood there dunking glassware into a basin of soapy water, holding each tumbler up to the light to ensure an absence of spots.

Miss Prim perched herself on a bar stool.

"Hello, Maude. How are you today?"

"Fine."

"I see you are experiencing a lull. It must be nice to have a respite from the flocks of hungry and thirsty villagers."

"Yeah."

"Maude, I hope you won't think me too familiar, but I have a bit of a sensitive topic to broach with you. Will you promise to consider with an open mind what I'm about to suggest?"

"Yup."

"Here's the thing, Maude. I was speaking with Valeska Reed over at the bookstore. She made the very good point that Greenfield's merchants should support one another, not work against one another's interests. I don't think anyone would disagree with that, do you?"

"Nope."

"Well, I'm afraid Mrs. Reed thinks that your willingness to provide free reading materials for the townspeople—over there, on your shelves—affects her ability to sell books. After thinking it through, I must say I agree with her. I don't think anyone is opposed to the sharing of good books with friends and family. But the truth of the modern world is that people seem to want everything for free, and why pay for something when you don't have to? Unfortunately, this philosophy greatly devalues books. Wouldn't you concur that the amount of pleasure given by a book is worth the few dollars one must spend for it? All those hardworking writers, editors, cover designers, and typesetters—these people must be paid to continue their work. With no revenue, how will anyone get paid? How will they feed their families and send their children to college? Books have tremendous worth, and we must not do anything to make them seem less valuable. Do you see what I am getting at, Maude?"

Maude nodded his head once.

"So, might you be willing to do something about those shelves of free books, Maude?"

"Well …"

"Thank you for considering it. I know Mrs. Reed will be most appreciative also." Miss Prim suddenly recalled a task she had been given. "While I'm here, Maude, it also occurs to me—I don't think I've ever seen a woman, other than Peg, working behind the bar with you. Yet New England has a long tradition of the tavern keeper and his wife working together to run the business. Is there a Mrs. Maude?"

"Nah."

"No special woman in your life?"

"Nah."

"So I see we have a great deal in common. We are both single and happy. Though perhaps it may be said that we are married to our careers."

Maude grunted. "Eh."

"Do you remember the woman I lunched with the other day—my sister Celia? She, too, is single."

"Yeah."

"Will you forgive me for being such an unrepentant meddler? I think she may have found you just the tiniest bit attractive."

"Hmmm."

"If you would like, I could arrange for a more formal get-together during her next visit. Is that an arrangement you might enjoy?"

"Yup."

"Well, then, Maude. Stay tuned for more details, if you please."

"Right."

Miss Prim took her leave, rose from the stool, straightened her skirt, and walked toward the tavern's front entrance. As she left, she saw Maude emerge from the back of the tavern carrying a large cardboard box. Outside, Miss Prim peeked through the window and watched as Maude began removing books from the shelves and transferring them into the box.

As Miss Prim began her stroll back to the Zap, she heard a loud but friendly bark. She looked up to see Bruno tied to a lamppost outside the Greenfield Post Office. She caught his eye and watched as he attempted to dislodge the lamppost in an attempt to reach her.

"Stay!" she commanded, walking to him and getting down on her haunches to receive his enthusiastic greetings. A moment later, the door leading to the building's second floor opened and Kit came running out.

"Miss Prim, what's up? Me and Bruno are getting a few things done."

Miss Prim looked at the lettering on the glass door: Greenfield Historical Society. "Oh, are you interested in history, Kit?"

"I have a project for school. I thought Gil could help."

"Gil?"

"Gil Fellowes. He's the old geez—I mean, he's the old guy—I mean, he's the guy who runs the place."

"Did you find the answers you sought?"

"No, he's not there. Or he's *pretending* he's not there. Sometimes he hides in the back room when he doesn't feel like talking to anyone. Sometimes he goes out for coffee and leaves the place empty. I'm gonna go over to Beantown to see if I can find him. You wanna come with?"

Kit untied Bruno's leash from the lamppost, Miss Prim locked her arm in Kit's, and the three began walking to Beantown. Miss Prim thought Kit seemed uncomfortable, so she released her grip on his arm.

"Do forgive me, Kit. I am sometimes too emotionally effusive. I am sure you do not want your friends to see you walking arm in arm through the town square with a woman old enough to be your grandmother. I should have considered that *before* I grabbed your arm like a drowning woman clutching at a life preserver."

"It's just that I never really walked around with an old la—I mean, a new friend, before."

"I shall be more cognizant of these things in the future, Kit. It's just that I've become so fond of you, in such a short time, and—as Miss Lavelle has noted, I can be much too forward in these matters."

"Don't worry about her, Miss Prim," Kit said. And then, in a moment Miss Prim would never forget, he locked his arm through hers as they continued walking through the square.

After Kit tied Bruno's leash to a bike rack outside Beantown, the two friends entered the coffeehouse. Kit spied a bowtie-wearing older gentleman with sparse white hair sipping from a steaming mug in a far corner.

"That's Gil!" Kit exclaimed and took off. Gil looked highly alarmed at being approached so rapidly and forcefully. Well, it is good for historians to experience the *present*, Miss Prim thought, as she felt a gentle touch on her arm from behind.

"Hello, Miss Prim," Detective Dawes said with that disarming smile of his. In one hand he held a cup of coffee; in the other, a prune danish. "Care to join me?"

"Detective! I don't mind if I do. Let me order myself a cup of tea and I'll be right with you."

"My treat. Lemon and honey?"

Miss Prim nodded in the affirmative.

"I remember that's how you fixed your tea the day we met. That's my table, right there. The one with the Lee Child book on it."

"How kind of you, Detective," Miss Prim said, settling herself at the detective's table and wondering if she should be drinking tea with a man she found so attractive—*especially* when she had not yet sorted out her feelings for Doctor Poe. She would sort those feelings out, she swore to herself, as soon as she could find the time.

A moment later Dawes placed a steaming cup in front of her.

"So, you are a Lee Child fan," Miss Prim said. "Tell me, do you wish you were Jack Reacher? Do not be reluctant to admit it. Many men do."

Was it Miss Prim's imagination, or did Detective Dawes appear to blush? "Well, Miss Prim, I wouldn't say I want to *be* him, but I do admire his ability to cut through the red tape that us real people have to deal with. And he's indestructible, isn't he? That would be nice, too."

"I see your point, Detective. But remember, Reacher is a fictional creation. Those of us who fight crime on a daily basis know that it is not quite so glamorous, and that not every case includes a wild sexual experience with the attractive person *du jour*. Such plot developments occur in fiction, not in the real world. Perhaps this is why one reads fiction to begin with—to live a more interesting reality than one's daily life. But on to more pressing matters. I've had no luck identifying the man in my basement. Have you?"

"None. It's really frustrating. I'm still waiting for the M.E.'s report, but I did get a copy of the guy's prints, and he isn't in any databases, anywhere. And nobody in Greenfield recognizes him or knows why he was here. Spike and Martin have checked all the hotels in a twenty-mile radius, and they've hit nothing but dead ends."

"Have you asked Valeska Reed about him?"

"Valeska? What would she know?"

"Yesterday I showed her the altered photo that you printed for me. She told me she'd seen the man peering in her store windows at closing time."

Dawes narrowed his eyes. "Why wouldn't she have told Martin about that?"

"I get the sense that he may not have shown her the photo. Perhaps he doesn't wish to bring his work home with him."

"Or he's afraid she'll yell at him. You say she told you all of this yesterday?"

Miss Prim nodded.

"Then I suppose she could have told him about it last night," Dawes continued. "I haven't seen Martin yet today, but still, he should have called to tell me. It's strange."

"I agree, it's all very perplexing," Miss Prim said, hoping to change the topic of conversation. She did not want to gossip about what might be the troubled marriage between Martin and Valeska Reed. "Tell me, Detective, what will be done with our unknown man, eventually?"

"We'll keep him—uh, I guess you would say in storage—until we find his next of kin. If we can't identify him or find his family, we'll have to bury him in a potter's field."

How tragic that would be, Miss Prim thought. If the man's family were not found, she would pay for a proper, dignified burial.

"While I have you here, Miss Prim," Detective Dawes said, somewhat hesitantly, "I did want to remind you that the speed limit in Greenfield is 25 miles per hour."

"Oh, dear," Miss Prim replied. "I do apologize for Celia's driving. I fear she has not been behind the wheel of an automobile for quite some time. For novelty's sake, I let her drive my Zap to the train station in Two Oaks. I realized she was poking along, but I hadn't realized she was driving at a speed so far under the required 25 MPH. I do hope she didn't inconvenience other drivers too much. We Prims were raised with a healthy respect for the rules of the road."

Dawes cleared his throat. "Uh, yes, well, that's good. And maybe you would like to make sure that you, too, abide by the speed limit? Greenfield is a small town and, uh, you know, I want to minimize complaints."

"Of course, Detective. I do not blame you for being vigilant. I, too, have noticed that the people of Greenfield drive quite poorly. Being neighborly, of course I would never dream of making a formal complaint, but I *have* noticed the sorry state of driving in Greenfield, and truthfully, I have occasionally found it frustrating. But look at the time! I simply must be going. Thank you so much for the lovely tea, Detective, and I shall be in touch as soon as I have any information worth reporting."

22

Drawing the Battle Lines

As Bruno settled in for a nap, Miss Prim loaded the groceries into her kitchen cupboards. At some point she would turn at least part of the basement into a pantry, but until the murder victim was identified, she thought it disrespectful to use the space as a larder.

Still, it might be worthwhile to have a look at the basement again, to see if she had missed any details. Hadn't fiction taught her that revisiting a crime scene, and viewing it with a fresh eye each time, might yield insights that had been overlooked in the initial rush of investigations? Prepared for a possible epiphany, she removed the wooden star from the cupboard and pushed it into the depression on the wall.

The door popped open quietly, and she felt a tiny tingle of fear. Miss Prim was not a fanciful woman—never had been, never would be—but the draft coming up the staircase seemed to carry a whisper of menace. Her rational mind told her that the basement must be empty, but even so, it did not pay to take chances—not when so many of the heroines in her beloved mystery novels had been led down the primrose path into the waiting clutches of a madperson. Those heroines almost always survived, which was a consolation, but Miss Prim saw no romance in being traumatized, not even briefly. She roused Bruno with a clicking of her tongue and felt somewhat reassured as he followed her down the staircase.

Standing in the center of the basement floor, she looked around. Neither she nor the members of the Greenfield PD had been able to deduce how the murderer and/or his (or her) victim had made it down the staircase without leaving footprints in the dust. Detective Dawes had said the crime-scene unit had found only one unidentified set of footprints, with those going *up* the staircase. But the basement was completely underground, with no outdoor access, and the space was completely without windows. Perhaps a trap door was hidden somewhere? No, that was sheer fancy. Nonetheless Miss Prim got down on her hands and knees (a professional criminal outsmarter must not be afraid to get her hands and knees dirty) and shuffled around the perimeter. The floor was hard-packed dirt, with patches of rough cement in places. The cement was uncracked and looked as if it had been poured decades earlier.

She was examining a small imperfection in the wood paneling that covered the walls when she heard her telephone ring. She ran up the stairs, Bruno close on her heels. She clicked the door closed behind her and picked up the receiver.

"Good afternoon, Rose Cottage."

A loud crackling. "Miss Prim? I … *crackle* … and … *hiss* … you."

"Oh, dear," Miss Prim said. "I'm afraid we have a terrible connection. This is Miss Felicity Prim. Would you kindly repeat what you just said?"

"Oh, blast it. Miss Prim—Felicity—Amos Poe here. It's this … *crackle, hiss* … cell phone that Norah has forced upon me. Hold the line, please. I will find a place with better reception."

As Miss Prim filled a teakettle and placed it on the stove, Doctor Poe returned, sounding frustrated. "Is this better? Yes? Well, that is a relief. In our day, phone connections were clear as a bell. Now we are perpetually jockeying around to orient ourselves to some unknown constellation, or to some fortuitous wind or data stream, in order to make ourselves heard. It is all quite maddening."

Miss Prim smiled. Although Doctor Poe was the gentlest of men with his patients, he had been known to become bristly when dealing with fools and/or newfangled, over-hyped technologies. Miss Prim knew that Doctor Poe's fit of pique would pass quickly, and he would return to his gentle self. In the meantime, she would be patient; Mrs. Charity Prim had taught her daughters that women must indulge men's conniptions, because males simply do not have the self-control, or maturity, of the female of the species.

"Anyway, Miss Prim, I had a quiet moment here at the office and I thought I would check in with you. Is all quite pleasant in Greenfield, Connecticut? We have had some humid weather, and just yesterday I was called to hospital unexpectedly. Mrs. Higgenbottom is having anxiety attacks and will be comforted only by me."

"Doctor, we have been saying for years that you must allow Mrs. Higgenbottom to stand on her own two feet. She quite rules you and I daresay she likes it. She finds attention from handsome men in short supply, and when she cannot earn it through charm, she will obtain it through guile."

"Why, Miss Prim," Doctor Poe said, his infinite delight evident in his voice, "are you implying that I am handsome?"

Miss Prim was grateful that nobody was in the cottage to see her blush. How had she made so adolescent a slip of the tongue? Was it one of those Freudian slips that one reads about, which seemed to occur much more in fiction than in daily life? Then again, why be coy? As Mrs. Charity Prim had often advised, there comes a time when one's cards must be laid on the table.

"You have caught me out, Doctor Poe," Miss Prim responded. "But you do not need me to tell you that you are an appealing man. Your female patients, as well as your staff, have always appreciated your countenance, and they are not going to stop now."

"Dear Miss Prim, you have made my day. I quite miss you. I cannot tell you how many times I turn to my left, or to my right, expecting to see you there; and each time you are not, I feel disappointed all over again. To speak with you on the phone makes me feel as though we are still connected, but I confess it is not the same as having you near, to advise and to—well, *entertain* is not the right word perhaps, but who, really, can match you in the art of conversation? You have no equal, and you have spoiled me. Norah is trying her best, but she is no Felicity Prim."

"Doctor, you must stop or I will grow quite conceited. Know, however, how much your words mean to me. Now, tell me about Zoroastria, and Viveca, and Dolly."

"Zoroastria is running wild, as always. And woe betide the man who succeeds in taming her! I suspect Viveca may be with child again. You know how her cheeks glow a bit after she has conceived? Well, they have been the color of McIntosh apples lately, but I am pretending not to notice until she is ready to share her secret. As for Dolly, I can only say she has seemed somewhat distracted, as if something is worrying her. She is staying at Zoroastria's apartment for a few days, perhaps for female companionship during a difficult period. I asked her if she is quite all right, and she assured me that she is, and you know I do not like to pry. I understand she will be visiting you this coming weekend? I was delighted to hear it. A jaunt may improve her spirits."

"Yes, we have planned a girls' weekend of fun and frolic. Greenfield has quite an active social scene, centered around Maude's, a local tavern."

Doctor Poe was quiet for a moment. "I hope you will not think me too forward, Miss Prim, but I am wondering when *I* will receive an invitation to Greenfield?"

"Doctor, of course you are welcome at any time! We have a local inn, which was once a brothel. I have not visited it yet, but I have been told it has a rich history."

"I cannot simply show up on your doorstep, Miss Prim. I must have a proper invitation."

"Then you shall have one, Doctor. The weekend is quite taken with Dolly's visit—but perhaps you would like to join us? You two could take the train together …"

The doctor sighed. "I wish I could. But I am on hospital rounds all weekend. May I call you next week so that we may set a date?"

"I would love that, Doctor. I truly would."

"I see you are still calling me 'Doctor,' not 'Amos.'"

"I continue to think about your very appealing offer, Doctor, and I reiterate my promise. If and when I consent to be your wife, I shall use your given name. And I shall call you very soon."

"The fact that you actively consider my proposal will have to be enough to sustain me for now," Doctor Poe replied. "And on that note, Miss Prim, I fear I have a waiting room full of surprises, so I must ring off. Until we speak again, my dearest Felicity."

As Miss Prim put down the receiver, the teakettle began to whistle. *How like Doctor Poe this teakettle is*, Miss Prim thought. *He is fairly boiling over with passion and steamy emotion.*

To her Earl Gray she added a packet of Mrs. Mallowan's Lemon Sugar and a teaspoon of honey. Then she gave Bruno a small treat (use of the bell was not necessary, as he did not drool) and took her teacup to the couch. She sat, picked up the phone receiver, and dialed Celia's number.

Celia answered the phone on the third ring.

"Miss Celia Prim here," said her sister.

"Sister!" Miss Prim said. "You sound quite exhausted. Is all well there?"

"Sister, your timing could not be better. I have run myself ragged all over this city since last we spoke. I had forgotten how much shoe leather is required in tracking down information from the various government agencies. Are you sitting down? I have a piece of very important news. I believe I have found Ophelia, and I am well on my way to finding the mysterious A. From there, it should be a simple matter to find Providence."

"I am all ears," Miss Prim replied excitedly.

"Where shall I begin? My first step was to pay a visit to Nathaniel Branson. Sadly, his mind is quite gone. Throughout our luncheon he called me 'Charity' and asked about my sisters, Faith and Hope. Eventually he admitted that he believed me to be a chimera sent by Samuel Taylor Coleridge to inspire him to write the epic poem he has long wanted to compose. I promised to serve as his muse if he would reminisce about his old friend Cornelius Prim, as well as any lady friend Cornelius may have had after the passing of his beloved wife. Mr. Branson said yes, he quite remembered arriving on the *Mayflower* with Cornelius Prim, who'd been deathly seasick throughout the voyage from England. I'm afraid I could not get him past the arrival at Plymouth Rock. He much prefers to discuss the seventeenth century, upon which he is fixated. For the record, he is convinced that John Milton stole his manuscript of *Paradise Lost* and made a complete hash of it."

"Dear Mr. Branson. He always did have those literary aspirations. He looked the part, didn't he, with that beautiful head of hair and those exquisite cravats."

"He still has both, which I suppose is some small consolation for the loss of his faculties. But my visit with him yielded nothing relevant to our inquiry. However, I was more successful with Miss Emily Spry, now Mrs. Emily Fielding of Valhalla, New York. Her mind is as sharp as ever, and she remembers Miss Ophelia LeFevre. Of course, Miss Spry knew exactly what was going on. At first she wondered why Papa kept finding excuses to call the office of Foster McGinniss, given his intense dislike of the man. It didn't take her long to realize that the person being called on was not Mr. McGinniss but rather Miss LeFevre. Of course, one does not become a trusted secretary by blabbing one's employer's secrets, so she kept her own counsel. In subsequent months, Papa dispatched her to pick up small gifts, to send flowers, and so forth. Finally, Papa could no longer keep the cat in the bag and admitted to Miss Spry everything she already knew."

"Go on, Sister," Miss Prim urged.

"Occasionally Ophelia would visit Papa at his office, and she and Miss Spry would sit and chat. Miss Spry said Ophelia was a lovely, intelligent woman with a sort of underlying sadness. She lived with her Aunt Ada on the Upper West Side, she told Miss Spry, and fervently wished to be independent from her. Apparently, Aunt Ada was a difficult woman, but of course we know this from Papa's journals. When Ophelia mentioned the name Ada, Miss Spry remembered that Papa had, on a number of occasions, sent tokens of kindness to a woman with this name. No doubt part of Papa's efforts to butter her up.

"Here is the best part, Sister. With a bit of prompting, Miss Spry recalled Ada's last name. It is Crenshaw. Ada Crenshaw. So tomorrow I continue my search. I shall go to the public records hall and search for Providence Prim, Providence LeFevre, and Providence Crenshaw. Surely she must have taken *one* of those names. I have read the cards and all signs point to the likelihood that she is among us. I feel confident she must be living here in New York, quite unaware that she has two sisters who will leave no stone unturned until she is found. Now, Sister, there is much to be accomplished, so I must ring off, but tell me—by any chance, have you ascertained Maude's marital status?"

"Quite single, Sister. You are free to conquer, if you so choose."

"Well, now. The cards indicated the likelihood of a new *amour* for me, but they implied that the man would have a full head of dark hair. The pentacles, you know. As far as I know, the cards do not specify baldness. I shall have to look into this. It is quite a necessity nowadays, what with all the men shaving their heads in an attempt to be chic. I shall call you as soon as I know more, Sister." With that, Celia told Miss Prim she loved her and hung up the phone.

As Miss Prim carried her empty teacup to the sink, she marveled, not for the first time, at her sister's ingenuity, energy, vigor, and zest. It was easy to understand why men found her so irresistible.

Bruno's ears pricked up. An instant later, Miss Prim heard a knock at her front door. Bruno seemed alert, but not aggressive, which meant the visitor was a friend. Miss Prim opened the door and Albert and Henry raced in, followed by Lorraine in a colorful headscarf and an even more colorful batik dress.

"Felicity Prim, you gypsy! Why are you never at home when I need to gossip? I call and the phone rings and rings. Or I get a busy signal. Who gets busy signals in this day and age? Ever hear of call waiting? And it's ridiculous that you don't have a cell phone. What is this, 1950? I stop by and my knocks go unanswered. You really should learn to be more idle. It's easier on the feet."

"Lorraine, forgive me. Every time I think I shall have a moment to myself, something comes up."

"Of course I'm jesting, Felicity. You have a life, and good for you! People who don't have lives are always getting into trouble, minding other people's business. I heard you had a cup of tea at Beantown with Ezra Dawes. Woof! You little minx, you. I thought I would have to pave the way for you, but here you are using your own devious techniques! Well, good for you. You were marvelous with Lucian, and rumor has it that you even sweet-talked Maude into dismantling his free bookshelf. You should write a book about handling men. You could make a million bucks!"

Write a book? *Oh, never*, Miss Prim thought. She simply wasn't capable of doing so, though perhaps this was not a tragedy, given the number of aspiring writers who have their egos brutalized and their dreams destroyed by callous literary agents and publishers.

"I'm glad you're here, Lorraine," Miss Prim said, seeing the opportunity to ask a few questions regarding the inconsistencies between Lorraine's memories and Elizabeth Saxe-Coburg's. "I like your new look, by the way."

"Isn't it grand? Erykah Badu meets Beyoncé."

"Who? Anyway, I visited Heavenly Pastures today, and …"

"Oh, yes, I wanted to ask you about that. Was Elizabeth as standoffish as ever?"

"No, she was actually quite welcoming. A very nice contrast to Miss Lavelle, whom I encountered as I was leaving."

Lorraine narrowed her eyes. "Did she make trouble again?"

"Well, let us say she was no more polite than she had been at Prothero's. In fact, she may have been *less* polite than she was during our first meeting, but we need not dwell on that, for as Mama always said …"

Lorraine stopped her foot furiously. "Albert! Henry!" she called. The dogs immediately returned to her side, Albert willingly, Henry reluctantly.

"That's it!" Lorraine fumed. "I've had it up to here with her. It's time for a showdown that's been brewing a long time. Don't you worry, Felicity. When I'm done with her, she won't so much as dare look at you cross-eyed." And out she stormed.

Miss Prim chased after her. "But Lorraine, there really is no need … please, I see no reason to …"

But Lorraine Koslowski did not hear, or chose not to listen.

23

The Break-In

Before settling in for the evening, Miss Prim suited herself up in her athletic clothing, stuffed the Laser Taser 3000 into her fanny pack, and dangled Bruno's leash tantalizingly in front of him. She really had been quite bad since removing herself to Connecticut. Prior to beginning her criminal outsmarting studies and leaving Manhattan, she'd engaged in a vigorous exercise schedule, and she'd made too much progress to allow a week in the country to undo all that hard work.

Was carrying the Laser Taser 3000 along on her jog a bit *much*? Perhaps, but the mysterious phone calls and hang-ups had disconcerted her; so had the unidentified creature skulking around in her backyard. Anyone who reads crime fiction knows that solitary runners create temptation for criminals, who often find it easy to waylay their victims. Bruno would likely ward off anyone threatening her, but an effective criminal outsmarter always has a backup plan. Miss Prim's backup plan was the Laser Taser 3000.

She soon congratulated herself on her decision. Disturbingly, Greenfield seemed more ominous at dusk. As Miss Prim ran through the streets of her neighborhood, she couldn't help but wonder if criminals with malicious intent hid in the rustling bushes, or whether a murderer watched her through binoculars from a distant window. These thoughts caused her to jog at a rather more rapid pace than usual, which made Bruno quite happy. As she passed the back of Lorraine's house, she could feel the street throbbing with the insistent bass beats of that awful music. (What was that musical genre called? *Dense iron?* Something like that.) Albert and Henry ran to the back fence to greet Bruno. For a moment Miss Prim thought they might join her and Bruno for the remainder of her run, but over the din she heard Lorraine scream, "Don't even *think* about it!" Henry and Albert slunk back on their bellies toward the house.

Back at Rose Cottage, Miss Prim drew a bath, emptied lavender bath salts into it, and bolted the doors. Into the bathtub she brought her book, the latest by English novelist Marjorie Eccles, whose work she adored. Such gorgeous settings, such lovely English manners, such independent women and dark but intriguing men! This was life as it was meant to be, and Miss Prim was so entranced by the narrative that she had to add hot water to the tub three times to prevent herself from freezing into an ice cube.

After tying Bruno to his tether in the backyard early the next morning, Miss Prim set off for the Greenfield Historical Society. Perhaps she might avoid a socially awkward question-and-answer session with Lorraine if the archivist, Gil Fellowes, could help her determine the year in which Rose Cottage had been built. It was quite possible that both Olivia Abernathy and Elizabeth Saxe-Coburg were mistaken, Miss Prim thought. Because, in the final analysis, can one *really* believe anything a real-estate agent says? And it was quite obvious that dear Mrs. Saxe-Coburg was almost completely out of it. Miss Prim understood a thing or two about senility, having witnessed its descent on her Aunts Phyllida and Prudence. In their dotage, both of those estimable ladies had recrafted the past to suit their needs and desires, putting new and unexpected spins on history. It thus seemed understandable that the aging Mrs. Saxe-Coburg would look back on her somewhat hermitic life in Greenfield with remorse. Such feelings could easily allow Elizabeth's mind to create a nonexistent friendship with the person whose friendly advances she had rebuffed.

As for the photo showing the Saxe-Coburgs and the Koslowskis together at a night club: It was likely that the people Mrs. S-C had identified as the Koslowskis were a different couple altogether. Miss Prim remembered back to those decades, when all women looked the same, and so did men. And while the man in the photo looked as if he might be a younger version of Lucian, the woman really did not resemble Lorraine all that much, except for a passing similarity.

As Miss Prim pulled open the glass door that would lead her to the Historical Society's headquarters above the post office, she noticed a Greenfield Police Department squad car parked at the curb.

She held onto the banister for dear life as she climbed the rickety stairs, which she feared might collapse under her weight at any moment. Perhaps this was to be expected, for has there ever been a historical society that can afford large, modern office space? As Miss Prim entered the society's large front room, her eyes took in a Jungian archetype of an archive: rickety wooden chairs lolling drunkenly on broken casters; bookshelves crammed with papers, folders, books, and newspapers; wheeled ladders to help truth seekers access hard-to-reach materials on upper shelves; rusty metal filing cabinets in military-looking greens and browns; a wooden card catalog; glass cases displaying flyers for carnivals and circuses that had visited Greenfield in the 1930s and 1940s; a large bulletin board featuring black-and-white photos with typed identification cards beneath each one.

Miss Prim heard a noise at the rear of the room. She craned her head around a large stack of desiccated magazines to see a man emerging from a back room, wringing his hands. He was followed by Officers Spike Fremlin and Martin Reed.

"Gil, relax," Spike was saying. "I don't know how you can even tell something is missing from this place. Gee whiz, it's a pig sty! I could write my name in the dust. I read somewhere you can get tuberculosis from breathing in too much dust. Plus I bet there's a lot of mold, too. That's even worse. It gets in your lungs. Miss Brim! What are *you* doing here?"

"Good morning, Officer Fremlin, Officer Reed. I was hoping …"

"Listen, Miss Brim, your timing isn't so good. Gil here thinks he had a break-in last night but he can't tell us what's missing. How do we find something if we don't know what we're looking for? You tell me that, Gil Fellowes. Because we have a lot of other stuff on our plates right now."

Martin Reed stood silently behind Spike Fremlin, seeming to accept his lot in life and perhaps thinking about the ways éclairs and crullers might ease the pain.

"Allow me to introduce myself, Mr. Fellowes," Miss Prim said. "I am Miss Felicity *Prim*." She slightly accented her surname for Spike Fremlin's benefit, though she didn't expect it to do much good. "You may have heard that I discovered a corpse in the basement of a house I purchased not too long ago."

"Oh, yes," Gil responded, shaking Miss Prim's hand. "It is tragic at a human scale, but important historically. We have almost no crime here in Greenfield, except for some crazy woman who has been drag racing through our quiet streets lately. All history is psychological, so I have begun a project to trace the emotional effects of your discovery on the lives and psyches of the locals. Such effects reveal themselves gradually over a period of years, perhaps even decades, so it is best to begin as soon as one can. But one needs *quiet* to examine the connections and interlinkages, and I'm afraid Officer Fremlin here does not have a healthy respect for silence."

"You've got your nerve, Gil Fellowes. You were the one who called the station with your knickers in a twist."

"I specifically asked for Officer Reed."

"Well, Reed and I are partners. You don't get one without the other."

"What happened, Mr. Fellowes?" Miss Prim asked, before Spike could commence another bout of hypochondriacal logorrhea.

"Miss Prim," Gil Fellowes began, "you appear to be an organized, well-put-together woman. I am sure you have experienced the phenomenon of walking into an accustomed space and knowing, simply *knowing*, that someone has been looking through your possessions. Many small details add up: A book is slightly out of place, a chair has been moved a tiny bit, a vase is a skosh to the left of where it should be. These were my impressions when I arrived at the Society this morning."

Spike rolled her eyes. "And so I ask you again, Gil, what exactly is missing? You don't even lock this place up half the time. Maybe some tourist walked in while you were getting a cup of something at Beantown."

"I've already told you, Spike. I was here late last night, and by the time I left it was quite dark. Anyone who entered the offices between the time I left for home and the time I returned this morning would *not* be a tourist. The hours on the door clearly state that we are open from 10 AM to 4 PM and closed an hour or two for lunch around midday. Anyone who enters outside those posted hours clearly has theft on his—or her—mind."

"Did you lock the door last night?" Reed asked.

"I'm not sure I did, Martin, and if it turns out that a thief has stolen a precious part of Greenfield's history as a result of my lapse, I will never forgive myself. But you see, I was intent on developing a blueprint for an oral history regarding the death in Miss Prim's basement. I had been wondering if and how geopolitics played into Miss Prim's voluntary relocation to Greenfield, as well as how recent events might be related to the ethnography of the Junusakey lemonade fad inexplicably sweeping the region, and I got so wrapped up in my ideas that I may have left the door unlocked. It's happened before, I'm afraid. Surely you understand, Miss Prim? You have a look of the scholar about you."

"I may have some insight into the Junusakey lemonade phenomenon, Mr. Fellowes," she replied. "Perhaps we might have tea sometime, and I will tell you all about …"

"Here's where we exit!" Spike interrupted. "Listen, Gil, if you can come up with something a little more concrete, call us back and we'll see what we can do. We're busy, you know? Come on, Reed, let's get a cup of coffee. And no, you can't have a donut. Don't give me that puppy dog look, it's not gonna work! I work hard at staying in shape for this job, and you should, too. You're getting to an age where you have to be careful about all that belly fat. It'll give you a heart attack. And I bet you're a prime candidate for gout, too. I read somewhere that gout is one of the most painful things a man can experience. Ha! It's nothing compared to childbirth, so don't look for any sympathy from *me*."

Miss Prim caught Reed's eye. The poor man looked utterly defeated, and Miss Prim had a flash of insight: With Spike's ongoing tirades, and Valeska Reed's dominant personality, perhaps sugary baked treats were among the few pleasures left in Martin Reed's life.

"Excuse me a moment, Mr. Fellowes," she said. "Officer Reed, might I have a word before you go?"

"Don't keep him too long, Miss Brim," Spike replied, moving toward the staircase. "Ezra will have a cow if we're late for the 'status meeting.' You tell me, Miss Brim, how we're supposed to do our jobs when we have to be in meetings reporting on progress we haven't made." As Spike continued down the stairs, Miss Prim could hear the running monologue becoming fainter and fainter: "God, these stairs! It's like being in a fun house. I'd better stop and buy some Vitamin C, I bet I'm gonna get sick after being in this place. Would it kill him to dust once in a while? Get a job with the police, my mother said. 'You'll have an easy life,' she said. Ha! … *mumble mumble mumble*."

Miss Prim touched Reed's arm sympathetically. "She's a bit of a handful, isn't she?"

"She means well. I think."

Miss Prim thought a moment.

"If you don't mind my asking, Officer, do you think your taste for baked goods helps you cope with the … shall we say *demanding* women in your life?"

Reed considered the question. "I guess it's true that something sweet takes my mind off things."

"Officer, not to give away the secrets of womanhood, but we women sometimes show concern, even love, in ways that men do not fully comprehend. The sexes have encountered these communication difficulties for millennia, with little progress made. However, as a woman, I can see that both your wife and Officer Fremlin care about you deeply, and they exhibit that care by focusing on your waistline. It is quite simply that they want you to live a long and healthy life, so that they are never denied your company. You must believe me, for I am quite positive it is the truth."

"Maybe," said Martin Reed, skeptically. "But they could be a little nicer about it."

"May I make a suggestion from my own experience? I have recently got myself into better physical shape after a fairly long period of indolence. In the process I discovered many recipes for tasty, filling snacks that are much kinder to the waistline. I have a friend, Dolly, visiting me this weekend, and I'm sure we will do some baking. If you'd like to stop at Rose Cottage on Sunday afternoon, I'd be happy to share some of my healthy treats with you."

"Well, everyone talks about your cinnamon rolls, and if you can make a diet version that tastes just as good, I'm willing to try them. So, sure, I'll stop by on Sunday. I'll see if Valeska wants to come, too, if you don't mind. I think she likes you."

As Miss Prim nodded her enthusiastic agreement, a voice from outside nearly shattered the windows. "Reed! What's taking so long?"

Reed sighed and made his way down the staircase, looking like a worn-out Atlas tired of balancing Earth on his shoulders.

Miss Prim turned back to Gil Fellowes. "Now, Mr. Fellowes, I'd like your help in determining the year my house was built. And about that Junusakey lemonade …"

As Miss Prim walked back to Rose Cottage, she found herself wondering if there might be a connection between Kit's visit to the historical society and the alleged break-in. Miss Prim remembered the stunts her brother Noel had pulled during his teen years, which helped her imagine the workings of Kit's teenage mind: *I need something from the historical society, it's closed right now but everyone knows the door is often unlocked, I could just borrow it and have it back before anyone notices it's missing …*

She was lost in thought as she passed Cambria & Calibri. A familiar voice snapped her out of her reverie.

"Miss Prim! Do come in."

The voice was Valeska Reed's. She held the door open and beckoned Miss Prim into the bookshop.

"Valeska, how nice to …"

Valeska Reed lost no time in grabbing Miss Prim's hand and arm, then pumping them up and down enthusiastically. Again Miss Prim felt an authentic affection in Valeska's greeting.

"You're quite wonderful, Miss Prim. I heard that you spoke with Maude, and I've had numerous reports that he took down his free bookshelves. You, my friend, are a miraculous lady."

"I can accept no kudos for any of this, Valeska. All credit goes to Maude. As I suspected, he is quite as community-minded as you are."

"You're too modest, Miss Prim. But you have my thanks. And you also have a 10 percent discount in perpetuity. I'd give you 15 percent, but the margins are way too thin and I have to pay the rent."

"That is unnecessary, Valeska, but I fear I would regret turning down your kind offer, so I accept. Still, it is Maude you should be thanking, not me. Promise me you will do so?"

Valeska nodded. "I promise, Miss Prim. I'll go there with a peace offering this afternoon. I have several nice titles on mixology that I will gift to him."

"While I'm here, Valeska, I do have one topic I'd like to discuss with you. I hope you won't consider me too forward ..."

"Say what's on your mind, Miss Prim. We are women who may speak freely with each other."

"This is difficult for me, in that, as a single woman, I have never had to manage a husband. However, I have observed many marriages, including the very successful one between my parents, and I think I have learned a thing or two about the factors that lead to happy couplehood."

"Is this about me and Martin? All right, I'm listening."

"Valeska, I cannot help but notice how much the people of Greenfield care for your husband. He is a sweet, gentle man, is he not?" Mrs. Reed nodded, and was that a tear forming in her right eye? "And of course we all wish him to be healthy and fit. His taste for calorie-laden sweets works counter to that goal, does it not?"

Valeska nodded again.

"I have had an insight into the situation, just suggested to me by your husband himself. He was talking about the stresses of his job, and he mentioned that 'something sweet' helps keep his mind off his troubles. I could not help but think that the phrase *something sweet* might be taken metaphorically as well as literally. You know how men are, Valeska. They respond well to compliments and to kindness, and they sometimes act passive-aggressively if they do not feel they are being sufficiently appreciated. Of course, as women, we know the depths of our love and concern for them, but they are not good at sussing out the deeper emotions. It is simply a limitation of their gender. Do you see what I am getting at?"

Valeska Reed lowered her eyes.

"I do, Miss Prim. I do."

24

The First Disappearance

Now that she was offering to cook for Greenfield—not only tasty meals for Kit, but also dietetic delights for Martin Reed—Miss Prim decided that yet another trip to Prothero's was in order. This time she would go by foot; it seemed silly to drive just a few blocks. She stuck her head out of the cottage's front door to determine the weather. The gray sky hinted at rain. As she grabbed her handbag and her umbrella, Bruno sprang to life.

"Not this time, Bruno," she said kindly, removing from a closet the wheelie-cart that had served her so well during her years in Manhattan. Negotiating that cart, which often seemed to have a will of its own diametrically opposed to hers, would require all her concentration and energy. She imagined she would look quite the fool attempting to steer the cart *and* Bruno simultaneously.

Walking to the market, the cart bumping obstinately behind her, Miss Prim thought the time had come to venture a *rapprochement* with Miss Lavelle. Her track record in improving human relations seemed to be quite good lately, given her successes with Maude and the Reeds. Perhaps she would approach Miss Lavelle, invite her for a cup of tea, and begin the diplomacy that would lead to the beginning of a *détente*.

As she entered Prothero's, she glimpsed Faye standing behind one of the cash registers. She'd tied her dreadlocks back to prevent them from falling in her face. Miss Gladys Lavelle stood behind her, training her on the finer points of cashier work.

"Now, dear," Miss Prim heard Miss Lavelle saying, "this is romaine lettuce, not chicory. Chicory is pointy. Romaine is sold by the pound, so you must weigh it and use produce code 4583. In contrast, iceberg lettuce is sold by the head. Therefore it does not need to be weighed. Be sure to bag produce separately and gently. Never bag it with canned goods or meats. It will be destroyed by the time the customer gets it home."

Miss Prim couldn't help but notice how gentle Miss Lavelle's voice sounded. She'd called Faye *dear*, and she'd said the word kindly, even affectionately. In contrast, all the terms of endearment Miss Lavelle had lavished on Miss Prim had been sarcastic, angry, bitter. Miss Prim noted, too, how very seriously Miss Lavelle took her job as head cashier, as demonstrated by the way she coached Faye on the finer points of bagging groceries for transport. A person so dedicated to her job could not be a bad person, Miss Prim thought. She also remembered Lorraine's contention that Miss Lavelle had engaged in a long-term extramarital affair with Ethan Prothero. Perhaps *that* explained her dedication to his business.

Miss Prim happily strolled the aisles, loading her cart with reduced-calorie ingredients, sugar substitutes, and low-fat cheeses. Then she made her way to the front of the store, where she caught Faye's eye.

"Miss Prim! Come to me!"

Miss Prim wheeled her cart to Faye's station and began unloading her items onto the belt.

"How are you enjoying your new job, Faye?" Miss Prim asked.

"It's great, Miss Prim. One of my screenwriting books says you have to be *in* the world to *write* about the world, and I think the author's right about that. I'm talking to so many people I've seen around town but never spoken to before. Of course, I could never set a screenplay in a grocery store. Just the way novelists shouldn't set scenes in a supermarket. Too mundane."

Miss Prim glanced up and noticed Miss Lavelle glaring at her. So much for the *rapprochement*. Miss Prim averted her eyes and continued chatting with Faye.

"You heard about the break-in at the historical society?" Miss Prim asked.

"Yeah, and I wonder if Kit had something to do with it. He was there the other day, for a school project or something, and he's always touching things. He might have moved something, which might have made Gil think someone stole it."

"What kind of project is Kit working on? I have a fondness for history and a somewhat deep level of knowledge on the subject. I may be able to help."

"He's looking for information about historic houses in Greenfield. It does sound kind of interesting, but he hasn't shared many details yet."

Miss Prim paid for her purchases and was attempting to negotiate her wheelie-cart through the market's sliding glass doors when she sensed a presence behind her. She turned around to discover Miss Gladys Lavelle an inch from her face. Complexion scarlet and nostrils flaring, Miss Lavelle attacked.

"You stay away from her, Missy, do you hear me? You want Heavenly Pastures? Fine, it's all yours. But Prothero's is *my* place. If you want to gad around town with crazy Lorraine Koslowski, that's your business. But don't think I'm going to let you charm Greenfield's young people into your web. Valeska Reed may have fallen for your shtick, but I won't let Faye and Kit fall into the same trap."

"Really, Miss Lavelle," Miss Prim sputtered. "You have quite the wrong idea …"

"Ha!" Miss Lavelle spat. "I know *exactly* what you're up to. I've dealt with women like you my whole life. I know a social climber when I see one."

Miss Prim could count on one hand the number of times she'd become truly furious. As Papa had always said, anger was not only counterproductive but also self-defeating. But to be called a social climber! This was the one and only type of person for whom Mama and Papa had no patience. "These people," Mama had pronounced, "live on the surface of life and make a habit of choosing the wrong priorities and the wrong people. They are parasites, and they will betray their closest friend for an invitation to the right party. Avoid them like the plague, children, and devote your time and energies to those with kind hearts and giving natures."

"Miss Lavelle," Miss Prim said slowly, "I am many things, but a social climber is not one of them. I simply try to enjoy my life and the relationships I have developed. If people choose to be my friend, it is because they sense I will be a devoted friend in return. And I daresay most, or all, of them would tell you that I have not disappointed them in that regard. If you ever decide to view me as a friend rather than an enemy, I will be most happy to reciprocate your goodwill. Until then, I would be grateful if you would not accost me viciously in public, for I do not deserve it. Good day."

With that, Miss Prim turned heel and left Miss Gladys Lavelle standing in the doorway of Prothero's market, white faced and speechless.

As Miss Prim began the walk back to Undercliff Lane, she worked at regaining her equanimity. Losing one's temper rarely accomplishes anything productive, but she'd had quite enough of Miss Lavelle's broadsides. To think, only minutes earlier, she had marveled at the softer side of Miss Lavelle, at her kindness toward Faye and her devotion to her career!

As she passed Cambria & Calibri, Valeska Reed hailed her from the door.

"Miss Prim! Come in for a chat?"

A pleasant *tête-à-tête* with a burgeoning friend was just what Miss Prim needed after the encounter with Miss Lavelle. She left her wheelie-cart on the sidewalk and entered the store.

"I was hoping to see you, Miss Prim," Valeska was saying. "I have a treat for you."

Valeska went into the back room and returned with a small packet wrapped in aluminum foil. She handed it to Miss Prim, who gently peeled back the edge.

"Oh," Miss Prim whispered. "Are these … ?"

"Kifli. Some apricot, some prune. For many years they were my specialty. I dusted off the recipe and made a batch last night."

"I thought you were adamantly opposed to selling baked goods here at Cambria & Calibri?"

"I made them for Martin. They've always been a favorite of his."

Unable to resist temptation, Miss Prim nibbled at one of the apricot treats.

"I can see why, Valeska. They are quite divine."

Valeska Reed smiled with satisfaction. "No one would guess they're made with low-calorie cream cheese and sugar-free apricot preserves, would they?" She winked, and the two women shared a knowing glance.

"Did Martin appreciate them as much as I do?"

"Once he got over the shock, yes. Then again, I think he was in a good mood after eating the meatloaf I'd prepared for dinner. A nice change, he said, from the salads and vegetables I usually force on him."

No words were necessary. Miss Prim simply grabbed and squeezed Valeska's hand. Valeska returned the gesture.

"As I said before, Miss Prim, you really are quite miraculous. I can't imagine how Greenfield survived with you. But there's another thing I wanted to tell you. Someone was in here a couple of hours ago looking for you."

"Someone?"

"I've never seen him before. Tall, young, unkempt, nervous. He wouldn't make eye contact. It wasn't just you he was asking about. He also inquired about someone named Dolly."

This was very strange. "Was it the same man who'd been inquiring after me a few days ago?"

"No. The first man was one of those plastic-surgery aficionados whose attempts to fight aging make them look highly artificial. *This* man was much younger and much taller. He had one of those straggly beards that I so detest. You know, the type that looks as if it is harboring breadcrumbs and microbes. I didn't like his looks or his demeanor, so I said I'd never heard of you, or of Dolly. Martin told me about your gracious invitation for Sunday—we accept, by the way—but I didn't want to tell a stranger that I know you, or that I'd heard of Dolly but haven't met her yet."

Miss Prim bit her lip. "I can't imagine why anyone would be looking for her in Greenfield. She lives in New York City."

"I agree, it's odd. There was something *off* about that young man."

Miss Prim shivered a little, not out of concern for her own safety, but out of concern for Dolly's. Had Dolly told Benjamin of her plans to visit Greenfield, and had Benjamin repeated the information to one or more of his unsavory contacts? The man Valeska described could not have been Benjamin, who was well-kept and academic, not unkempt and slightly crazed.

"Well, it is a bit of a mystery, Valeska, but I'm sure the truth will reveal itself." She added, "At some point."

Miss Prim was placing her purchases in the refrigerator when the telephone rang.

"Hello, Rose Cottage."

"Dolly?" A voice she didn't recognize.

"No, who's calling please?"

Click.

Miss Prim replaced the receiver. The hang-ups were becoming more and more nerve-racking, part of a disturbing pattern. So many wrong numbers and intentional or unintentional disconnections; two men asking around Greenfield about her and Dolly's whereabouts; the intruder she'd seen in her yard. Her heat beat just a bit louder and faster.

Perhaps it was time to take these concerns to a professional. Should she call Detective Dawes and share her concerns with him? No, she would not. She refused to become one of those hysterical women who overreact to bumps in the night. She would keep a close eye on the situation and involve the authorities when she had something more than vague suspicions and irrational fears to report. In the meantime, she had both Bruno and the Laser Taser 3000.

As she was calming herself with soothing thoughts, the doorbell rang, not once, not twice, but three times in rapid succession. Sensing danger, Bruno let out several intimidating woofs and bounded to the front door.

"Who's there, please?" Miss Prim yelled over Bruno's woofing.

"It's me. Lorraine."

Miss Prim opened the door to find a dripping Lorraine Koslowski. Miss Prim had been lucky enough to miss the rain, but the drops had begun falling almost as soon as she'd arrived at Rose Cottage.

"Lorraine! Do come in. I almost didn't recognize you." Today Lorraine wore a form-fitting black dress and a shoulder-length brunette wig. She'd also applied a shockingly large amount of lipstick. The effect made her lips seem twice their normal size.

"Do you like the new look, Felicity? I'm going for the Angelina Jolie effect. Long lines and easy on the eyes. With that *glow* you see on the silver screen."

"It becomes you, Lorraine. It really does." Which may not have been perfectly true, but as Mrs. Charity Prim had often said, a tiny lie that pleases a friend is usually a lie worth telling.

"Say, Felicity, I don't suppose you've seen Lucian, have you?"

"Lucian? No, I haven't. I guess I had the impression that he doesn't leave Ridgemont much."

"He doesn't. But he's gone, Felicity. Gone." And with that, Lorraine Koslowski did something Miss Prim never would have expected. She burst into tears.

25

Tea and Sympathy

As Miss Prim brewed the tea, Lorraine explained.

"I thought I had Lucian's wandering under control, Felicity. I told him I'd introduce him to the King of Siam if he promised not to leave the house without telling me. He's not good with time, but he remembers that particular promise, and I keep the ruse going by telling him the King is expected any day now. But when I got home from running my errands downtown, I couldn't find him anywhere. Not in the house, not in the attic, not in the basement, not on the property. God, I hope he isn't naked somewhere! One time he left me a note saying he'd gone to visit the sulfur baths in Saratoga Springs. We found him frolicking *au naturel* in the woods near Lake Greenfield."

"How long were you out of the house, Lorraine?" Miss Prim asked.

Lorraine raised her wrist to consult a watch that wasn't there. "No more than a couple of hours."

In her most comforting voice, Miss Prim said, "That's good news. He can't have gone far in two hours. Finish up your tea, and we'll go to the police station and ask for their help."

Lorraine grimaced. "It won't be the first time. Fortunately, Lucian likes Ezra and Martin. Spike reminds him too much of my sister Lorna, so he steers clear of her. Says she gives him a headache. Spike does that to a lot of people."

As the two women scurried to the police station, Lorraine tried to console herself. "I don't think he'd do anything dangerous or hurt himself. But Felicity, as I'm sure you've noticed, his mind isn't it what it used to be. He gets confused more easily, and sometimes he thinks the Hessians are stalking him. And let me tell you, he does *not* like the Hessians. He won't let them take Ridgemont, he says, while making threatening gestures. If someone approached him the wrong way, I don't think he'd hurt them, but ..." Her voice trailed off.

They found the full complement of the Greenfield police squad viewing something on Ezra Dawes' computer screen. Dawes and Spike munched on crullers while Martin Reed—surprise of surprises—snacked on miniature carrots from a small Ziploc bag.

Lorraine got straight to the point. "Ezra, Lucian's gone again."

Ezra removed his half-moon glasses and stood up. "How long?"

"Two hours max."

"Any ideas where he might be?"

"Let me think for a minute." Lorraine turned to Miss Prim to explain. "Sometimes Lucian will store up conversational details that he'll get fixated on. The time he took off for Saratoga, for example, it was because a few days earlier I'd bought some new bath salts."

"I've heard that bathing in Epsom salts can help if you're constipated," Spike put in. "Can someone explain how that works? I mean, sit in salt water and all of a sudden ..."

"Spike, *not now*," Dawes said, more sternly than Miss Prim had ever heard him speak. "Lorraine, you were saying?"

"Before I left Ridgemont, I told Lucian about the break-in at the historical society. But I'm afraid that's not much to go on. For Lucian, references to history can spur thoughts of anything from ancient Ur and Mesopotamia to the Arab Spring."

"Anything else?"

"I bought him a book of English crossword puzzles, which he's quite enjoying, even if the words he's writing into the blocks are strictly of his own coinage. I hadn't realized he likes puzzles so much, so I told him about tavern puzzles and promised to get some for him."

"Tavern puzzles?" Miss Prim had never heard of these.

"You know, Felicity. Those puzzles that have two pieces of metal intricately intertwined, and you have to separate them. Lucian is quite hopeless at anything like that, so I thought they might keep him occupied and out of trouble for a few weeks."

A light bulb seemed to illuminate in the heads of Lorraine and Ezra simultaneously.

"Tavern puzzles," Ezra said. "Maude's."

Ezra and Lorraine took off—really, Miss Prim thought admiringly, Lorraine was as spry as a much younger woman—while Martin Reed, Spike Fremlin, and Miss Prim brought up the rear.

Ezra sent Lorraine and Spike into the tavern, directing Reed to join him as he unlatched the gate leading to the tavern's rear yard.

"Any time Lucian's disappeared, we've found him outdoors," Ezra explained. "Miss Prim, you'd better wait here. Come on, Reed." The detective and the police officer disappeared into the rear yard.

Wait here? Miss Prim should have known this moment would come: the moment in which the professionals direct the *amateur*, the *neophyte*, the *tyro* to mind her own business and not interfere with an official police investigation. Miss Prim wondered at Detective Dawes's naïveté. Did the man *really* believe that this particular amateur would behave as directed? Minding one's own business is *not* the way to develop experience in criminal outsmarting.

She tiptoed quietly into the yard and watched as Dawes and Reed inspected the dumpster and storage shed. Another gate in the rear of the yard gave onto a service road running behind the businesses on the square's north side. But the gate was locked and the fence too high for Lucian to climb.

Miss Prim nearly jumped out of her shoes when she felt a stirring in the pine trees behind her. Could Lucian have sneaked up behind her? She wheeled around and crouched into a self-defense pose only to discover a calico cat rubbing against her leg and meowing loudly. She suspected Bruno would not appreciate this interloper's efforts to charm her, but she could not stop herself from getting down onto her haunches to pet the cat, which rolled happily on her back and grabbed Miss Prim's hand gently with her paws. It was surprising, Miss Prim thought, that it had taken so long for a cat to show up; everyone knows that cats are a staple of locked-room mysteries taking place in New England villages populated by kooky individuals, and they (both cats and kooky individuals) are frequently the chosen companions of aging spinsters.

"He's not here," Miss Prim heard Dawes say. "Let's see if Spike and Lorraine have had any luck."

They hadn't. Maude had helped the two women inspect every inch of the tavern, from the basement through the cramped attic, but Lucian Koslowski was nowhere to be found.

The members of the police force regrouped in front of the tavern. Dawes gave the orders. "Spike, you and I will check the lake. Reed, check the square. Lorraine, Miss Prim: Go back to Ridgemont. Call us if Lucian comes home. We'll be in touch as soon as we find him. Try not to worry, Lorraine. He always manages to take care of himself."

"Thank you, Ezra," Lorraine said sincerely. "I've been thinking about getting him one of those GPS-type devices so that we can track him when he gets loose. This time I'm going to do it. I'll tell him it's a secret crystal offered to special humans chosen by the inhabitants of Atlantis. That'll give him incentive to wear it."

"Lorraine," Miss Prim said, "may I meet you at Ridgemont? I have a few things I need to discuss with Detective Dawes."

Lorraine winked at Miss Prim knowingly. "I'll leave the door unlocked, Felicity. I'm going to search the house again, starting in the basement. If you could take care of the second-floor rooms and the attic, that would be so helpful. Come get me if you find him. He might be disoriented, and I'll know how to deal with him."

As Lorraine began walking quickly toward Ridgemont, Miss Prim turned to Dawes.

"Detective, I know you are busy, and I won't take too much of your time, but I wonder if I might ask your advice. I don't wish to be alarmist, but I have seen too many people"—and by *people*, she meant *characters*—"ignoring danger signs and not informing the police. I don't wish to be one who discounts ominous portents, only to regret my decisions later. At first I thought I should not bother you with these matters, but I am growing increasingly concerned."

"You don't strike me as the alarmist type, Miss Prim. I'm all ears."

So Miss Prim told him about the telephone calls and the hang-ups, the person (?) she saw lurking in her backyard, and the unknown/unnamed men who had been asking about her and Dolly at the bookstore.

Detective Dawes narrowed his eyes. *Here it comes*, Miss Prim thought. Here is where a law-enforcement professional discounts everything I have just said, implying that I am fanciful, perhaps paranoid. Here is where Detective Dawes, in keeping with genre traditions, suggests that I am lonely and inclined toward the dramatic; that the telephone calls were simply random wrong numbers with no meaning; that the creature in my yard was a deer, not a person; that I will soon discover the identities of the men asking about me and Dolly, and that they will turn out to be well-wishers. In short, that I am rather silly, even though the mounting evidence shows that some person, or persons, may have malicious intent toward me.

To Miss Prim's surprise, Dawes did nothing of the kind. Instead, he said, "Hmm. If just one of those things happened, I'd say it was no big deal. But there seems to be a pattern. Can you think of anyone who might … ?"

Miss Prim knew he was thinking of a polite, non-scaremongering way of saying *want to hurt you.*

"I can think of two possibilities, Detective." She told him about Dolly's impending visit and the unresolved situation with Benjamin and his possible clandestine activities. "As for the other," she continued, "I fear I have made an enemy of Miss Lavelle. She is compelled to believe the worst about me and has taken to haranguing me, quite loudly, in public places. During our most recent donnybrook, she accused me of trying to coax Faye and Kit Cotillard into my 'web,' to use her infelicitous phrase, when in reality I have hired Kit to walk Bruno, and Faye, Kit, and I are fast becoming friends."

"That's Gladys for you. She's so unhappy here, I don't even know why she stays. She should go somewhere else, make a fresh start."

"Yes, Detective, but as my mother used to say, *Wherever you go, there you are.*"

"I'll talk to her, Miss Prim. She's a bully, and she's jealous of you. She hates that an attractive woman has moved into town and has made more friends in a week than she has in a lifetime. She thinks of herself as Queen of Greenfield and she doesn't like having a rival."

Miss Prim's cheeks became rosy. Being called attractive often has that effect on a modest woman.

Dawes handed her a card. "This has my cell number on it, Miss Prim. Call me, or 911, if you feel seriously threatened. Will you be all right in the meantime?"

"Thank you for your kind offer, Detective," Miss Prim responded, taking the card and tucking it into her pocket. "And thank you for taking me seriously. That kind of respect is not often given to people in my position, at least not in fiction."

Dawes smiled. "Fortunately, this isn't fiction."

Henry and Albert greeted Miss Prim as she walked tentatively through Ridgemont's front door. Both dogs seemed subdued; perhaps they understood intuitively that something was amiss. Miss Prim patted them as they stuck their heads out the door, searching for Bruno. To reward their good behavior, she made her way to the kitchen and gave each a treat from the jar.

She carefully climbed the junk-laden staircase and began methodically searching each room of Ridgemont's second story. At the head of a staircase was a large office with a leopard rug in the center of the floor. Miss Prim wondered if Lucian had killed the animal on safari; she hoped not. Lucian's diplomas hung on the wall behind the desk, but the other walls had been stripped of their adornments; bright, unfaded bits of wallpaper stood out in marked contrast to the remainder of the faded and peeling wallpaper. A closet held a suit of chain mail and a ball of twine about two feet in diameter, but no Lucian.

Two other rooms appeared to be unused guest bedrooms. The first room held hundreds of jars of nuts and bolts, with each jar containing one specific type or size. Someone—Lucian, surely—had arranged the nuts and bolts so that each lay at the bottom of the jar, in the same position, with no two touching each other. The second bedroom held what appeared to be the world's largest pillow collection: round, square, overstuffed, beanbag, triangular, patterned, monochromatic, multicolored. As a child she would have loved playing in the room, jumping on the cushions for hours alongside Celia and Noel; now, however, she feared she might sink into the cushions and never emerge, like a character in an Edward Gorey cartoon.

The large room at the end of the corridor was clearly Lorraine and Lucian's bedroom. Lorraine had asked Miss Prim to search the second story, and she hadn't declared any room off limits, but Miss Prim's decorum and modesty prevented her from entering and searching the homeowners' private suite.

The door to the attic was open on its hinges. As she began climbing the stairs, Miss Prim pushed back thoughts of Tippi Hedren in *The Birds* entering an attic space she knew she should not have entered. She expected to find a dusty, musty attic filled with old steamer trunks and dressmaker's mannequins. Instead she found a movie paradise. Luxurious pink couches and divans sat along the walls; fluffy white rugs appeared to float over the floor like clouds. Movie magazines sat neatly stacked on shelves and on small tables.

And the walls! A veritable *Who's Who* of Hollywood's most beautiful, from Theda Bara and Clara Bow, through Lauren Bacall and Katharine Hepburn, to Meryl Streep and Anne Hathaway. On the men's wall, Clark Gable and Buster Crabbe and Johnny Weismuller and Brad Pitt, all in glorious black and white to maximize their glamor.

"I see you've found my sanctuary," said Lorraine, who had miraculously materialized. Miss Prim nearly jumped out of her skin.

"Lorraine! It's simply stunning. What a beautiful space."

"I come here when I need a break from reality. It's relaxing to be surrounded by beauty. Inspiring, too. I don't suppose you've found Lucian, have you?"

"Sadly, no. I checked all the rooms on the second floor, except your bedroom of course."

"He's not on the main floor, in the basement, or in the yard, either. Come on, let's have a cup of coffee. Or tea. Then I'll get the car and we can go out searching until it gets dark. Maybe he'll be home by then. He's pulled that trick before. I'll look up, and there he is, as if he'd never been gone."

"I'd be happy to drive, Lorraine, so you can focus on the search."

"Thank you for the offer, Felicity, but my nerves are much too frazzled as it is."

In the kitchen, Miss Prim took notes while Lorraine brainstormed a list of Lucian's possible whereabouts. The women hastily drank their beverages and then climbed into Lorraine's huge black Cadillac.

26

Things That Go Bump in the Night

Lorraine and Miss Prim spent two hours driving around Greenfield in search of Lucian, but their efforts met with no success. As dusk descended, Miss Prim suggested that Lorraine might be better off at home, waiting for the police to call and Lucian to return.

"Would you like me to stay with you tonight, Lorraine?" Miss Prim asked. "If you'll leave me at Rose Cottage, I'll pack an overnight bag and meet you back at Ridgemont."

"That's sweet of you, Felicity, it really is. But it would only make more work for me. I'd have to get one of the guest rooms ready, and I'm stressed enough as it is."

"As you wish, Lorraine. Please call any time you need me, and I shall be there. And do let me known as soon as Lucian is found. I will rest so much easier."

Lorraine promised to call, dropped Miss Prim at Rose Cottage, and waved in the Cadillac's rearview mirror as she turned the corner and headed up the ridge.

I fear I have lost my opportunity, Miss Prim thought. She had so many questions to ask Lorraine, but the timing could not have been worse. All of those questions would have to wait until tomorrow, when Lucian was safely home. Perhaps some in the criminal outsmarting profession would criticize her decision to delay interrogating Lorraine, arguing that the holders of important information should be questioned even when the timing is inauspicious. However, such axioms ran counter to the practices Mrs. Charity Prim had so carefully inculcated in her children: to be sensitive to others and to value kindness over cold, grim efficiency.

With the remainder of the evening stretching ahead of her, Miss Prim saw an opportunity to catch up on her telephone calls. First she placed a call to Doctor Poe, but the call went unanswered. That was strange, Miss Prim thought; the doctor was usually home by this hour, reading his newspaper and enjoying his nightly port.

Replacing the phone receiver in its cradle, Miss Prim thought, *I must examine my feelings regarding Detective Ezra Dawes more closely.* Certainly he was handsome and certainly he was appealing—and, to a certain extent, he was *expected*. For is it not commonplace for the new criminal outsmarter in town to meet an attractive member of the police force and to fall head over heels in love with him while denying the attraction to herself and everyone else?

Not that it had come to that; at least not in her case, and at least not yet. Miss Prim was self-aware enough to understand that attraction to a rugged detective does not have the same emotional value as a long-standing relationship with a dear friend and confidant, but she was also human enough to admit that Ezra Dawes made her pulse race and her pupils dilate. And hadn't the detective, earlier that very day, openly admitted that he found her pleasing to the eye? Though this likely meant the attraction was mutual, mature reasonable people know that a mutual attraction does not necessitate the pursuit of a romantic relationship.

Her attempts to raise Celia were equally unsuccessful, so Miss Prim left a brief message. "We're having a bit of excitement here, Sister," Miss Prim said into the hissing air of Celia's answering machine. "Lorraine's husband has gone missing and a manhunt is ongoing. Please call when you get a moment. I am anxious to hear about your progress in locating Providence and her aunt."

Remembering that Dolly was staying at Zoroastria's apartment, Miss Prim dialed Zoroastria's number. Someone answered on the first ring.

"Sup?" Zoroastria yelled over a throbbing electronic beat in the background.

"Zoroastria? Is that you?"

"Yo, girl! Hey everyone, it's Miss Prim! How you doing, baby?"

"I'm quite well, Zoroastria. I can't believe it's only a week since I've seen all of you. It seems so long ago."

"Life's a drag without you, Miss Prim. That's why we had to have a party."

So that explained the noise in the background …

"Is Dolly there, Zoroastria? I don't wish to interrupt your party, but I've been a little concerned about her and, well, I suppose I am just checking in."

"She's all mopey, Miss Prim, and I've had enough of that! Viveca's mixing up the cosmos right now, even if she can't have one. Hint, hint!"

"But Dolly's all right? She told you what's happening with Benjamin?"

"Benjamin Smenjamin. Just a guy, Miss Prim, just a guy! We both know they're a dime a dozen, but D ain't with the program yet. Don't worry, me and my girls are gonna teach her what to do when a man messes with your head. When I get done with her, you'll be calling her Zoroastria the Second!"

Oh dear, Miss Prim thought, *one Zoroastria is more than enough.*

"Would you put her on the line for just a moment?"

"Sure. YO! DOLLY! MISS PRIM WANTS TO TALK TO YOU! Here she is, Miss Prim. Make it quick, girl, we gotta get this party started!"

After having her eardrums assaulted by several unpleasant noises, Miss Prim heard Dolly's voice.

"Miss Prim, thank God! I can't believe what I've gotten myself into." She lowered her voice. "You know how we always suspected that Zoroastria's life is one big party? Well, it *is*. I haven't slept a wink in two nights."

"Oh, dearest, enjoy this time with your friends! You may not be sleeping much now, but you will look back on these nights with many smiles when you are my age."

"I don't know about that," Dolly said, skeptically. "But I'll admit that all this … um, stimulation … has kept my mind off my troubles."

"Any word from Benjamin?"

"None at all. I'm really worried."

"You do need some time away, dearest," Miss Prim said. "Is our plan now cemented? I shall pick you up tomorrow evening at the Two Oaks train station?"

"Absolutely, Miss Prim. The train gets in at 7:12. It'll be good to have some peace and quiet." Miss Prim heard whooping in the background. "Because those two things are definitely in short supply around here. I'd better go, Miss Prim. Zoroastria is waving a pink drink at me."

"Go, go," Miss Prim ordered. "And I do promise you a restful, relaxing weekend in Connecticut."

As Miss Prim hung up the phone, she fought to resist an urge that had been a source of much consternation to Mama:

specifically, Miss Felicity Prim's intense desire to matchmake. While Miss Prim had liked Benjamin when she met him, she had now decided he was thoroughly unsuitable, and a substitute must be found. Her mind wandered to the tall young man who'd carried her books from the moving truck into her attic. Josh. Certainly a polite young man, though one who made too-frequent use of the informal vernacular; but someone with such good bones could be brought along gently with the right coaching.

Yes, on the morrow she might make a few discreet inquiries about Josh's current relationship status. And what the heck. One more person at her upcoming Sunday gathering would only make it merrier.

An hour later, her shower taken and her nightly ritual complete, Miss Prim turned in. As always, Bruno stretched himself alongside her bed and began snoring, a sound not unlike a pig attempting to sing opera. Miss Prim found the noise charming and endearing; in a strange way, it made her feel safe.

With the racket emanating from Bruno, was it any wonder that strange dreams should take hold? The dreams had no images associated with them, but rather took the form of urgent whisperings, struggles, and frustrations. But … how odd that Bruno should seem to hear them, too, for intimidating growls began to replace his snores.

Miss Prim's eyes sprang open when she realized the sounds were not emanating from a dream but rather from somewhere in the cottage.

She swung her legs out of bed and put her hand on Bruno's collar to quiet him. The sounds were unmistakable: angry murmurs and entreaties. The noise was not coming from the cottage's main floor or from the attic. No, it was below her, in the hidden basement.

What should she do? Common sense dictated that she get out of the cottage immediately and drive directly to the police station. Alternatively, she could lock herself into her bedroom to protect herself from anyone who might wish to harm her. But there was no guarantee that the person or persons in the basement would not be able to break down the bedroom door. In just two dozen steps she could reach the phone in the parlor and call for help, but dialing a phone seemed like the wrong course of action in an emergency. Fleeing or barricading herself would expose her to less danger.

Or—perhaps this was her opportunity for a trial by fire? As she'd prepared for her career in criminal outsmarting, she'd known that she might find herself in dangerous situations. This was one of the reasons she'd trained in self-defense. Now she had Bruno to protect her, too. *And* she was the proud owner of a Laser Taser 3000.

Gathering her resolve, she retrieved the Laser Taser 3000 from the drawer of her nightstand. She then donned her slippers, switched on the lamp next to her bed, and made her way slowly and quietly to the kitchen.

To her surprise, the secret door was firmly closed, the wooden star in its assigned place in the cupboard. Now she could hear no noises in the basement, none whatsoever. Had her footsteps silenced the intruder? Or had the noises been the sounds of the house settling—or the product of an over-active imagination?

Quite possibly the latter, but it would not hurt to double check. Ensuring the emptiness of the basement, she decided, would allow her to sleep better (but not wonderfully) for the rest of the night, so she removed the star from the cupboard and pressed it firmly into the indentation. The door popped open. Miss Prim listened and heard nothing.

"Come, Bruno," she said, flipping the light switch at the head of the staircase. She placed her foot on the first stair and Bruno moved into place behind her. She grabbed the Laser Taser 3000 with both hands, thinking how foolish she must look: a crazy lady, gripping an electrical shock device, descending the basement stairs in her nightie.

She descended three more steps and lowered herself onto her haunches to get a wider view of the basement.

A man stood in the corner. Their eyes met.

"Well, if it isn't Miss Serendipity," said Lucian Koslowski. He was carrying a box overflowing with springs, switch plates, and extension cords. "Why are you pointing that thing at me? Come down here and help me, if you please. I seemed to have misplaced my copy of the *Bhagavad Gita*, and Lorraine is no help whatsoever."

27

The Second Disappearance

What a night it had been, Miss Prim reflected the next morning. Despite Lorraine's warnings that Lucian might be dangerous when agitated (perhaps another of Lorraine's exaggerations or not-quite-true statements?), Miss Prim had found her neighbor quite pliant. She'd invited him upstairs for refreshment. As he sat sipping tea, munching happily on oatmeal cookies and reminiscing about his friendship with Charlemagne, Miss Prim had placed two telephone calls, the first to Lorraine and the second to Ezra Dawes.

Five minutes later, Lorraine had shown up, this time wearing elaborate (some might say *garish*) face make-up and a wig of wild curls. Miss Prim was horrified, for Lorraine had managed to make herself look quite deranged. Lorraine, noticing Miss Prim's aghast expression, had rushed to explain.

"It's the Dee Snyder look, Felicity."

"Dee Snyder?"

"The lead singer of Twisted Sister. A classic metal band from the eighties. Some music critics called them 'hair bands' because they sported long, fabulous locks. I've been wanting to go curly, and I couldn't think of any really wonderful modern celeb to use for inspiration. Maybe Minnie Driver, but she's not exactly A-list, is she?" Then, to her husband: "Lucian, what *are* you doing here?"

"What?"

"I SAID, WHAT ARE YOU DOING HERE, LUCIAN?"

"You need to put on your glasses, Lorraine. Anyone can see I am enjoying a cup of tea with a delightful hostess. I say, Miss Simplicity, have you seen my Fabergé eggs anywhere? I had them just a moment ago."

As Lorraine hurried Lucian to finish his snacks, Detective Dawes had arrived. He took Miss Prim off to the side.

"Any idea how he got into your basement, Miss Prim?"

"The only thing I can think of, Detective, is that he somehow got into the cottage while Lorraine and I were out searching for him. I don't understand how, though. I recently changed all the locks, and there were no signs of a break-in. Also, the secret door in the kitchen was closed tight, and the wooden star that's used to spring the door open wasn't in its indentation. I suppose Lucian could have pulled the door closed behind him, but I don't know how the star could have been returned to the cupboard in which I keep it. And I'm absolutely sure the door was closed before I left the cottage."

"I need to take a *much* closer look at your basement, Miss Prim," Dawes had replied. "But I'm exhausted and not capable of clear thought right now. The key thing is that Lucian's back. I'll stop by later or tomorrow, after I've had some sleep."

"If there's anything further I can do to help, Detective, please let me know. I hate to ask the same question over and over, but I don't suppose there's been any progress on discovering our victim's identity?"

"None whatsoever. We're at a complete dead end. And I *still* don't have the M.E.'s report, so we don't even know the official cause of death yet. Everything takes way too long because we're so understaffed."

After seeing Lorraine, Lucian, and Detective Dawes off, Miss Prim had brewed herself a cup of chamomile. She'd been feeling stimulated, perhaps even nerved up, by the evening's events, and she thought a cuppa would help her fall back asleep. The chamomile had worked its usual magic, and she'd risen later than usual, feeling grateful that Lucian's disappearance had been followed so quickly by his return. However, the fact that he could find his way into her locked house, and somehow get past her vigilant watchdog, remained unnerving.

Miss Prim consulted her watch. Dolly would be arriving in just a few short hours.

An idea struck her. The last time she'd visited Cambria & Calibri, she'd noticed the newest title by one of Dolly's favorite writers. Dolly'd had a difficult week. What would make her happier than the latest Cecelia Ahern novel, purchased with the aid of the ten percent discount so generously granted by Valeska Reed? Miss Prim attached the leash to Bruno's collar, locked up the cottage, and began her stroll to Cambria & Calibri, where Valeska welcomed her with open arms.

"What a night, Miss Prim. Martin was out until 5 AM looking for Lucian Koslowski. Quite a bit seems to happen in your basement, doesn't it?"

Miss Prim agreed that yes, the basement of her tiny cottage saw more than its share of action. The two women chatted amiably as Miss Prim browsed through the shop's newest offerings, feeling relieved that the Cecelia Ahern books were on the shelves reserved for acceptable, worthy books.

As Valeska rang up the purchase, she said, "I had a flash of insight last night, Miss Prim. Remember the retouched snapshot you showed me? The photo of the man in your basement, but without facial hair? I think I've made a connection."

Miss Prim's ears perked up. "Oh?"

"I told you I saw him looking in the window once or twice at closing time. Well, last night—or should I say, early this morning—when Martin got home, he showed me a recent photo of Lucian, the one they'd been showing around when they were out trying to find him. And it hit me. It was Lucian's face I'd seen at the window."

"This is extraordinary, Valeska. But how could you not have recognized Lucian when you saw him looking in the window?"

"Nobody really sees him, Miss Prim. Lorraine keeps him out of harm's way in Ridgemont. The way I understand it, the two of them used to be quite the gadabouts. But as Lucian has gone downhill, Lorraine has found it increasingly difficult to manage him in public. Apparently she's concocted enough stories to keep him happily at home most of the time. Martin and I have lived in Greenfield only about two years. By the time we moved here, Lorraine had already confined Lucian to quarters, so even though I've heard that he 'escapes' from time to time, I've never met him. Until Martin showed me the photo last night, I hadn't realized I'd encountered him face to face.

"And I need to thank *you* for that epiphany, Miss Prim," Valeska continued. "I have spent too many years expecting Martin to volunteer information. When he didn't, I got angry and thought he didn't want to share his life with me. But men want us to show interest in their lives, don't they? We do that by asking questions rather than waiting for them to start talking. That's why Martin showed me Lucian's photo—because I asked him to. It's been a valuable lesson, Miss Prim, and one I won't soon forget."

"I'm so delighted to hear this, Valeska. It looks as if Martin has been making healthy choices, too; I noticed him snacking on carrots at the police station. Of course, if he likes the low-cal treats I'll be preparing on Sunday, I shall be happy to share the recipes with you." Miss Prim paused for a moment. "Oh, Valeska, please do not think, though, that I am in any way trying to ingratiate myself with, or steal, your husband! I made the offer to prepare healthy snacks for him spontaneously, and I am sometimes too impetuous. I'm afraid Miss Lavelle has made me aware of that fact, and how interfering I can be. I really am not trying to mind everyone's business. I just wish to have friends and relationships in Greenfield, and I may be trying too hard." To her surprise, she felt a tear trickling down her right cheek.

"Now stop that right now, Miss Prim," Valeska ordered. "Gladys Lavelle is a bitter, angry woman without a friend in the world. Even her lover, Ethan Prothero, doesn't like her any more, and most of us are surprised he ever did. Don't let her get to you. And don't change, either. Greenfield quite likes you the way you are."

"Valeska, thank you. You could not have said anything kinder. I shall see you and Martin on Sunday. Until then, I must consider why you thought the man in the photo looked so much like Lucian Koslowski."

"There's only one reason I can think of, Miss Prim. The man is probably his son."

"But Lorraine and Lucian have no children."

"I didn't say he was Lorraine's son, Miss Prim. I said he was Lucian's son. They're not the same thing."

As Miss Prim and Bruno arrived at Rose Cottage, Miss Prim noticed Bruno's tail beginning to wag rapidly. When she unlocked the front door and placed her book purchase on the small table in the entryway, she understood why. On the floor was a slip of paper:

Hey Miss P,
Came to walk Bruno but you guys are gone.
Listen I have something pretty interesting to tell you.
I'll tell you when I see you.
Stay cool,
Kit

After wrapping Dolly's gift, Miss Prim lay down for a brief nap. It had been a tiring night, so she felt no guilt about closing her eyes for a restorative siesta. When she opened them again, it was almost time to meet Dolly at the train station.

She grabbed her handbag and Dolly's gift and jumped into her car, making excellent time as the Zap easily passed the distressingly sedate drivers of Connecticut. She arrived a few minutes early and went into the depot, where a new copper sign gleamed near the refreshment stand:

WELCOME TO TWO OAKS, CONNECTICUT
Birthplace of Junusakey Lemonade

After waving in greeting to Deb, Miss Prim spent a few moments looking through the tourist brochures while she awaited the train's arrival. A few minutes later she heard a whistle and walked to the platform. Dolly was the first passenger off the train.

The two friends flew into each other's arms.

"Dolly!" Miss Prim exclaimed. "I can't tell you how good it is to see you."

"I'm so glad to be here, Miss Prim. Staying with Zoroastria is fun, but taxing on the nerves."

And Dolly *did* look just a bit tired, Miss Prim reflected. But one need not *say* that.

"Come, Dolly, I cannot wait for you to see Rose Cottage." She presented the wrapped gift to her friend. "Here's a little something to help you pass the time, dearest."

"I brought something for you, too, Miss Prim," Dolly said, handing Miss Prim a paper sack with Veneiro's Pastry Shop printed on it.

"Dolly, you didn't!"

"I couldn't resist, Miss Prim. And yes, it's exactly what you think it is. Two bear claws. One chocolate for you, one vanilla for me."

On the return trip to Greenfield, Dolly attempted to open her gift but seemed to have difficulty with the wrapping. Miss Prim apologized. "I'm sorry for the roughness of the ride, Dolly. While the Zap is certainly fuel-efficient, I'm afraid its suspension sometimes makes for a tooth-rattling journey. You look a bit nauseated, dearest. Was the train journey that difficult? Do not worry. A cup of tea will settle your stomach nicely."

Back at the cottage, Miss Prim introduced Dolly to Bruno—the two took to each other instantly—and then showed Dolly to the guest room. As Dolly unpacked, Miss Prim put the tea-kettle on the stove to boil and placed each bear claw onto a pastry dish. She couldn't blame Bruno for drooling, as she was practically doing the same. But the dog's training must not be allowed to lapse, so Miss Prim distracted Bruno by throwing his bone, ringing the bell, and then providing him with a small treat when the drooling stopped.

Dolly watched Miss Prim from the doorway. "Miss Prim, what was *that* all about?"

Miss Prim explained that she was attempting to use Pavlov's method in reverse to train Bruno, reporting on her animal companion's excellent progress to date. Dolly complimented Miss Prim on her mastery of psychology's main precepts, and the two sat down to enjoy their tea and pastries.

"Oh, but I'm forgetting Mrs. Mallowan's," Miss Prim said, rising from the table to retrieve the lemon sugar.

"That reminds me, Miss Prim. I brought you a new brand that I found at Zabar's. It claims to have not only lemon but also undernotes of lime and peach. Let's try it instead of the same old lemon sugar."

Miss Prim bit her lip. Could Mrs. Mallowan's Lemon Sugar really be improved on? Why add those additional flavors when lemon served quite nicely on its own? But she did not wish to appear closed-minded, and when Dolly returned from her room with a box of Miss Meredith's Blended Sugar, Miss Prim eagerly opened the box and removed two packets. She tried handing one to Dolly, who said she'd prefer to drink her tea "straight," so Miss Prim ripped the packet open and poured it into her own tea.

Miss Prim sipped tentatively. Hmmm. Not quite the same as the tart lemon she so loved, but the peach did add an interesting sweet note to the somewhat mellower lemon of Miss Meredith's recipe, and the lime kicked in after she swallowed the first sip. The taste was not unpleasant at all, and Miss Prim decided Miss Meredith's product would have a permanent place in her cupboard. It would never substitute for Mrs. Mallowan's, but it would make for a lovely alternative when one felt the need for novelty.

Miss Prim gingerly broached the subject of Benjamin.

"Tell me, Dolly, has there been any word from, or about, Benjamin?"

"Nothing at all, Miss Prim. I'm starting to think he's in deep trouble. I want to help him if I can, but I'm also afraid to get involved."

"The key thing is to proceed cautiously, Dolly. And to rest while you are here."

Fortunately, relaxation was easy for the two friends. Within an hour of drinking their tea, both declared themselves exhausted. They agreed to turn in early, with the goal of sleeping in and then taking Bruno for a morning walk. As Miss Prim fell asleep, she thought she heard Dolly talking on the phone—perhaps to Zoroastria or Viveca? *The young*, she thought, *so dependent on the telephone*; and promptly lost consciousness.

The next morning she rose feeling rested and refreshed. As always, Bruno seemed to know when she opened her eyes, and he was quickly on his feet, waiting for her to get out of bed and start her day. Walking past the guest room, she saw that the door was still closed, so she tiptoed around the cottage so as not to wake her slumbering friend. When Dolly had not risen by 10 AM, Miss Prim let Bruno into the yard, promising to take him for a good, long walk later.

By 10:15, Miss Prim thought she might just check on Dolly. She knocked on the door and received no response. She then turned the handle gently and caught her breath when she saw that the bed had not been slept in.

28
Revelation

Do not panic, Miss Prim commanded herself. But, even as her mind turned over the possibilities—Dolly had returned to New York due to some unexpected emergency, Dolly had gone out for a walk—her logical side refuted each explanation. Dolly would not leave without telling her. And if she'd chosen to return to Manhattan, why would she have left her weekend bag in the guest room?

But wouldn't Bruno have alerted her if something dangerous had been afoot? She'd slept quite soundly, but she would have heard Bruno's growls if he'd sensed danger.

What was her next course of action? Call Detective Dawes and report a missing person? She knew he'd say what detectives in crime fiction (and in reality) always say to concerned friends and relatives: "A person must be missing 48 hours before we can do anything." She had to tread lightly. Detective Dawes had listened sympathetically when she'd recounted the mysterious events that had befallen her since her arrival in Greenfield. If she called the police every time something out of the ordinary occurred, would the Greenfield PD begin to see her as a silly, easily spooked woman with paranoid delusions who was on her way to becoming the town nuisance? No, that would not do. She was not a silly-goose character in a poorly plotted novel, and she did not want to be treated as such.

Her first step, then, was to conduct a thorough search of the cottage and the grounds. But she could not find Dolly in the basement, in the attic, in the barn at the rear of her yard, or anywhere else on the property.

She must calm her nerves, she simply must. She put the kettle on and brewed a cup of chamomile. But which should she choose, the multiple flavors of Miss Meredith's Blended Sugar or the comfort of Mrs. Mallowan's Lemon Sugar? The decision was made for her because she could not remember where she had placed the box of Miss Meredith's recipe. She would have sworn she'd left it on the top shelf of the cupboard, but it was nowhere to be found.

As she sat on the couch to sip her tea, she noticed something from the corner of her eye. There, next to the telephone, was a small rectangular business card. Miss Prim recognized it instantly.

OLIVIA ABERNATHY
Abernathy Realty
Greenfield's Premier Realtor

You know you want to live here.
860-555-CHARM
OAbernathy@abernathyrealty.com

Miss Prim remembered hearing Dolly's whispers the night before. She'd assumed Dolly was chatting with Zoroastria or another friend. Why on earth would Dolly have been talking with Olivia Abernathy? There was only one way to find out.

Miss Prim returned to her bedroom to grab her handbag. It was not on the settee, where she'd left it; nor was it in any of the closets or anywhere else in the cottage.

Taking a deep breath, Miss Prim opened the drawer of her nightstand, fully expecting the Laser Taser 3000 to have gone missing along with Dolly and the handbag. But there it was, in all its electrical, protective glory. She grabbed it, stuffed it into a spare handbag, and then retrieved a spare set of car and cottage keys from her jewelry box. She noted that none of her jewelry was missing, but she wouldn't have cared if it was. Dolly was much more important than baubles, bangles, and beads. She returned to her closet, retrieved the small photo album in which she kept her favorite snapshots, and thrust the album into her handbag.

Bruno must have sensed her worries. He followed closely on her heels, as if not wanting to let her out of his sight. She tried patting his head to reassure him, but he did not seem mollified.

She threw the front door open to find Kit standing on her doorstep, his finger on her doorbell. He jumped back.

"Miss P! What's up? You don't look so good."

"Oh, Kit, it's a long story. I'm afraid I don't have time to chat. I know Bruno will be happy for your company while I'm gone."

"Is everything all right?"

At first Miss Prim thought that she should not draw Kit into her problems, but a lifetime of reading mystery fiction had taught her that teenagers often know more than they let on. So she decided to take Kit into her confidence.

"Kit, I think you know that my friend Dolly is visiting …"

"That tall lady you picked up at the train station yesterday? The one you think me and Faye will like?"

"That's her, Kit. I don't suppose you've seen her anywhere?"

"No, sorry. Is she missing?"

"That's what I'm afraid of, Kit. I'm sorry, I must be on my way …"

"Miss P, before you go, I need to talk to you about something."

Miss Prim looked at her watch helplessly. "Kit, can it possibly wait? My mission is really most urgent."

"But this might have something to do with your friend being gone. I've been trying to tell you for a couple of days, but I haven't seen you."

"All right, Kit. If you think it's important, let's talk now."

Out of sheer habit—she simply could not invite someone into her home without providing a beverage and a snack—Miss Prim poured Kit a glass of iced tea and buttered a slice of cinnamon-raisin bread for him.

Kit tucked into the bread like a hyena into a fallen zebra. "The other day, when the detective was here. You guys were talking and I went around back to say goodbye to Bruno. I guess I sorta heard what you guys were talking about." Miss Prim looked at Kit fondly, admiring his ability to admit to eavesdropping without using that word. "Detective Dawes said something about a locked-room mystery, how you two couldn't figure out how that dead guy got into your basement. I thought that was pretty cool. Not that the guy was dead but that nobody could figure out how he got there. So I started wondering about a few things. So I went to see Gil Fellowes …"

Miss Prim listened closely as Kit finished his story. Suddenly all the pieces of the puzzle fell into place: her visit with Mrs. Saxe-Coburg, Lorraine's half-truths, Lucian's disappearance and mysterious reappearance.

As she climbed into the Zap, Miss Prim thought, *I believe I have just cracked my first case*. Perhaps arrogant detectives, such as Hercule Poirot, took their epiphanies for granted; but for her, the sensation was entirely new, and she found it most agreeable.

It was Saturday afternoon, and Greenfield Town Square was filled with weekenders walking through the streets, snapping photographs, and visiting the shops. Abernathy Realty was located on the square's north side.

Olivia emerged from her glassed-in office to greet Miss Prim. "Miss Prim, what brings you here? Looking to trade up already? I don't blame you, not one bit. You have been bitten by what I call the 'Greenfield bug.' It happens to everyone, sooner or later."

"Olivia, might I have a word with you in private? It's rather urgent."

"Of course, come right in," Olivia Abernathy said dubiously. For her, the only truly urgent matters concerned getting the right listings.

Miss Prim sat opposite Olivia at the latter's large, imposing desk. "I think you may be acquainted with a friend of mine, Miss Dolly Veerelf?"

Olivia shook her head. "No, I don't know anyone with that name."

"But I feel confident that she has spoken with you."

"Miss Prim," Olivia said in a disapproving tone, "it's my business never to forget a face or a name."

"So you did not speak to anyone named Dolly Veerelf yesterday or last night?"

"No, I did not."

"I wonder if I might ask you to look at a few snapshots? You may recognize her."

Miss Prim removed the small photo album from her handbag and flipped to a photo showing her and Dolly, taken by Zoroastria at Doctor Poe's office a few months earlier. The two friends smiled broadly at the camera, their arms around each other's shoulders.

Olivia recognized the younger woman instantly. "Her? Oh, yes. But her name's not Dolly. It's Nellie. Nellie Oleson."

Nellie Oleson? Wasn't she the snippy girl from *Little House on the Prairie*?

"I'd be most grateful if you could tell me a little about your dealings with her, Olivia."

"Not much to tell. She came in with her husband a week or so ago. They were looking for a short-term rental. The husband has a temporary assignment in Litchfield, I believe. I have a few properties that are stubbornly not selling, and the owners have agreed to rent them by the month. I set the Olesons up in a nice little farmhouse. Between you and me, it's on the wrong side of town, or it would have sold long ago."

"Do you remember her husband's name?"

"As I said, Miss Prim, it is my job never to forget a face or a name. It was Benjamin. Benjamin Oleson."

Benjamin Oleson? Could this be the secret identity of Benjamin Bannister, graduate student of magical realism at Columbia University?

"This may be a strange question, Olivia, but did the couple look ... content? Happy? Or was there a strain?"

"Most definitely content, Miss Prim. When you've been in this business as long as I have, you know who's happy and who isn't."

Miss Prim's head was spinning. First Kit's revelation, now this.

"You don't happen to have a photo of Benjamin Oleson, do you?" Miss Prim asked.

"Of course not, Miss Prim. I take photos of houses, not of people." Her tone implied, *Because houses matter.*

"I think you may have misunderstood, Olivia. You may have assumed his last name was Oleson because that was the woman's last name, but I don't believe they are married. I believe his last name is actually Bannister."

"I suppose you may be right, Miss Prim, though I do not usually make mistakes like that. You wouldn't believe how *sensitive* people can be."

"Oh, dear," Miss Prim sighed. "If only there was a place we could go to find a photo of him. Then you could confirm his identity so much more easily."

"Do you know what he does for a living?"

"He's a graduate student at Columbia University."

"Let's see if we can pull him up on the Internet. There's bound to be a few photos."

"The Inner Net?"

Olivia Abernathy looked at Miss Prim as if to say, *Are you mad, woman?* But she held her tongue and instead began clacking on her keyboard.

"Here he is," Olivia said. "Benjamin Bannister, Ph.D. candidate. Yes, that's him, all right."

"Olivia, would you mind giving me the address of the house you rented to Benjamin and Dol—Benjamin and Nellie? That would not be a breach of professional ethics, would it?"

"I don't think so. I mean, you're not exactly the dangerous type, Miss Prim. Wait a minute—is Nellie the woman you picked up at the Two Oaks train station last night?"

"It's a long story, Olivia. But I promise that once I get to the bottom of things, I will return and give you all the details."

Olivia Abernathy seemed satisfied with this assurance.

"The address is 50 Pierced Arrow Lane. Pick up Milford Road off the south side of the square and take it about a mile into the country. Look for a dilapidated red barn—the town really *must* do something about that—and then make the next right onto Iroquois Road. About half a mile down, you'll get to Pierced Arrow. Make a left, and it'll be the last house on your left."

29

Trapped

There *had* to be a reasonable explanation, Miss Prim reasoned, throwing the Zap into a lower gear to pass a Hummer that was blocking her way. She hoped with all her being that the explanation would be innocent and harmless, but as she raced through the streets of Greenfield, she felt less and less hopeful. For years she and Dolly had been the best of friends, the closest of confidantes. There was no good reason for Dolly to hide her plans to rent a house in Greenfield or to give Olivia Abernathy a phony name. No, Miss Prim feared that Benjamin was in quite a bit of trouble and that he had somehow pulled Dolly into his difficulties.

Was Dolly being held against her will? Miss Prim thought the possibility quite likely and applied her foot more forcefully to the Zap's gas pedal.

She would proceed with caution and would *not* get herself into any situation from which she could not extricate herself. But Dolly's safety was paramount, and Miss Prim would do whatever was necessary to ensure it.

Pierced Arrow Lane dead-ended at a picturesque field. From her seat in the Zap, Miss Prim looked at the house Dolly and Benjamin had rented. It was a small, charming red farmhouse, probably built in the 1920s or 1930s, its windows adorned with white lace curtains. A barn sat at the end of the driveway, its huge wooden doors tightly closed. A line of pine trees separated the driveway from the adjoining property to the left. The house was neither pristine nor dilapidated. While it did not appear to be lived in, nor did it appear to be deserted or neglected.

No car sat in the driveway, a fact Miss Prim found heartening. The farmhouse was not walking distance from the Greenfield town square. To live here, one would need a car; and the fact that there was no car in the driveway meant that Dolly's captor was likely not present.

Unless, of course, the car was in the barn.

Miss Prim turned the Zap around and parked it halfway down the road. This way, anyone looking out of the front windows of 50 Pierced Arrow Lane would not see the car. She grabbed her handbag, slung it over her shoulder, and began briskly walking toward the farmhouse. Oh, how she wished for cover of night, which would have allowed her to remain undetected! But it was broad daylight, and strategies must be adjusted accordingly. She pulled her shoulders back and adjusted her gait to give any onlookers the impression that she was simply a New England matron out for her daily constitutional.

Remaining alert to her surroundings, Miss Prim used the pine trees lining the driveway for cover as she made her way to the barn. The structure had no windows in the front or along the tree line—Miss Prim began to feel disappointed—but two windows near ground level at the back of the barn allowed her to peer in. She'd expected to find—what? Drug dealers divvying up cash? A flotilla of antique cars? A counterfeiting operation?—but instead she saw an empty barn through sparkling dust motes.

What should her next move be? The rules of criminal outsmarting required her to scope out the remainder of the property, but skulking took time. Why not just go to the front door, ring the bell, and see what happened? Maybe Dolly would open the door and answer all her questions. Or, perhaps, the front door might be unlocked, and she could enter the house easily.

She purposefully strode toward the front door, again to convey the impression to passersby, or nosy neighbors, that she was a resident, friend, or invited guest. With a quick stab of her finger, she rang the doorbell. She heard its deep chime resounding through the house, but nobody answered.

Miss Prim put her ear to the doorjamb to listen for footsteps. But the only thing on the other side of the door was silence.

But wait—what was that sound? Not whispers, not talking, but—a muffled, prolonged scream? Was someone locked in the recesses of the house? Had the captive heard the doorbell, and was she now screaming to get the visitor's attention?

She tried the doorknob. Locked tight.

Her sense of urgency increased, Miss Prim walked along the driveway, looking for possible points of entry into the house. There was one window, but it was much too high for her to reach, and the side entry door was securely bolted.

At the rear of the house, a set of wooden steps led to a good-sized outdoor deck. Miss Prim climbed the stairs and looked through the door into the kitchen. Deserted. She tried the doorknob. It wouldn't budge.

Miss Prim looked around helplessly at what she would have, under other circumstances, considered a charming outdoor space. Clay flowerpots along one side of the deck were abloom with zinnias and marigolds. A table with a folded patio umbrella sat in the center of the deck, awaiting guests for a summer barbecue. Even the milk box was charming, a throwback to more innocent times.

Then it her: what every person intent on criminal trespass remembers, if she has a brain in her head. Rare is the homeowner who does not hide a house key somewhere on the property. She glanced at the barn, but no—that would not be the best hiding place for a spare key. She hadn't hidden her spare key in the barn on her own property. If she'd been locked out of the cottage at night, she would not have wanted to stumble through the dark yard and into the barn (an archetypally creepy place) to retrieve the key. To avoid such a scenario she'd hidden the key close to Rose Cottage.

First she searched the milk box. Dozens of clothespins, but no key. She looked under the welcome mat in front of the door: earwigs, but no key. She felt around the window frame and was rewarded with small chunks of dry, broken putty, but no key. She got on her knees to look under the picnic table, hoping to find a key taped there, but she found only spiderwebs.

As she rose to her feet she spied the flowerpots.

The spare key was not under the first flowerpot, nor under the second or third. It was under the fourth.

Rejoicing at her luck and/or intelligence, Miss Prim grabbed the key and returned to the door. She slid the key into the lock—it went in marvelously easily—and twisted it. The bolt disengaged with a satisfying *click*, and within a moment Miss Prim was inside the house.

The house's interior was much like its exterior, neither well kept nor neglected. It was really quite impossible, Miss Prim thought, to determine whether anyone was living here. A refrigerator stood to her right. She opened the door to see if it held any food. It did. The light blinked on when she opened the door, so the utilities were live, which meant the house was most likely occupied.

She paused to listen. Yes, she still heard desperate noises. They emanated from somewhere farther into the house and below her feet. The basement?

Following her ears, Miss Prim tiptoed into a hallway. The wooden floors were creaky, but she felt sure that she and the captive were quite alone. The air was much too dead for someone to be watching her from close by.

Along the hallway she encountered a substantial door locked with a heavy padlock. A door to the cellar?

She knocked on the door. "Dolly? Dolly, can you hear me? It is I, Miss Prim."

Miss Prim heard a sob. "Oh, Miss Prim! How did you find me? You've got to get me out of here."

"I shall, dearest. There's a padlock on this door. I must find a way to get it open."

"Hurry, Miss Prim. Please."

Miss Prim examined the padlock. It was large, heavy, and intimidating. Perhaps steroid-crazed bodybuilders might be able to crush it with their bare hands, but she lacked the necessary brute strength.

How convenient it would be if she could find a spare key to the padlock. But would a captor really leave the key to his captive's cage accessible to anyone who decided to snoop through the house? This was one of those situations where criminals were inconsistent, Miss Prim thought. On the one hand, criminals were highly intelligent and would never do something so stupid as to leave a key in plain sight. On the other hand, criminals were also human and could be expected to slip up eventually. On balance, Miss Prim decided that searching the house for a key was a good idea, mostly because there was no other way she could defeat that heavy lock.

She returned to the kitchen and began opening the cupboards. She gave a small yelp of joy when she found a key rack attached to the inside of the door to the broom closet. Five keys dangled from the rack. She gathered them quickly and returned to the basement door.

None of the keys worked.

She returned to the kitchen and began going through the cabinetry. A drawer filled with cutlery; a drawer filled with plastic bags; a drawer filled with dishrags and towels. A junk drawer filled with ladles, plastic spoons, and tools: a screwdriver, a wrench, a hammer.

Eyeing the screwdriver, Miss Prim flashed back to the 1970s. At that time, Doctor Poe had stored pharmaceuticals in a cabinet in one of his examination rooms. When certain patients discovered its contents, that cabinet had experienced a rash of thefts. Doctor Poe had solved the problem by purchasing a latch, screwing it into the cabinet doors, and then padlocking the doors through the hasp. The system had worked marvelously until the office manager (Miss Prim's precursor) lost the key. Everyone had wrung their hands helplessly, until Doctor Poe found a solution to save the day. He'd retrieved a screwdriver, unscrewed both sides of the latch, and removed it from the door, thus triumphing over the padlock.

Miss Prim grabbed the screwdriver and returned to the door that kept Dolly a prisoner. Working slowly and cautiously, Miss Prim began unscrewing the screws from the latch. One—two—three—four—five—six—seven—eight. All the screws were removed, and the latch with its intimidating padlock lay on the floor.

Miss Prim unlocked the lock on the doorknob and swung the door open. Contrary to her expectations, the basement was not dark; several light bulbs shone from below. She began walking down the stairs tentatively.

"Dolly?"

"Over here, Miss Prim."

Dolly, looking pale and frightened, sat on the basement floor, her wrists and ankles bound with rope.

"Oh, Dolly," Miss Prim cried, "are you all right?"

"I'm OK, Miss Prim. We have to get out of here."

Miss Prim began working at the knotted ropes.

"Wait," Dolly said. "What was that?"

"What was what?" Miss Prim had been working the ropes so frantically she hadn't paid attention to anything else.

"*That*," Dolly whispered.

Miss Prim listened as the basement door was slammed shut and the door lock was engaged with a sickening *click*.

Miss Prim rushed up the stairs. Yes, the door was sealed tight. She returned to Dolly and continued working the ropes.

"What are we going to do, Miss Prim? Now we're both locked down here."

"This is completely my fault," Miss Prim said, enraged with herself for not having foreseen this twist in the plot. "I thought the house was empty. I should have been more careful."

"He went out a few hours ago, Miss Prim. I guess he's back now." Miss Prim thought she had never heard Dolly sound so bitter.

"Are you hurt, dearest?" Miss Prim asked, as the ropes binding Dolly's ankles came loose.

"I'm OK. I don't think he wants to hurt me. He's just using me to get to Benjamin. How did you find me?"

Miss Prim told her about finding Olivia Abernathy's business card, about her interview with Greenfield's premier real-estate agent, about locating the hidden key under the flowerpot and releasing the padlock by using a trick Doctor Poe had taught her.

"I'm impressed, Miss Prim," Dolly said with awe. "You really *are* cut out for your new profession."

"Perhaps, but that's the last thing on my mind right now. Dolly, why ever did you rent this house and give a phony name to Olivia?"

"He made me do it, Miss Prim. I didn't have a choice."

"Who is 'he'?"

"It's such a long story. His name is Everett Mansour. He's in the graduate program with Benjamin. It all started with a book."

"Go on," Miss Prim said, working at the ropes binding Dolly's wrists.

"One day, Benjamin and Everett stopped in a used bookstore on the Upper West Side to kill some time. The way Benjamin tells the story, he and Everett began on opposite sides of the room and found their way to the middle at the same time. They were looking through a pile of dusty old books and they both reached for the same book at the same time. That's where the problem started. Benjamin says he got the book first, but Everett says he had his hands on it and Benjamin grabbed it from him. Anyway, Benjamin started paging through it. He couldn't believe his eyes. The bookstore owner had no idea and sold it to him for five dollars."

"What was it, Dolly?"

"Miss Prim, you won't believe this. It's one of the original copies of *Songs of Innocence*, printed by William Blake himself in 1789, with all of his original artwork. Benjamin felt pretty sure it was authentic, but he brought it to one of his professors to get his opinion and asked him to keep it a secret. The professor said yes, without a doubt it's an original. Benjamin was overjoyed, but then the professor started gossiping and Everett found out. Everett thought Benjamin stole the book out from under him, and he started making threats. The book's worth a lot of money, Miss Prim. It's hard to make a living at magical realism, and Everett realized how much he could make by selling it. He confronted Benjamin and demanded that they sell the book and split the money, but Benjamin wanted to keep it. He said he'd found it and paid for it and it was his."

"How did Everett get you and Benjamin to rent a house up here?"

"Benjamin? No, it was Everett who wanted to rent the house. I was posing as Everett's wife when I met that awful real-estate agent."

The ropes gave and Dolly's hands were free. "But, Dolly, Olivia Abernathy pulled up a photo of Benjamin on her computer. She said that he was the man you'd rented the house with."

"That's totally untrue, Miss Prim. It was Everett, not Benjamin. From what I can figure out, Everett broke into

Benjamin's apartment to find the book, but Benjamin had already hidden it somewhere else. So Everett waited for me outside Doctor Poe's office and he told me if I didn't help him and keep my mouth shut, he'd make sure Benjamin was hurt really badly … or worse. So I did what he told me to do. He wanted me to rent this house with him, so I did. And now I know what he's planning. He's holding me hostage until Benjamin gives him the book. Then he'll let me go. At least, that's what he says."

"But why rent a house in Greenfield, of all places, Dolly?"

"I can't figure that one out, Miss Prim. And I've had a lot of time to think about it, being tied up in this basement."

"I don't understand why Olivia Abernathy should have lied to me about this," Miss Prim said, puzzled and frustrated.

"I have to assume that Everett bribed her, Miss Prim. You know real-estate people. They'll do anything for money."

Miss Prim could not dispute the veracity of this assertion, though she supposed she understood the motivation. A real-estate agent must live in the very best neighborhood to have professional credibility, and living in the best neighborhoods costs a pretty penny.

"Did he kidnap you from the cottage?" Miss Prim asked.

"In a way yes, but in a way no. I left voluntarily. Everett waited until you were asleep and then he showed up at the cottage. He told me Benjamin was at the house and wanted to speak with me. He very specifically told me to take my purse with me, which I thought was strange. I told him I didn't have a purse, but he didn't believe me, and I was scared so I took yours. I *think* he believed I was holding a key to a safety deposit box, or something like that, for Benjamin. As soon as he got me down here, he opened your bag and shook everything out. When he didn't find what he wanted, he just left everything on the floor."

Miss Prim looked over her shoulder and saw her favorite handbag upended, its contents spread along the floor: rain bonnet, change purse, cosmetics case, hair brush, even the bell she'd been using to train Bruno. *How had the bell found its way in there?* she wondered. She distinctly remembered leaving it on the credenza after her last training session with Bruno.

Delighted to have recovered her handbag and its difficult-to-replace contents, she began gathering the items and transferring them to her backup bag, which (due to the necessity of keeping the Laser Taser 3000 close at hand) remained firmly slung around her neck and shoulder.

"Do you know where Benjamin is, Dolly?"

"No, and I'm starting to think Everett has other guys helping him. Oh, Miss Prim, how are we going to get out of here?"

Miss Prim pursed her lips. "I wish I knew, Dolly."

As day turned into evening, Miss Prim and Dolly exercised the few options available to them. They hoped Everett would leave the house, listening for the sounds of footsteps and closing doors, which they heard about two hours after Everett trapped them in the basement. Together they threw their weight against the basement door, hoping to break it or damage the lock, but their efforts were unsuccessful.

Like the basement of Rose Cottage, the basement of 50 Pierced Arrow Lane had no egress, so there was no hope of escape via such a route. Unlike Miss Prim's basement, however, their current prison was only partially underground, and it had four small windows—two on each side of the house—that allowed light to filter into the space. Dolly boosted Miss Prim up the wall, and Miss Prim used her dainty fist (which she'd wrapped in layers of old rags she'd found in the basement) to attempt to smash through the filthy windows. But the windows were made of sturdy plastic and seemed unbreakable.

By nighttime, the two women were feeling thoroughly discouraged. Everett and his henchmen had not returned. Miss Prim and Dolly listened carefully through the floorboards and the windows for any indicator that help was on the way, but no such aid was forthcoming.

Around midnight, as Dolly and Miss Prim were nodding off to sleep, Miss Prim thought she heard a noise: a car door slamming? A moment later they heard the doorbell ringing. Both instantly began screaming at the top of their lungs, trying to make themselves heard.

As they screamed, Miss Prim saw a glow emanating from somewhere behind the basement's dirty windows. And that sound—a gruff woofing—was that Bruno?

"Bruno," she screamed. "Bruno, down here, boy. Bruno! Bruno!"

But Bruno did not appear to hear her. Based on the decreasing volume of Bruno's woofs, Miss Prim thought he was moving *away* from the house rather than *toward* it.

"Dolly," Miss Prim shouted, "grab the bell from my handbag. Ring it! Ring it like a madwoman!"

It must have been quite a sight, Miss Prim reflected later, as she and Dolly screamed like lunatics while Dolly rang the dinner bell with all her might. Then, magically, the sounds captured Bruno's attention. The Boxer began barking loudly and furiously. Within seconds, several circles of light appeared outside the window.

Miss Prim heard a hard thud. She looked up at a window to see it bulging as someone attacked it from outside. Two minutes later, one of the windows cracked. A black boot continued kicking at the window until a hole opened.

"Miss Prim, are you down there?"

Miss Prim recognized the voice immediately.

"Detective Dawes! Yes, Dolly and I are being held down here quite against our will."

"Hold tight, ladies. We'll be right down. Are you all right?"

"Yes, we're fine. Please be careful, Detective. There might be unpleasant men around."

"There's no one here, Miss Prim. Just us."

"Who is with you?"

"Me, and Spike, and Martin, and Lorraine. And Kit, Faye, Maude, Valeska, Josh, Jedediah Mason, Ethan Prothero, and a few others. And Bruno, of course. Everyone was worried about you, Miss Prim."

The door was unlocked and Kit came flying down the stairs, directly into Miss Prim's arms. Bruno followed close on his heels.

"Jesu—I mean, God, Miss Prim," Kit said. "Don't make us worry like that."

Faye joined their embrace, as did Valeska, Lorraine, Dolly, Maude, Josh, Jedediah Mason, and Spike.

"How did you find us?" Miss Prim asked.

"We have Kit to thank," Dawes said. "Everyone started getting worried when we didn't see you for a day. By night-time, Kit decided something was wrong. He remembered you were going to see Olivia, so he came to see me, and we went looking for her. But she was out somewhere and didn't get home until about an hour ago. She told us about your conversation. By that point half the town was out looking for you, and they followed me here even though I told them not to. Why doesn't anyone in this town *listen*?"

"I suppose we should be grateful for a defiant populace, Detective," Miss Prim said. "Now let us get out of here immediately, if you please."

They filed up the stairs, out the door, and into the waiting police cars.

"Oh, I've forgotten my handbag," Miss Prim said, unbuckling her seat belt. She had removed her handbag from her shoulder when she and Dolly had attempted to get some rest, but she'd kept it close at hand until the rescue. "I must retrieve it. Life would be much too inconvenient without it."

"I'll go with you, Miss Prim," Kit volunteered.

"That's quite all right, Kit. I am not one of those fearful women who is easily traumatized. I know exactly where it is. I'll be back in a jiffy." That promise made, she returned to the house, descended the stairs into the basement, and retrieved not only her preferred handbag but also her backup bag.

Of course Detective Dawes wouldn't have allowed her to return to the house on her own; she saw his shadow out of the corner of her eye.

"Detective, how kind of you to …"

The man looming over her was not Ezra Dawes. It was a man wearing a rubber face mask crafted to look like Richard Nixon.

She had not come this far to be defeated. She'd been mugged on the streets of Manhattan, and this hulking figure appeared even more intent on harm than the man who'd knocked her down on Lexington Avenue, taking her handbag and her dignity with him.

In one fluid motion Miss Prim reached into her bag, grabbed the Laser Taser 3000, released the safety, and shot 50,000 volts into her tormentor.

As the man lay twitching on the floor, she thought, *I must see what this arch-criminal Everett Mansour looks like.* She reached out, grabbed the mask, and pulled it over Everett's head to reveal the face of Doctor Amos Poe.

30

The Murderer, Discovered

Spike conducted Miss Prim and Bruno home while Ezra Dawes drove Doctor Poe to the hospital and Martin Reed brought Dolly to the police station, at Dolly's request.

"But Dolly," Miss Prim had asked, "why do you need to go to the police station tonight? Detective Dawes said we can give our statements in the morning. And I truly would prefer not to be alone right now."

"Oh, Miss Prim," Dolly had replied through tears. "This has all gotten so completely out of hand. I have to talk to the police about Doctor Poe *tonight*. He's one hundred percent innocent. I know how it looks, Miss Prim, but he loves you. He wouldn't harm a hair on your head. You have to believe me."

"Until tonight," Miss Prim had responded, "I *would* have believed you. But the events of the evening have proved otherwise, I think."

"No, no, no. I promise, I'll explain everything after I talk to the police."

Lorraine had jumped into the conversation. "Felicity, I'll be happy to keep you company until Dolly returns. Let me go home first to check on Lucian—I gave him a very tricky logic puzzle to work, one with no solution—and then I'll meet you at the cottage."

Now, after enduring Spike's worried monologue about all the mold spores to which Miss Prim and Dolly had been exposed in that dank basement, as well as her predictions that both women would end up with gangrene, tuberculosis, or rickets, Miss Prim was installed in Rose Cottage, awaiting Lorraine's arrival. Bruno remained one step away from her at all times. His eyes reprimanded her: *Please do not ever do* that *again.*

She was working to recover her equanimity; being kidnapped and held captive had been upsetting in the extreme. The experience had not been the romantic, suspenseful adventure that novels had led her to believe it would be. True, there had been no bomb ticking in the background, no load of nitroglycerin or TNT ready to blow her and Dolly to kingdom come, no weird contraption to keep them immobile, as in some of those disturbing Scandinavian thrillers. But the experience was still humbling, especially as she considered the possibility that she might have spent her last days on Earth in that basement. Was that *likely* to have happened? No. As fiction had taught her, the amateur/cozy sleuth always lives to see another day, another case, another book in the series. But *could* it have happened? Yes, it could have.

Still, none of it was nearly as frightening and surreal as the revelation that Doctor Poe, who had professed love for her, had plotted against her and Dolly. She simply could not fathom the reason. Doctor Poe loved literature, as all good doctors do, but it seemed highly unlikely that he had teamed up with Everett Mansour to steal Benjamin's copy of *Songs of Innocence*. After many years of successful practice in Manhattan, Doctor Poe was quite well off; thus money could not have been the motivating factor. Or could it? Perhaps the doctor was a drug addict or an inveterate gambler who had squandered his fortune and who saw the original book of Blake's poems as an easy, lucrative sale on the literary black market?

And what had Dolly meant when she said she'd explain "everything"? Hadn't Dolly already explained "everything" while they were stranded in that basement? What more could she have to say?

Well, all would be revealed shortly. In the meantime, Miss Prim saw the opportunity to close another aspect of the investigation. Given the intensity of the day's events, she'd had to put aside the piece of information Kit had given her. (Was it only this morning? It seemed so long ago.) Now, finally, the time had come to discuss her theories with her neighbor and sidekick.

She didn't have to wait long. Shortly after she'd set the tea to steep and tied Bruno to his tether in the backyard, the front door opened and Lorraine breezed in. She'd changed out of the getup she'd been wearing at the crime scene (Pippi Longstocking braids, denim overalls) into a dark-brunette pageboy wig and a long, flowing gown.

"Well, Felicity," Lorraine said in her forthright way. "Here you've just had a brush with something violent, and there you are, looking as put-together and as calm as ever. You really are a marvel."

"As are you, Lorraine," Miss Prim replied. "I must say I prefer this—Louise Brooks?—look to today's earlier *ensemble*."

"Oh, that. Sometimes I don't feel like putting in the work it takes to be glamorous. The overalls are my way of saying to the world, 'Don't expect the elegant Lorraine Koslowski today. Today, she's just a Pandora in blue jeans, like Grace Metalious.' I see the tea and coffee are ready, so let's have at it and you can tell me what in God's name happened to you today. I'll say this, you had all of us damned worried, Felicity."

"Lorraine, if you don't mind … I am going to relate this story many, many times over the coming weeks. I'm hosting a small gathering tomorrow—well, actually, later today—and I'll provide all the details then. Will you and Lucian join us?"

"Of course."

"Lovely. Now, for tonight, I would love nothing more than to listen rather than to speak. All of that screaming in the basement has made me rather hoarse."

"You got it, kid. What should we talk about? Lucian's recent discovery that the Garden of Eden was located in Lubbock, Texas? The extortionate prices that Prothero's has started charging for produce? Oh wait, I'll tell you about an interesting little tidbit I recently picked up …"

Miss Prim thought, *Now is as good a time as any*. She jumped in with both feet.

"All of that sounds most interesting, Lorraine. But what I would really love to hear about is the secret passage that connects your house and mine."

Lorraine, not usually lost for words, remained silent.

Miss Prim rushed to reassure her friend. "I'm not angry, Lorraine. I know you have very good reasons for keeping the passage a secret. But there *is* a passage connecting our houses, and it explains how Lucian found his way into my basement. The night Lucian disappeared, I heard whispering down there, and I would have sworn I heard two voices whispering, not one. The first one was Lucian's. The second was yours. Wasn't it, Lorraine? You were pleading with him to come home, but when I started down the stairs, you fled."

Lorraine nodded. "I knew you'd figure it out sooner or later, Felicity. The first time I met you, I knew you were a clever one."

"It wasn't I who figured it out," Miss Prim admitted. "It was Kit. He overheard Detective Dawes and me talking about the 'locked-room mystery' in my basement. Having a typical teenage boy's adventurous imagination, he took it on himself to research our houses at the historical society, where he found a copy of the houses' original plans. Ridgemont was the master house, and Rose Cottage was originally intended as a guest house or a residence for Ridgemont's domestics. Olivia Abernathy said she didn't know about the hidden basement, and I believed her; and I now see how mistaken I was in trusting her. Perhaps she sought to cover her prevarications by telling partial truths. She told me that our two homes had been built around the same time, after you told me that Rose Cottage had been built many years after Ridgemont. I tried to ask you about it, but we kept getting interrupted. In the meantime, Gil Fellowes confirmed that our houses were built around the same time, but he didn't mention anything about the secret passage."

Lorraine shook her head. "No, Felicity. Olivia wasn't lying. At least not about that. She's only been in Greenfield about six or seven years. Lucian and I have been back about three. We came back after his condition made it impossible for us to travel. I suppose Olivia could have talked to some of the Old Timers, who might have mentioned that Ridgemont and Rose Cottage are about the same age, but I doubt she would have known about the passage or about your basement. The only people who know are Lucian, I, and Elizabeth Saxe-Coburg. I certainly haven't told anyone about it, though I suppose Elizabeth might have babbled indiscreetly about it. I doubt it, though, because she has a few skeletons in her own closet. And Lucian was always extremely secretive about it, too. You have to remember, Ridgemont was built after the war, and everyone was still feeling upset, paranoid, and threatened by a world that had spiraled out of control."

"But if Lucian kept it a secret, how would Kit have found a copy of Ridgemont's plans at the Historical Society?"

"I'll tell you how," Lorraine said with a huff. "I'm sure Gil Fellowes tricked Lucian into it when I wasn't watching or during one of Lucian's escapes. Gil may appear to be an absentminded scholar, but he's single-minded in his pursuit of cataloging absolutely everything that has happened in Greenfield. You know academics, Felicity. They know how to sweet-talk people into sharing top-secret documents. I'm sure Gil played on one of Lucian's delusions to convince him to share the house plans. And Gil isn't always forthcoming with information, even when you ask him directly. It's that academic thing."

Miss Prim looked into her friend's eyes. *These are not the eyes of a criminal*, she thought. *They are the eyes of someone who is protecting the man she loves*. But the time had come to solve the mystery of the body in her basement. She forged ahead.

"Now, Lorraine, what I'm about to say is likely to upset you. Before I say it, I want you to know that you have a true friend in me, and that I would not say or do anything to hurt you or harm you. Do you believe me?"

"Yes," Lorraine said, simply.

"Then I am going to outline a possible scenario. Will you tell me, truthfully, if what I suggest is what really happened?"

Lorraine cast her eyes down and nodded.

"I think it was Lucian who killed the man I found in my basement. And you hid the body down there. Am I right?"

"He didn't mean to. It was an accident."

"That is exactly what I thought, Lorraine. You yourself hinted that Lucian can turn violent when he feels threatened. I think this stranger somehow threatened him and Lucian felt the need to protect himself. So he picked up something within reach—the chisel—and drove it into the man's stomach.

"I think you came home and saw what Lucian had done, and you needed to hide the body until you could dispose of it properly. My basement was the ideal hiding place. The body could have stayed down there a good long time, and I never would have found him because I didn't know the basement existed. But I kept asking myself, If you didn't want me to know about the basement, why would you leave the wooden star in a box of old magazines in my attic? It wouldn't take me long to realize that the star matched the impression on the kitchen wall, and then discover the basement and the body.

"But you weren't the person who put that box in my attic, Lorraine. Lucian was. He likes to carry boxes around. He was carrying one at Ridgemont on the day I met him, and he brought one into my basement on the night I found him down there. And of course the box in my attic was filled with Hollywood gossip magazines, which are your favorite reading material, as well as the inspiration for much of your wardrobe."

"What can I say, Felicity? You have everything more or less correct. Lucian said the man lunged at him. I was desperate to hide the body while I thought of some way to bury him with dignity. I knew about the wooden star, of course, and I searched through the cottage until I found it, so that the new owner—you—wouldn't find it or the basement. Who knew you'd be moving in so quickly? I pressed Olivia for information, and she's usually pretty free with it, but for some reason she doesn't like me. Maybe it's because I told her that if we ever decided to sell Ridgemont, she'd be the last agent I'd list with, because I find her venal and tacky. I found the star on one of the bookshelves and brought it home. I hid it, and the chisel, in a box in my Hollywood attic room, thinking Lucian would never find them. But of course he did, and when I wasn't looking he must have used the hidden passage to move the box from Ridgemont into your attic, as a way of getting rid of the evidence. I nearly panicked when I heard that you'd found the body. I went looking for the box in my Hollywood room, and it was gone."

Miss Prim made her voice as kind as she could make it. "That's why you descended on me so quickly, yes? To begin damage control?"

"It's true, Felicity. I had an ulterior motive. I was trying to protect Lucian, and I befriended you as an element of that plan. I'm a pragmatist, Felicity, and I'm not ashamed of it. But never in my wildest dreams did I imagine what a lovely, kind person you would be, or that I would come to value your friendship as deeply as I have. I'm sorry; I can't tell you how sorry I am. I didn't mean to hurt you."

Miss Prim placed her hand over Lorraine's hand and squeezed.

"I believe you, Lorraine. And I understand what motivated you. You were trying to protect your husband. But Lorraine, the victim is still lying unclaimed in the morgue.

His family needs to know what happened to him. Do you know who he is?"

Miss Prim could see the conflict in Lorraine's face. After a moment, Lorraine said, quietly, "It's his son. Lucian's son."

Miss Prim blinked her eyes once. "Oh, Lorraine," she said quietly, "I cannot even imagine the pain of knowing that your husband killed your child."

"He wasn't my child, Felicity. He was Lucian's. And Elizabeth Saxe-Coburg's. His name was Alexander."

Miss Prim's visit with Mrs. Saxe-Coburg at Heavenly Pastures came flooding back to her. Elizabeth had hinted at secrets, at troubles she would rather forget. And another piece of the puzzle clicked into place.

"That was why she went away," Miss Prim said. "To have her baby. Did her husband know?"

"Of course he knew. He was sterile, so the baby couldn't have been his. But he loved his wife and he forgave her. I don't think the Old Timers ever suspected, either. In those days, girls went 'to the country' for only one reason, but Elizabeth wasn't exactly a blushing teenager when she got pregnant with Alexander. She went to take care of an ailing aunt, she said, and she wrote lovely letters to her friends while she was gone, and nobody suspected a thing. Then she returned to Greenfield and picked up her marriage, but she was never quite the same, they say. She'd been perky and upbeat, but giving her child away took something out of her. She became a recluse, more or less. But I've heard that she's reverted to her old self again. Maybe senility has its blessings."

Miss Prim thought for a moment about Elizabeth Saxe-Coburg's sacrifice. To have been denied the joys of a child, a family—it was tragic, pure and simple.

"But I don't understand, Lorraine," Miss Prim said. "Why would Alexander come back to threaten Lucian? I would think he would be overjoyed to find his birth father."

"This is where it gets a little Gothic, Felicity. He wasn't threatening Lucian."

"I don't understand … ?"

"Lucian had found ways to send money to the family who adopted Alexander, of course. But he never planned to contact the boy. You know how it was in those days, Felicity. Children were given up for adoption and the records were sealed. There was no such thing as a parent looking for a child or a child looking for a parent. But Alexander's adoptive parents died, and he went through every last paper they had, and he somehow figured out his father's identity. Then he came to Greenfield to meet him. But he watched us first, and some of the things he saw didn't quite match the facts he'd uncovered in his research. He was convinced that someone was swindling Lucian, and he threatened to expose her. And the *her* he threatened to expose was *me*."

"I really am not following you, Lorraine …"

"You know what, Felicity? I'm tired of Lorraine. Lorraine, Lorraine, Lorraine. I loved her dearly but she's become too much effort."

With that, Lorraine pulled off her wig. A gorgeous mane of thick, curly, auburn locks spilled down her shoulders and back.

Miss Prim was shocked. Why would this gorgeous creature choose to hide behind those outrageous wigs and Hollywood getups?

"This is the real me, Felicity. My name isn't Lorraine. It's Lorna."

"Lorna? As in Lorraine's sister, Lorna?"

"The one and only."

"But Lorraine … Lorna … why?"

"Because I loved my sister as much as you love yours. She knew she was dying, and she knew Lucian was slowly but surely losing his marbles. She adored him, Felicity. She forgave him for his affair with Elizabeth because she couldn't conceive, and she saw the affair as her fault. But I hated him. I hated him for cheating on my brilliant, beautiful sister. And I didn't disguise my hatred. So he hated me in return, and because I was so stubborn, I didn't see my sister for years and years. Because she had to take his side. That's how it is with husbands and wives. Stanley and Stella Kowalski, right?

"And then, out of the blue, I got a call from her. I was living quite happily in South Africa. She tells me she has only a few months to live. Can she come to South Africa for a visit? Of course I say yes. It's only when she arrives that she tells me the rest of her plan. She wants to die in South Africa, and she wants me to take her place. To take care of Lucian. She couldn't bear the thought of him getting locked away in some loony bin, or being swindled out of his money by unscrupulous people.

"*But he hates me*, I said. *And I hate him*. And she said something I'll never forget. She said, *But I love you both*. That was all it took. I buried my sister in Pretoria, packed up my bags and her passport, and I flew to London, where they were living at the time. Lorraine and I had always resembled each other, but we were hardly doppelgangers. That's when I started with the wigs and the kooky clothes. It was meant to be a temporary solution, but it took on an element of fun, and by the time we returned to Greenfield, so many years after Lorraine and Lucian left, the masquerade became reality. And there you have it. There are so few Old Timers left, and most of them are as dotty as Lucian. No one suspected a thing."

Miss Prim's thoughts turned to Ridgemont's bare walls. "And this is the reason you removed all photos of Lucian and Lorraine from Ridgemont's walls?"

"Right again."

"This is why Henry doesn't like you. Because he knows you are not Lorraine."

"He's always known. From the moment I arrived in England."

"Lorraine … Lorna … I am quite overwhelmed by this. And touched. You did all this for your sister?"

"I did. And something strange happened along the way, Felicity. I've come to love Lucian. I see why my sister found him so wildly attractive. Of course, there's nothing physical between us; never has been. But he's special and unique. What I thought would be a massive personal sacrifice has turned into the most rewarding and enriching relationship of my life. Would I do it all over again? You bet I would."

"Am I understanding you correctly? Are you saying that Alexander found out that you were actually Lorna, not Lorraine? That he thought you were stealing from Lucian or mistreating him somehow? And he threatened to expose you?"

"That's exactly what happened. He waited for me to leave the house, and then he knocked on the door and invited himself in. Imagine being Lucian and having your long-lost son showing up at your house, looking all bearded and disheveled, ranting and raving about your giving him up for adoption and how your wife is an impostor who's robbing you blind. Lucian's not good with intense emotion. It frightens him, and when he's frightened, he can get worked up. When I got home, I found Alexander crumpled up on the floor and the chisel in Lucian's hand. You know what happened after that."

Miss Prim rose from her chair and walked to Lorna's chair, draping her arms around her in an affectionate embrace.

"Lorna, this is going to be difficult. But we must tell the police about Alexander's identity. And we must determine what to do about Lucian. He is a big man, and if he is dangerous, he might harm you. We must make sure you are protected."

Lorna looked at Miss Prim helplessly. "I can't turn him in, Felicity. He's too old. I can't let him spend his last days in prison. I just can't."

Miss Prim heard a small noise, as if one of the floorboards had settled. She looked up to see Lucian Koslowski standing in the kitchen doorway.

"The secret passage strikes again," Lorna said.

The doorbell rang and Miss Prim went to answer it. Through the closed door, the visitors identified themselves as Ezra Dawes and Dolly.

As Miss Prim opened the door, Dolly rushed in and hugged her. Her friend looked as if she'd been crying for hours, Miss Prim thought.

"I'm such a mess, Miss Prim," Dolly said.

But Dolly'd had her wits about her in the basement of the house on Pierced Arrow Lane. Why would she go to pieces now?

"Now, dearest, you are fine, and I am fine, and that's all that matters. Why don't you freshen up and then join us for tea? Oh, and allow me to introduce you to Lucian Koslowski."

Lucian bowed deeply and kissed Dolly's hand. "*Enchanté*, Mademoiselle. Any friend of Miss Multiplicity is a friend of mine."

Dolly blushed and fled into the guest room, closing the door behind her.

"How is Doctor Poe?" Miss Prim asked Dawes. Decades of caring about the man could not be eradicated in just one day.

Dawes rubbed his eyes. "What a night it's been, Miss Prim. I've been doing this job for longer than I like to admit, and what I heard tonight … Let's just say, it's one for the books." He smiled.

He *smiled*? A smile did not seem appropriate at the moment, but Miss Prim was tired, so perhaps she had misread the detective's physiognomy?

"But to answer your question about Doctor Poe," Dawes continued, "he had a nasty jolt—we'll have to talk about that toy of yours, Miss Prim—but he'll be fine by tomorrow. He and Miss Veerelf have made me promise that I'll let them provide you with a full explanation of the evening's events."

These statements were most curious, but *time reveals all*, as Mrs. Charity Prim had been fond of saying; and Miss Prim was not one of today's youths, who demand instant gratification. So, rather than press Dawes for details, she simply invited him to the gathering she and Dolly planned to host later that day (for it was now the wee hours of the morning). The detective accepted her invitation and turned to go. "I almost forgot, Miss Prim. Remember I told you that the medical examiner's office hadn't finished the autopsy on the body yet? Well, it was waiting for me when I got back to the station tonight. The man died of natural causes. It's still a mystery how he ended up in your basement, of course. But Simon—the M.E.—told me in no uncertain terms: The man we've been seeing as a murder victim actually suffered a massive heart attack."

"But … what about the chisel with the blood on it?"

"The man's skin was punctured by the chisel, but it was a surface wound. There was some blood, but it had nothing to do with the way the man died."

As Miss Prim closed the door behind Detective Dawes, Lorna exhaled deeply.

Such grace under pressure, Miss Prim thought. *It really is quite remarkable.*

"Come along, Lucian," Lorna said, "It's time to get you home."

"Yes, my dear," Lucian responded. "May I meet you outside? I wish to thank Miss Mendacity for her hospitality."

"Very well, Lucian. But do hurry. President Roosevelt awaits us at Ridgemont."

Lucian shut the door behind Lorna, then bent to kiss Miss Prim's hand.

"Thank you, Miss Loquacity. I am most appreciative of your friendship, as is Lorna."

"Lorna?" Miss Prim sputtered.

"Did I say Lorna? I meant Lorraine. My wife Lorraine. Yes, my wife. A most clever woman. Always trying to outsmart me. I have a feeling she has played a rather large trick on me, and sometimes I think I know exactly what it is. But then I say to myself, 'Lucian Koslowski, why are you wasting your time thinking about such things, when you have a lovely wife, as well as the world's largest collection of emerald doorknobs?' I may have my quirks, Miss Grandiosity, but my wife does, too. Her self-esteem is dependent on believing that she has put something over on me. It does no harm to let her believe she has succeeded."

31
The Lost Children

Miss Prim had hoped to sleep in, to rejuvenate after the stressful events of the previous day. But she hadn't been able to relax, and her sleep had been fitful and unsettled. So she rose early, dressed, and began preparing the cottage for the afternoon gathering.

Dolly woke shortly thereafter and offered to take Bruno for a walk.

"Oh, Miss Prim," she said sadly. "I hardly slept a wink. I feel so awful. I just can't believe how badly everything went awry. I want to confess, but I promised Doctor Poe I'd let him tell you the whole story. Detective Dawes told me he'd bring the doctor here this afternoon, after he's recovered from the tasering."

Miss Prim wondered why the detective would bring Doctor Poe to her home rather than asking her to visit Doctor Poe in prison. But all would be revealed soon enough; and so, for now, Miss Prim had to be content to wait.

After Dolly and Bruno returned, Miss Prim and Dolly worked side by side in the kitchen, preparing the canapés and other comestibles in companionable silence, enjoying their freedom and each other's company.

Lorna and Lucian arrived at one o'clock. Miss Prim almost didn't recognize Lorna, who wore a bald cap and a white smock.

"I see you looking, Felicity. Think of it as a cross between Sinéad O'Connor and Demi Moore during her bald period."

"Felicitations, Miss Complicity," Lucian said, kissing Miss Prim's hand in greeting. "We thought we'd show up a bit early to help with the preparations."

"Come in, come in," Miss Prim said. As Lorraine—for surely that name and identity were her preference—walked past her, Miss Prim whispered jokingly in her ear, "So good of you to use the front door instead of the basement."

Lorna smiled. "Dolly, would you mind looking after Lucian for a bit? Lucian, I know Dolly would love to hear about the war."

"What?"

"THE WAR. TELL HER ABOUT THE WAR."

"Which one?"

"WHICHEVER ONE YOU WANT."

"Well, it is the Civil War on which I had the greatest impact," Lucian said. "Quite fascinating, actually. Miss Polly, you sit right there and I will tell you about the espionage methods I used to infiltrate the camp of General Ulysses S. Grant."

"Let's go to the basement while Lucian and Dolly talk," Lorraine said.

Nodding her agreement, Miss Prim used the wooden star to pop the door open. She then led the way down the stairs as Lorraine followed.

At the bottom of the staircase, Miss Prim saw the door of the secret passage gaping open. Located against the basement's rear wall, the one nearest the ridge on which Ridgemont perched, the door began at the ceiling and ended at the floor, thus preventing any seams from showing at the top and bottom of the door. The wood paneling on the basement walls had camouflaged the door's vertical seams at the left and right.

Miss Prim examined the door.

"Most … revealing," she said. "But how does someone in Rose Cottage get the door open?"

"That's the thing, Felicity. You don't. Lucian had the door designed to be one-way only. You could have looked for a hidden mechanism until the end of time, and you never would have found one. Now that you know where the door is, I hope you'll put a bolt on your end to prevent unwanted intrusions."

"I shall do that, Lorn—I mean, Lorraine, yes?"

"Yes. Thank you."

The two women shared a moment of silent understanding. Then Lorraine continued.

"We've just come from the police station. I've told Ezra everything. Now that he knows Alexander's identity, he's begun looking for his adopted family. I've arranged to have him buried in the same cemetery in which the Saxe-Coburgs own a plot. I hope I made the right decision. I kept asking myself how Ralph Saxe-Coburg would have felt about it. But he loved Elizabeth, he really did; all the Old Timers know that. I truly think he'd be OK with it, so I made the arrangements. There will be a service tomorrow evening. Will you join me and Lucian? We'll pick you up about seven."

"Of course."

"Lucian had a good morning. I got more information out of him. He picked up the chisel when he thought Alexander was about to spring on him. 'He bent his knees, like he was getting ready to throw himself at me.' That's what Lucian said. But I think you and I know what really happened. Poor Alexander suffered his heart attack, and he started to crumple. Lucian mistook it as aggression and moved to defend himself."

"But what now, Lorraine? What did Detective Dawes say about all of this?"

"He said Lucian isn't a murderer and that, given the circumstances, he would let the matter drop, on one condition. I can't leave Lucian alone, ever again. This means I have to find a full-time nurse for him. Truthfully, one side of me hates the idea, but the other side feels relieved. I'll start looking for someone this week. I don't suppose you'd be interested?"

Miss Prim's eyes widened in panic. "Oh, Lorraine, I am of course flattered and honored …"

Lorraine laughed heartily, and Miss Prim was delighted to hear these sounds of merriment emanating from her friend. "Relax, Felicity! I was just kidding. I'd never do that to you."

Miss Prim smiled. "This is for the best, Lorraine. With an aide to watch over Lucian, you and I will have more time to spend together. And I predict that the two of us will engage in quite a number of escapades over the coming years."

"From your lips to God's ears," Lorraine responded, clicking the hidden door shut.

As Miss Prim added the finishing touches to the diet cinnamon, chocolate, and apricot rugelach that she was preparing for Martin Reed, Bruno jumped up and ran to the front door, his tail wagging frantically. Miss Prim dusted her hands on her apron and opened the door to find Kit and Faye standing on her doorstep. The latter carried a box bearing the Sweetcakes Bakery logo.

"I thought you might like these, Miss Prim," Faye said. "I've heard they're very popular in New York."

Miss Prim took the box and opened it to reveal several dozen black-and-white cookies. Their waistline-increasing charms must be guarded against, of course, but they could be placed on a serving platter and offered to guests while Miss Prim indulged in one or two as a sort of reward for having survived Doctor Poe's nefarious plot.

Miss Prim brought her cup of tea and a black-and-white cookie to the couch. Faye sat on one side of her, Kit on the other, and the assembled Greenfieldians listened raptly as Lucian relived his days of serving as one of King Arthur's knights. He found Lancelot to be an inspiring leader, he said, but thought Guinevere was overrated. He'd just begun regaling his audience with stories about the unpredictable effects of Merlin's potions when the front door burst open.

The latest visitor to Rose Cottage was Miss Gladys Lavelle. The smoke pouring from her nose and ears hinted that she was not pleased.

"I knew it!" she hissed venomously, pointing a long, bony index finger at Miss Prim. "It's not enough for you to get yourself kidnapped to elicit the town's sympathy. No, you won't be happy until you've put *everyone* in Greenfield under your spell, you … you … witch! If the adults of Greenfield allow you to enchant them, there's nothing I can do about it. But I will not—I repeat, I will *not*—stand by while you try to charm unsuspecting children. Faye! Kit! Come with me this instant."

"Miss Lavelle, please," Faye said, embarrassed. "I don't know why you think such bad things about Miss Prim, but you're wrong about her."

"Listen to me, Faye," Miss Lavelle said. "I've been on this planet a lot longer than you have, and I know evil when I see it. You and your brother are too young, and too naïve, to understand what's happening."

As Miss Prim watched the proceedings in desperation, Lorraine sprang to her feet.

"Gladys Lavelle, I've had quite enough of you. Nobody invited you, so why don't you take yourself back to the hole you crawled out of?"

"Don't order me around, Lorraine Koslowski. If that's who you are, underneath that ridiculous wig and all that makeup."

"Gladys, this nonsense is going to stop *right now*," Lorraine shot back. "You're incredibly threatened by Miss Prim. Anyone with two eyes can see it. Most people in Greenfield think they know why—because you're an angry, bitter, jealous old cow. But I know the real reason."

Miss Lavelle stared daggers at Lorraine. "You don't know anything, Lorraine."

"That's where you're wrong, Gladys. I did a little checking around, and you know what I discovered? Something interesting about the house that Faye and Kit live in. *You* bought it twenty years ago, and you and your lawyers concocted a story about their mother and father leaving it to them as an inheritance. Gil Fellowes keeps a copy of all the property records in Greenfield, in case you didn't know. He left the doors unlocked one night, and I found all the documentation I needed without asking for his help. So the question is: Why would Gladys Lavelle, who wouldn't throw a life vest to a drowning man, buy a house and give it to two strangers? I'll tell you why." Lorraine's voice lost its volume and became gentler. "Because they're *not* strangers. Faye and Kit are your children, aren't they?"

Miss Gladys Lavelle appeared lost for words.

"I've heard the rumors, Gladys. So has Lucian. We know you took extended vacations around the times that Faye and Kit were born. You knew Ethan Prothero would never leave his wife, so you went to the country and gave birth to the children, and then you paid a relative to raise them. You waited for Faye to become an adult so that you could bring them here and finally be close to them. And it's making you insane that your children like Miss Prim more than they like you."

Miss Lavelle stood silent, the burning fury in her eyes turning to something softer as she gazed upon the shocked faces of Faye and Kit.

Faye spoke quietly. "Is it true, Miss Lavelle?"

Miss Lavelle blinked her eyes once and nodded. Miss Prim thought she'd never seen a woman so valiantly fighting back tears.

"I sensed it, Miss Lavelle," Faye said, wonderingly. "I just knew it, somehow, somewhere, without really knowing why." And with that she rose from the couch, walked to her mother, and embraced her. Without a word, Kit joined the embrace as Miss Lavelle stroked her children's hair.

"I'm a fool," Miss Lavelle said quietly. "I chose a man over my children, and I've done nothing but regret it for the last two decades. I just wanted to be near you for a few years, to have some time with you before you went into the world. It was selfish, I know. As always, Gladys Lavelle thought of herself first, and everyone else second."

She reluctantly extricated herself from her children's embrace. "Miss Prim, I don't blame you for not wanting me here. I'll go now." She turned to leave.

"Don't go," Miss Prim said. "Please stay. Can't you see, your children want to be with you? Everyone in this room wants you to say. *I* want you to stay."

Miss Lavelle couldn't take it any more. She dissolved into tears. Of joy.

Miss Prim's other guests began to trickle into Rose Cottage. First Spike Fremlin arrived on the arm of a quite handsome but rather short man. "Hey, Miss Slim. I think you forgot to invite me! No worries, I'm not offended. This is Killer. Killer Abramowitz." Killer smiled at Miss Prim. "He's an accountant down at the courthouse," Spike explained. "Not bad looking, eh? Killer, get me something to eat, would you? Those cookies look good. Hey, Miss Slim, did you ever get all that dust taken care of in your attic? Cause I'm highly allergic and I'd hate to have to leave early …"

Miss Prim got a reprieve when the doorbell rang again. She detached herself from Spike to welcome Martin and Valeska Reed. Valeska cast a skeptical glance at Miss Lavelle (who was sitting on the couch, deep in conversation with Faye and Kit) and raised her eyebrows questioningly at Miss Prim. "Very long story," Miss Prim whispered. "But, suffice it to say, a happy ending."

"Do I smell rugelach, Miss Prim?" Valeska asked. Miss Prim nodded. "I don't suppose you have cinnamon-raisin?

You do? That's Martin's favorite. Wait here, my love, while I fetch us some."

Martin Reed looked at his wife with affection and just a bit of puzzlement.

"You look a bit … dazed … Officer Reed," Miss Prim observed.

"It's my wife," Reed said, in an astonished tone of voice. "When I wasn't looking, she turned back into the woman I fell in love with. Isn't she something?"

"She certainly is," Miss Prim agreed, as Valeska returned. Martin took a piece of dietetic cinnamon-raisin rugelach in one hand and his wife's hand in the other.

Miss Prim had just unveiled a plate of dietetic cinnamon rolls, to the *oohs* and *aahs* of her guests, when the doorbell rang again. Dolly rose to answer it. A moment later, a familiar scent wafted across Miss Prim's nose. She looked up to find two unexpected guests: her sister Celia on Maude's arm.

"Sister!" Miss Prim exclaimed. "Whatever are you doing here?"

"I simply couldn't wait, Sister," Celia said. "This was something to tell you in person, not on the phone, so I hopped on the train and took a cab into town from Two Oaks. After such a journey, I was feeling quite thirsty, so I thought it could not hurt to stop at the tavern for some refreshment." She winked at Miss Prim. "And Maude here, being a true gentleman, insisted on escorting me to Rose Cottage. Well, I certainly could not turn down such an inviting offer; so here we are. Maude, would you mind mingling for a bit while I talk with my sister? I shan't be long."

Maude nodded graciously and unlinked his arm from Celia's.

"Oh, my," Celia said. "It's such a relief to be out of physical contact with him. He *quite* distracts me."

"Sister," Miss Prim said with a grin, "you are simply incorrigible."

"Yes, I am," Celia agreed. "And in addition to being incorrigible, I am tenacious. I have the most wonderful news. I have found our sister."

Surviving the kidnapping attempts of a suitor was a good reason to be happy, but this—*this* was cause for even greater celebration.

"Oh, Sister!" Miss Prim exclaimed. "I have so much to tell you about what has happened since we last spoke. But all of that can wait. Tell me everything."

As Dolly rooted around in the refrigerator behind them, Celia launched into her tale. "After hours of combing the Manhattan records hall, I located Aunt Ada. She had lived for many years on the Upper West Side, but she died about ten years ago. I went to the building in which she had lived for so many years and began knocking on doors, hoping to find a neighbor who would remember her. And I was successful. Across the hall lives a delightful old lady, still quite sharp, who was happy to reminisce about Ada. Her reminiscences were not exactly fond, however. Apparently, Ada was widely disliked. The phrase Mrs. Berry used was 'hypocritical old prude.' You know, the type who complained about everyone in the building, minded everyone's business but her own, and didn't tip servicepeople at Christmas. In short: one of those spinsters who gives mature unmarried women a bad name.

"But Mrs. Berry also remembered the niece who had lived with her. She had only lovely things to say about the young woman. Apparently, the two of them had bonded when Mrs.

Berry had happened upon the young lady crying in the elevator. She invited Ada's niece in for a cup of tea, and the niece revealed her life story, which had taken her many years to piece together. And a most revealing story it is.

"We wondered why Ophelia would not marry Papa. She could not, Sister, because she was already married! She had lived on Long Island with her husband, an abusive man who beat her regularly. In desperation, she fled to her only relative, the aforementioned Aunt Ada, who reluctantly took her in. Ophelia filed divorce papers, but her husband was insanely jealous and he refused to grant her the divorce. And Ophelia feared that her husband would hurt or kill Papa if he were to discover his identity. She was trying to *protect* Papa, Sister! In the meantime, she got pregnant, which enraged her puritanical aunt, who then took against Papa for having compromised Ophelia's virtue. Ophelia was thus in a no-win situation. She feared that if she accepted Papa's offer, her estranged husband would hunt him down and kill him. So she was forced to accede to her aunt's wishes, because she did not want to be turned out onto the streets with an infant.

"And we know what happened after that. Poor Ophelia died, and Aunt Ada had to care for the child. Before she died, Ophelia had begged the aunt to change the baby's last name so that her husband could never find her daughter. So, rather than giving the child the surname Crenshaw, she simply took the letters of Ophelia's last name, LeFevre, and rearranged them into Veerelf. And—this is the best part, Sister—I have located a Miss Providence Veerelf living on the Lower East Side! I tracked down her home phone number, and I have left several messages, which she has not yet returned. But when

I return to Manhattan, I shall go to her apartment building and sleep on her doorstep, if need be, until she returns."

Before Miss Prim could say a word—for the stunning truth had destroyed her ability to speak—she heard a bowl crash to the floor behind her. She and Celia turned to see Dolly standing there, an inscrutable expression on her face.

"Celia," she said slowly, "*my* last name is Veerelf. And my given name is Providence. My second-grade teacher nicknamed me Dolly, and I've used it ever since."

Miss Prim struggled to find her voice. "Dolly, how can we have known each other all these years, and yet I never knew that Providence is your given name?"

"I don't tell anyone, Miss Prim. I just don't like my name, and I never have. It brings back horrible memories of growing up with my great aunt Ada. I put that name on a back shelf when she died, and I never thought it would see the light of day, ever again."

It was Celia's turn to be shocked.

"But, can this mean," she sputtered, "that … that … *you*, Dolly, are our sister?"

"I think that's exactly what it means," Dolly said. Then she added, touching Miss Prim's and Celia's arms simultaneously, "Sisters."

Oh, what a joyous day, Miss Prim thought, her eyes sweeping over her guests. Celia and Dolly stood in one corner, talking animatedly and occasionally embracing, while Maude stood protectively over Celia, gazing at her with alarmingly adoring eyes. Spike Fremlin and Killer Abramowitz inspected the bric-a-brac as Spike engaged in a running monologue that Killer appeared to find simultaneously fascinating and incomprehensible. Martin Reed stood with his arm around Valeska's waist as his wife leaned into the crook of his arm. Miss Gladys Lavelle looked transformed; in the space of an hour, her face had shed twenty years. Lorraine and Lucian watched the proceedings like elder statespeople, with Lucian prattling to Lorraine, who responded to her quasi-husband's stories with lingering glances of adulation.

Miss Prim lowered her head for a moment—the whole day had been overwhelming. So many plot turns in such little time! How had she not picked up on the anagram of LeFevre into Veerelf? This was perhaps one of the most overused, hackneyed elements of crime fiction, and any savvy reader would have seen it coming. But the epiphany had eluded her completely. Which meant, she supposed, that she still had a lot of learning to do before becoming an expert criminal outsmarter. Why, she'd even done the worst thing a criminal outsmarter could do—she had jumped to conclusions! All along she'd assumed that Alexander had been murdered, but he'd died of natural causes. She made a mental note: *Guard against trusting circumstantial evidence in the future.*

"Penny for your thoughts, Sister," Celia said, as she entered the kitchen to prepare a cup of tea for Maude.

"I wouldn't call them *thoughts*, Sister," Miss Prim replied, "but rather *feelings.* Feelings of deep happiness and gratitude."

"We are indeed lucky, Sister," Celia replied. "As always, the cards predicted all of it. It is indeed comforting to know in this unpredictable world that the cards never lie."

"As grateful as I am," Miss Prim said quietly, "I cannot help but feel that everything is just a bit too … *coincidental.* Surely, if these events took place in a novel, readers would complain about too much coincidence. Even those lovely readers who willingly suspend disbelief."

Celia considered this. "Sister, what you call *coincidence*, I call *cosmic alignment*. All the events of the past week have been leading us here, inexorably. We cannot, should not, and must not fight Fate, especially when it has been so good to us. Now, I'll hear no more of this *coincidence* nonsense. Come, sit with me and Dolly."

32

The Things We Do for Love

Miss Prim and her guests had settled in a circle in the parlor, talking about everything in general and nothing in particular, sharing anecdotes from their childhoods, travels, and life experiences. From the peals of laughter emanating from Rose Cottage, a bystander would not have guessed that just 24 hours earlier two of the inhabitants had been held captive in a quasi-deserted farmhouse.

When the doorbell rang, Miss Prim's heartbeat accelerated slightly. Only two guests had yet to arrive, and she was not sure she truly wanted to see one of them. She excused herself from the conversational circle and opened the door to find three men standing on her doorstep: two expected, one unexpected. The expected guests were Detective Ezra Dawes and Doctor Amos Poe. The unexpected was Benjamin Bannister.

Before she could say a word, Benjamin rushed to take Miss Prim's hand. "Miss Prim, I expect I'm the last person you want to see right now. But I wanted to help Doctor Poe and Dolly explain everything to you."

Dolly, a.k.a. Providence, appeared at Miss Prim's side. "Benjamin, Doctor Poe, something incredible has happened here today," she said. "I'll tell you about it later, but now we have to come clean with Miss Prim. Let's get it over with."

Doctor Poe stepped forward. Miss Prim noticed he was not wearing handcuffs or the orange jumpsuit that would have branded him as a criminal. He looked a bit dazed; but more than that, he looked embarrassed.

"Dolly, Benjamin, I appreciate your offer, but I need to talk with Miss Prim alone. This was my idea, and I conscripted the two of you into it. I bear all responsibility in this matter." He looked directly at Miss Prim. "Miss Prim, I fully expect you will never wish to lay eyes on me again after you've heard my story. But it is a tale that must be told. May we speak somewhere in private?"

Looking at Doctor Poe—the man for whom she had held more affection and esteem than she held for any other man on Earth, except Papa—Miss Prim's somewhat angry heart melted.

"Yes, Doctor Poe. Let us sit in the backyard, and I shall listen to everything you have to say. Detective, Benjamin: Help yourself to refreshments. Come, Doctor. I shall show you the backyard, though I suspect you have already seen it. It was you running through it several nights ago, was it not?"

Doctor Poe nodded and followed Miss Prim to the rear of the cottage.

Doctor Prim approached the patio table and pulled out a chair for Miss Prim, as was his wont. After she'd settled into it, he took a seat facing her.

"I must say, Doctor Poe, you are looking a bit the worse for wear," Miss Prim began.

"While you, Miss Prim, look as radiant as ever. Leave it to you to come out of a kidnapping ordeal looking even younger and more lovely."

Doctor Poe cleared his throat. "Ahem. So, here we are, Miss Prim; and I must confess, it is not the place I had hoped to be. Now let me explain what happened to you, and then I will be on my way.

"We have known each other many years, Miss Prim, and I think you know I have never been a man given to exaggeration. I daresay we have long complemented each other in that regard: unimaginative me and creative, enterprising you.

"As you know, I was quite beside myself with grief when you announced not only your impending retirement but also your desire to enter the field of criminal outsmarting. I suppose I could have lived with both those decisions, but the idea of your moving out of the City and up to Connecticut—*that* I simply could not accept. Dear Miss Prim, you were the light of the office and the light of my life. And I am not the only one who feels this way. Dolly and Viveca were devastated, and even Zoroastria, not a woman given to tears, became quite morose. As for Norah—well, let's not talk about Norah, as she is an outlier.

"The night after you announced that you'd purchased this cottage, Dolly and I were working late and commiserating. Dolly put into words what all of us were feeling. She said she wanted you to be happy, and to have the adventures and experiences that you so strongly desired; but at the same time, she feared for your safety, and she could not bear the thought of being so far away from you. Then she said the words that will live in infamy. 'Oh, Doctor Poe. If only *we* could give her the adventure she wants! We could do it safely and ensure that she comes to no harm. Then she'd realize that it's not much fun being in danger, and that she really does *not* want to pursue a career that puts her life at risk!'

"I began ruminating on those words, and before I knew it, I had approached Dolly with my idea. The idea was this: We would find a way to create your first case in a controlled way. Thus you would have your experience of outsmarting a criminal, after which you would wish to return to us in New York. And life would return to normal, but with one change. You would return to the City as Mrs. Amos Poe, not as Miss Felicity Prim.

"Dolly had her cavils, but I overcame them. Thus we sat down and hatched this plot.

"To begin creating the sense of menace that we believed you desired, I rented a car and drove to Greenfield, where I applied some makeup to my face and color to my hair in order to disguise myself. Then I began asking about you in town, with the hope that word would get back to you that an unknown man had been making inquiries. Dolly and I took turns calling your home phone and then hanging up when you answered. And, as you suspected, it was indeed I who was lurking in your backyard that evening."

Miss Prim thought a moment. "I should have realized something was not quite right when you called me from a cell phone. I know you are as adamantly opposed to those horrific devices as I am. It would have taken much more than pressure from Norah to make you purchase and use such a thing."

"Of course you are absolutely correct about my detestation of those devices. But I needed you to think I was in New York City, when I was actually here in Greenfield. A cell phone was the only way to accomplish that. You may have heard about a second man inquiring about you here in Greenfield. That was Benjamin. He was miserable seeing Dolly so lost without you, and he promised his help in our endeavor.

"After we had achieved our goal of making you feel somehow uneasy, but not truly threatened, in Greenfield, we moved forward with the next part of the plot. This, of course, involved Dolly becoming increasingly uneasy over the fictional situation in which Benjamin found himself.

"Dolly read a few mysteries by some of your favorite writers, and from the contrived denouements of those novels we thought we understood how the rest of the plot should unfold. We wanted you to aid, and save, a friend who was in danger, and then narrowly escape from the dangerous situation in which you found yourself embroiled.

"After rejecting several ideas, we decided on a kidnapping. Dolly would come to Greenfield and mysteriously disappear. You would be the one to find her and save her, and you would then get trapped yourself. You'd get rescued by the police, find yourself thoroughly tired of criminal outsmarting, and return home to New York, where you belong.

"So Dolly and Benjamin came to Greenfield to rent a house for a short period, giving phony names to the real-estate agent. Both Dolly and I felt that using a real-estate agent's services in this manner would work perfectly, in that they are inveterate gossips who cannot keep a secret to save their lives. Dolly and Benjamin rented the house and we arranged it so that you would find a way inside. We know how enterprising you are, Miss Prim, and we knew you'd find the hidden key. And I felt sure you'd remember how to get that padlock off the basement door, as we had used that technique in the office a number of years ago. In that expectation, I was not disappointed.

"But we had to get Dolly to disappear from the cottage mysteriously. How would we accomplish that? We all know of your fondness for Mrs. Mallowan's Lemon Sugar, so Dolly purchased a new brand. We steamed the packages open and

I added a safe, mild sedative to them, a gentle tranquilizer that would provide a night of very sound sleep. You drank your tea with the sedative, slept through the night, and found Dolly missing when you arose."

"So this is why I could not find the box of Miss Meredith's Blended Sugar," Miss Prim stated. "You and Dolly feared that I might use another packet and knock myself unconscious."

"Exactly. I picked Dolly up at the cottage and brought her to the farmhouse. To add some verisimilitude to the scenario, Dolly suggested that we take your purse. She'd mentioned that you were using a bell to train your dog, and she thought that the bell might prove useful at some point. She had the idea that she might start ringing the bell to get your attention as you searched the farmhouse. That seemed like a neat novelistic or cinematic trick that you would enjoy. It didn't quite work out that way, however. When I tied her up, we realized she could not ring a bell with her wrists bound. So we concocted the story Dolly told you, and I emptied the contents of your handbag onto the floor.

"To provide you a clue to her whereabouts, Dolly left Olivia Abernathy's business card near the phone. We knew you would call on Olivia, who would inform you about the rented house, and we knew that you would soon be on your way.

"The plan was simple. You would untie Dolly and rescue her, but the evil Everett Mansour—who, by the way, does not exist—would lock you in the basement as well."

Miss Prim had a flash of insight. Dolly had been tied up, but she had not been gagged. Why would any respectable kidnapper tie up the kidnappee but leave her free to scream at the top of her lungs? Why had she not considered this question earlier?

"So I locked you in the basement and returned to the Two Oaks Inn, at which I had rented a room. I was going to wait a few hours and then place an anonymous call to the police, tipping them off to the location in which you and Dolly were held captive. The police would arrive and you would be liberated. Benjamin would decide that an original copy of *Songs of Innocence* is not worth imperiling the lives of his girlfriend and her dearest friend; and that would be the end of it. You would have had your adventure and decided to return to Manhattan, and life would go on.

"But I made the mistake made by too many fictional villains. I decided to throw in one final plot twist. I'd planned to call the police around midnight. But then I thought: No, *I* will be the one to rescue Miss Prim and Dolly. I had concocted a realistic story about how I'd ascertained your whereabouts. I thought that once you saw me as your savior, you would accept my proposal of marriage instantly. I had hoped to pull off the mask and reveal myself as your hero, thus stunning and delighting you simultaneously.

"With my story ready, I returned to the farmhouse, parking my rented car on a different street. But no sooner had I entered than I became aware of the Greenfield police, and your friends, descending on the house. Not knowing what else to do, I hid in the attic. I watched through the windows at the front and rear of the attic as you and Dolly were rescued. Then I watched you climb into the police car and return to the house to retrieve your handbag.

"I thought: Here is my chance. I will surprise you and say I had shown up at the same time as the police. I decided to keep the mask on to give you the 'big reveal' that I knew you would so enjoy. It would not be quite the tale of the knight in shining armor that I had hoped it would be, but it would still demonstrate how deeply I care for you. I had planned to come up behind you and say, 'Miss Prim, I knew I would find you,' and then peel off the mask. You would say, 'Doctor Poe, what a night I've had,' and we would walk out of the house, arm in arm. Instead, you turned around, pulled a taser out of your bag, and shot 50,000 volts into me. But I suppose I deserved it.

"And there, my dear Miss Prim, is the entire tale. I had hoped the events of the past week would make you my wife; instead, I fear they have inserted a wedge between us that I shall never be able to overcome. I have committed the most egregious error of my life, and I will never forgive myself for it. Miss Prim, you *belong* in Greenfield. In just one week you have made your mark on this town, and it is easy to see that the people of Greenfield love you as much as Dolly and I do. We have been selfish, Miss Prim. We did not want to share you. We thought only of ourselves, not of you. Never speak to me again, Miss Prim; I shall understand and go home to lick my wounds. But I beg you, do not desert Dolly. She will be inconsolable without you."

Doctor Poe stood. "With that, Miss Prim, I must take my leave. Before I depart, however, I wish you to know that I have considered it not only an honor, but also a privilege, to be a part of your life. I offer you my deepest, sincerest apology, as well as my best wishes for your new career and your life in Greenfield."

The doctor turned to leave.

"Wait," Miss Prim said. As she looked into Doctor Poe's eyes—his deep, brown, sad, loving eyes—she felt cleft in two.

On the one hand, the man she'd trusted fully and completely had plotted and schemed against her. He'd attempted to manipulate her, and he'd almost succeeded. On the other hand, his actions had been driven by love. As Jane Austen and countless other novelists had demonstrated, the course of true love never did run smooth; and, as Mama was fond of saying, all men make mistakes, and they make them quite often. The key to forgiving them is to look in their hearts, to examine their motives, and to understand that men behave in strange ways as a result of testosterone and societal expectations.

Miss Prim was amazed to find herself feeling suddenly quite light-hearted. In a way, wasn't it rather adorable, and endearing, that Doctor Poe should go to such lengths to give her the adventure that she had so obviously wanted? He might see his actions as selfish—and perhaps they were, to a certain extent—but weren't his methods also extremely … thoughtful? How many men, she wondered, would go to such extremes to concoct a mysterious, well-executed plot in which to embroil his beloved?

What would Mama have done? Miss Prim asked herself, looking to the heavens. And the answer came to her, as clear as a bell.

"Wait," she said again, as Doctor Poe looked at her quizzically.

"Leaving would be most unseemly at this point," Miss Prim continued. "With everyone gathered under one roof, this is the perfect time to announce our engagement." As Doctor Poe gasped with delight, Miss Prim added, "Amos."

Epilogue

From on high, Mr. Cornelius Prim and Mrs. Charity Prim watched the proceedings.

Mrs. Charity Prim sighed.

"Our daughter is a most remarkable woman," she said, beaming with pride.

"Well, my dear," her husband replied, "how could she be anything *but* remarkable? You are her mother, after all."

Mrs. Charity Prim inclined her head to rest on her husband's shoulder.

"I do so love a happy ending," she said. "And I think this will be a good lesson for Felicity. Happy endings are not limited to fiction."

"And to see all my daughters under one roof," Cornelius said. "I find I just do not have the words to express my feelings. But my heart seems to be glowing. How I wish Ophelia were here."

Ophelia LeFevre appeared at Cornelius's side and locked her arm in his.

"I am, Cornelius. And I do believe my heart is glowing as brightly as yours." She turned to Charity. "I owe you a debt of gratitude, Charity, for taking such good care of Cornelius for so many years."

"Not at all, Ophelia," Charity replied. "It is *I* who must thank *you* for loving Cornelius so much after my departure."

A bell pealed three times in the distance.

"Time for Junusakey lemonade," Cornelius Prim said.

The three of them walked, arm in arm, into the light to enjoy their afternoon refreshment.

Junusakey Lemonade

Simple syrup
2 cups fresh lemon juice
1/2 cup mint leaves

To make simple syrup: Place 2 cups sugar and 2 cups water in a saucepan and bring to a boil. Stir until sugar is dissolved and let cool.

Place lemon juice in a large pitcher, then add 4 cups water and 1 cup of simple syrup. Stir in mint leaves and refrigerate for 1 hour. Serve over ice.

For a special treat, dip rims in honey and sprinkle with Mrs. Mallowan's Lemon Sugar before serving.